Happy Before After

By

Dave Jeanes

Contents

Solomon pulled into the vacant space and applied the handbrake.

'All good. Well-done car! Now, you rest here quietly while I go to the butchers. Hmm, doing this out loud lately. Have to watch that.' He exited the vehicle and walked carefully through the fallen beech leaves, some green, some brown, owing to a few inclement nights. The church building gazed down at him from years of indifference. He reached the less-afflicted streets, turned left, and headed for the butcher's shop.

The bell on the door frame announced his arrival.

'Morning Sam.'

'Morning Solly. How's it hanging?'

'Like a picture.'

Sam removed a carrier bag filled with produce and products from the refrigerated shelf and placed it on the glass counter.

'All in order and to order.' That is a favourite remark.

'Good man. Pay Tuesday?'

'Not a problem. Playing today?'

'Yep. Up the Downs for eleven-thirty. It should be okay. Walloped them at theirs back in the spring.'

'All the best then.'

Solomon's attention was drawn to the builders' lorries across the street.

'Hello, what's going on at the Methodist church?'

'Pulling it down, ain't they? A few months down the line, and that'll be city flats. All filled with starving commuters. Every day. Lovely.'

'Sad loss for the community though.'

'No congregation, no funds. Business is business.'

3

'I suppose so. I used to play five-a-side football at Sunday school there - when I was in the choir. They were supposed to be rehearsing for one thing or another, but nobody ever said anything. All played in complete silence on the basketball court.'

'Why would the Methodist church have a basketball court?'

'Who knows? Some Americans were over here, saw it was an unused room, and made them an offer. Didn't last long. Father used to play on it. With best friend, Howard.'

'Basketball? In church?'

'Football.' As if that was alright then.

'Oh.'

'Won the Churches Cup one year. All awarded pictorial penknives - I still got mine somewhere. Got the suspension bridge on it.'

'Would have. But knives, though? Wouldn't be allowed nowadays.'

'No. S'pose not. Well, this won't get the baby washed. Cheerio Sam.'

'Laters.'

'See you on the ice.'

He scrunched back over the leaves to his car, got in, made himself comfortable, and reversed over the carpet of nuts and leaves. The vehicle poked its head out between the impressive stone pillars, and he pulled out onto the Gloucester Road and headed home.

'Did you get it?'

A female voice shouted. Solomon thought of all the things he should have remembered.

'No. Didn't have any.'

4

Boots off. Slippers on. The stink of marzipan for birthday cakes is in the air. He couldn't stand it - she knew. He wondered if he'd ever be a father.

He strolled gently down the corridor to the kitchen and handed her the carrier bag.

'There you go.'

'Oh, you devil! You said they didn't have any.'

'They don't. Now. Expecting company?'

'It's alright, don't panic. It'll be all done and dusted by the time you return.'

'Aw, I'll miss Sharon.'

She put a powdered fist on her patterned overall.

'You like her, don't you?'

'Not as much as she likes me.'

'I'll have to get you a T-shirt – "Hands Off. He's Mine."'

'Good idea. She'd never shut up about it afterward. "Who'd have thought?" she'd say. "You and me." Don't worry. Never happen.'

'You'd exhaust her. Pretty little thing.'

'Always too much scent. I can smell her coming from a mile off. And what about you, my bigger and brighter second half? Couldn't I exhaust you?'

'Other half - not second. Football brain on again. It must be Saturday. Now, push off. You have a match to win, and I'm up to my eyes and ears in the cake mix. Where are you playing?'

'Don't know yet. Depends who shows up.'

The Downs League provides for about fifty amateur clubs— Ragbag, ramshackle teams who kept together just because they already had. There was an implied history to all of them. All of them are virtually the same. The Dog and Duck, for example, was named after a public house used by hunters. Or poachers. Who could tell?

Nearest to the road on this misty morning, a track-suited man with a deerstalker cap prowled the touch-line nervously. Around his neck was a whistle on a bootlace - but he never used it.

Solomon surprised him.

'Morning, Graham.'

The man whirled around.

'That man! That man! Good morning, Solomon. It's lovely to see you. Boots?'

They hung loosely over his shoulders. Solomon tapped them together confidently. 'Good, good. A pair?'

Solomon nodded.

'Worn them before?'

'Yes.'

'That's it then. You're in the team.'

Graham was the team's Manager. That didn't involve planning any tactics or strategies or anything like that. Just a series of telephone calls the night before a match to ensure eleven men would turn up. It didn't always work out okay, but the team muddled along happily enough, and Graham continued to be their Manager player once. He had dislocated a knee in a rock-climbing accident - which he'd be only too happy to tell anybody about. It meant he couldn't take to the field anymore. Besides this, nobody else wanted to do it.

'Nice weather for frogmen.' said Solomon, indicating the mist and frost.

'Proper taters.'

'Who else is playing?'

'Don't know. Early yet.' The Manager glanced at his Hunter fob. 'I told everyone eleven-thirty. What did I tell you?'

'Eleven-thirty.'

'There you are then.'

Once underway, the game progressed calmly enough. Stuck out on the right wing, his preferred position, Solomon watched as another twenty men were almost lost in the mist.

Graham stood close by, kicking every ball.

'Look at 'em, look at 'em. No grouping, I said. No grouping.' He hollered across the desolate pitch. 'No grouping! No grouping! Keep your shape! Oh, what's the use?'

'Should I go over and help, Manager? Might be a bit of a nuisance.'

'No, no, no. Chances are some idiot defender will hoof it clear any minute now, and there you will be - through on goal. Superior tactics. Brain beats brawn.'

'Where is the goal anyway?'

'Down that end somewhere. Think of their keeper, poor sod. That could be you. Where's our Aiden?' He swiveled around. 'Oh, it's alright. There he is. Leaning against the goalpost, eating an apple. Very unprofessional. I'll have to have a word with him later. Aiden. Aiden. Funny name. Irish, by the sound. Never play for England.'

'Fellow last week smoking a cigarette.' said Solomon.

'A cigarette! In goal? I should never do that. Ruin your gloves.'

There was the sound of crunched bone and a scream known only to men.

'Which one's your first-aider, Graham?' asked the referee, appearing ghost-like from the mist.

'We thought you were one.'

7

'Afraid not. Harry is, but his youngest is having her third, so they asked me to step in. I could hardly refuse. You know, all teams must have a first-aider. It's in the league rules.'

'Break, is it?'

'Seems so. Sounded like it.'

'Solomon!'

'Oh, what?'

'You got your car with you?'

'Down The Ladies Mile. Give me two minutes, and I'll nip and get it.'

'Good fella. Right. Off you go. Oh, and Solly - remember you can't drive in football boots.'

'Trifle squares.' said Sharon. 'Any wet wipes?'

'Plenty about. Me and Trifle squares are sworn enemies.'

'Ah, well. Love your trifles, Franny. That is the only reason I come sometimes. Not having any kids of my own.'

'Could always adopt?'

'No, no. Too much trouble. Think how they might turn out. A pair of mini me's. No, no, no. The best thing about kids is handing them back at the end of the day. Perfectly happy with your trifle squares now and again. All home-made?'

'Of course. Proper Cornish girl, me.'

'Dab hand.' The two looked at each other. 'Suits you. No Solomon today?'

'Playing football. You know, blokes. Must be freezing up The Downs today.'

'He'll need some warming up come the time. Hot soup. Warm hands on a fevered brow. Or thereabouts.'

'Don't worry. I'm a dab hand at that, too.'

'Comfortable?'

'Not bad. Thanks. Should never have gone for that tackle. The guy's an animal. What did you think?'

'Couldn't see.' said Solomon. 'What's your name?'

'John.'

'Glad to know you, Johnny boy. Sorry about your injury.'

'Could have been one of my team for all I know. Couldn't see a thing half the time.'

'Noticed that, noticed that. You couldn't see out; I couldn't see in. I asked the Manager if I should get involved, but he said no.'

'Good job, too. At least you were, well, on hand.'

'True, true. Listen, Johnno. Roads are rough between here and there, so feel free to scream. I won't stop, though. Just get you there in one piece. Well, several pieces. All set?'

'Yeah.'

'Okay.'

'Lucky escape, really. In-laws for lunch. Pains in arse.'

'Got one for keeps now, ain't cha? A pain, I mean. Well, not for keeps. Depends on your recovery. Busy at work?'

'Office days mainly. Drive sometimes. Glass warehouse out at Avonmouth. Recycled five hundred tonnes this last year.'

'Not lucky, though. Never say that. Can't see you walking this one off, fella.'

'No. What's the splint made from?'

'Old bus stop timetable somebody picked up. It'll be fine as long as it keeps the limb straight, well, straight-ish. Trooper's Hill. Nearly there.'

'Mm.'

'Used to be a sign on the station wall when I was an apprentice. Said Trouper's Hill. Disappeared one day. New Manager in, I guess. Said to the men, "Take that down, it's wrong."'

'Aha. Ouch!'

'Of course, back in the day, most people spoke French anyway. English wasn't a proper language.'

'That a fact?' John wondered. A little knowledge is a dangerous thing.

'When I was young,' Solomon continued. 'I used to think there was only one vowel. Because there's only one in my name - Solomon. See?'

'Yeah.' said John. 'Mine too.'

'Here we are. More lumps and bumps, I'm afraid. Speed bumps. Man's most stupid invention.'

'Agreed.'

'Come the alien invasion, our little green friends will look at each other and say, "What the hell are these for?"'

'Probably.'

They pulled up.

'I'll just go and get someone. It took half the team to get you in, but I can't get you out alone. Stay there.'

John smiled weakly.

'Solomon entered through automatic doors and, making apologies to anyone in a uniform, eventually detailed three orderlies to approach the car with a stretcher trolley.

'Hello, hello!' said the first. 'What's been going on here then? Deliberate foul?'

'Straight Red.'

'Obvious Yellow by the look.'

'VAR!'

'No time. We'll appeal.'

'He's shamming! Soon run that off.'

'Blood on socks, though.'

'Alright, alright.' said John. 'Drivers have been rattling on about nothing the whole way. Don't you lot start.'

'Trying to keep his mind off it.' said Solomon.

'Sound.'

To John: 'This your driver? He does this to you?'

'No, no. He was out on the wing. Happened to have his car parked nearby, so here we are.'

'Took half the team to get him in.'

'No doubt, no doubt. Okay, fellas, here's the plan. One on the legs, one on the body, and I'll be head and shoulders when I can. Just like in training. All clear?'

Various nods. 'Right.'

Moments later: 'Success! Well done all. Strap him down, then. In case he tries to escape.'

'Oh, this is odd.'

'What is?'

'Come and see.'

His colleagues crowded around the leg.

'Oh yes. So it is. Well, I never.'

'What?' asked Solomon, alarmed.

'The six and seven buses both stop at the White Tree roundabout.'

'Never. Get out of here!'

'It's true, it's true. It says so on this small blue panel.'

'I usually get off at the lights. Whitecoat is handy in a bag. Tell driver I'm a doctor, off to deliver a baby.'

'Nine months waiting.'

The first drew himself up to his full height.

'Now then, lads. Duty first. Let's get him inside before it rains. Don't want the trolley going rusty, do we?'

'No sir.'

'Yes, sir.'

'Right, you are, sir.'

'Better move the car, Mr Samaritan. You know what they're like round here.'

'Right.'

After doing so, Solomon approached the reception desk again. There was not another soul about. Unusual, he thought. His footsteps echoed on the linoleum floor.

He noted the nurse's rank - a Sister, marking notes in a folder. Nurses were always filing. What was in all of those?

'Can I help you, sir?'

'I imagine so, Sister. You have a friend of mine. I wondered where I should wait.'

'Nurse Carshalton will see to you. Nurse Carshalton!' She glanced at her breast pocket watch. 'It's my round.'

She glared at him like she'd heard them all before. He said nothing. She closed folders and scurried off briskly.

Nurse Carshalton was filing, too. She made a few entries and came across him, a pretty nurse in a cute uniform. He liked the way her hips moved as she walked. Her badge said her name was "Edie."

'Now then.' she began. 'Father? Maternity, is it?'

'No, no. Good Lord, no. Nothing like that. Just a friend with a broken leg. Well, it sounded broken. Of course, I'm no doctor.'

She smiled. 'Who is?' Rhetoric.

'I say, "Friend". More of a team-mate, actually.'

'Thought you might be.' She smiled as she read. 'John Wilson?'

'Could be, could be. First name John, in any case.'

'Upper or lower?'

'Leg?'

'Upper Case. Joke. Never mind. I knew he was in your field, so to speak. Although, different-coloured shirts. He's in twelve. Just down the corridor. Doctor with him at the minute. If I was you, I'd wait.'

'Wait! Yes. Good idea. Where's best?'

'Waiting room, generally. Just across there.' She indicated with her nail-polished fingers, clear. 'Tea and coffee on tap. Honor system. I'll come and tell you when he's free.'

'Thank you.' he said. 'Very much.'

She smiled again. 'Thank you.'

The party ended in a comfortable mess, as usual. The women waved "Bye-bye!" to all of the children and got about the inevitable cleaning chores.

'When, when, when, will we ever learn? said Fran.

'Kids are kids.' said Sharon.

'I suppose so.'

'What about you, Francesca?' said Lizzie. 'Ever see yourself as the motherly type? The clock's ticking.'

13

Fran and Sharon laughed. 'So's yours! Anyway, maybe, before very much longer. We'll see. And I don't want any daily inquiries. Let me enjoy myself.'

'Oh, don't worry.' said Lizzie. 'We won't disturb you.'

After a while, the nurse reappeared. He had sprawled himself on one of the easy chairs, an uncomfortable plastic piece in hospital blue. There was nobody else in the place.

She was in blue, too.

'Everything alright?' she asked with wide-eyed innocence.

'Oh, yes. Lovely. Thanks.'

She shook her head. 'You're just being kind. I hate those chairs. Horribly lumpy things. One slip, and you're on the floor. I wouldn't have one in my house.'

'House?'

'Well, flat then. Share with some of the other girls - all nurses. You must drop in sometime.'

Must.

'Uh, thanks.'

'Of course, you'd never get away again. You know what nurses are. Mmm, you've got lovely footballer's legs. Must be a lovely footballer. Where do you play?'

'Up The Downs.'

'I meant, what position?'

'Oh. Sorry. Out on the right wing, generally.'

'Very manly. No! Don't sit up. You'll give me ideas.' He grinned sheepishly. 'Don't see many men in here. Makes a nice change.' She leaned closer and whispered in his ear. 'What about it then? Think you've got a chance with me? Don't tell the Sister — she'd have me sacked. Doesn't trust me.'

'I'm not sure I do.'

'I would invite you to the flat, but it's better here. Like it in my uniform. Makes me feel sexy. How about you?'

'Very attractive.' said Solomon.

'More dangerous, you know?' she continued. 'Turns me on.'

'Sure it is. Dangerous, I mean.'

She straightened up, her voice not much more than a whisper. 'Come into my back office. Ooh! Sounds rude, dunnit? You'd have to do me standing up, but that's okay. You with your footballer's hands all over me. I'd like it like that. Come on. You should see what I've got on under this uniform. All black today. Bra, panties, suspenders, stockings. Yes, stockings. It makes more sense than tights. Can always change one if there's an accident. Is there going to be an accident?'

'You'd make a noise.' he said.

'I'll bet I would. Always make a noise, me. Doesn't have to be full penetration. Just enough to get us hot and bothered. Sister won't be too long.'

'I'm hot and bothered already.' he said.

'Alright for you. You can say you've been playing football. I can't. I have to be all prim and proper. Like a good nurse, eh? Go on. Last chance?'

'Extremely kind offer, uh, nurse. However, I am happily spoken for.'

'Oh, come on. How often do you get propositioned by horny nurses? Hmm, by the look of you, quite often. In your colourful kit. Go on. Imagine the feel of my bare naked skin under your hands. You could rub them all over me. Pull my skirt around my waist and even take my knickers off.'

'Steady now. What if the Sister comes?'

'Hmm, the only one who will come this afternoon is me. Have to go down to the staff toilets and sort myself out. All wet down there now.'

'I can imagine.'

'Go on then.'

'Do this a lot, do you?'

She shrugged. 'Enough. Liked the look of you, that's all. It's boring in here when it's quiet. "Hello. Who's this?" I thought. "Nice-looking man. Whatever next?"' She smiled. 'Some other time, maybe. After all, you know where I work. You're okay to see your friend now. Tell him what you just turned down. Watch me walk away and think what you could have had. Bye, sweetie!'

Despite himself, he watched her totter away.

He got home late. She told him so.

'You're late.'

'I know.'

'Missed your fancy woman.'

'She ain't fancy. Not like you.' He kissed her.

'What happened then? Penalty shoot-out?'

'One of theirs broke a leg, and I had to drive him to hospital.'

'You?'

'Well, I was on hand, and Greybags asked me if I had my car.'

'Could have said no.'

'Could have, yes. But I was freezing already. Anyhoo, you know how it is in any of these social emergencies. Everybody does what they can.'

'My hero.' she said fondly. 'How is he then?'

'Yeah, proper broken. Below knee, which is a good thing, apparently.'

'Less stress to the knee."

He thought about this.

'I guess so.'

'Having him out at yours? Picking and packing?'

'Said I'd ask. Doctor says plenty of rest for the next two weeks.'

'Your busy time. Might be alright.'

'Apart from all the pain and the agony, yes.'

'Good. Now, get your feet off the good sofa. There's leaves to sweep.'

Leaves...

'Did you know they're pulling down the Methodist church over St Andrew's? Across from Sam's?'

'Not surprised. No one ever goes in there. We haven't. Not since the wedding of those two with the same name.'

'All married couples have the same name. Idiot.'

'Not always. Can decline. Anyway, no. Same Christian names.'

'Oh - Michael and Michelle.'

'That's them. Micky and Micky.'

'Odd pair.'

'Wonder if they're still together.'

'Not them. This was seven or eight years ago.'

'True. Seven is pretty much the achievement, isn't it? After that, everybody stops loving each other.'

'Not us.'

'Not us, no. We'll be together forever.'

'Forever? Sounds like a long time.'

'Well, as long as we want to.'

'Okay then, yours forever. Now, come on. Get those leaves up. I'm not slipping over and risk breaking a hip.'

'I love your hips.'

'I know you do. Maybe later. Come on.'

He struggled to his knees and stood.

'See?' he cried. 'I can do it when I try! It's those scientists. What do they know?'

'You hungry?'

He checked his ribs.

'Will be, will be.'

'I was going to make sausage sandwiches, but we're all out.

'Really? It's not like kids to demolish bangers. How many did you get through?'

'How many did you order?'

'A pound. Same as always. Didn't check it, though. Maybe he ran short?'

'No use asking me. Meat's easy. Lay it all out on the roasting pan. A quick dash of oil - sunflower, of course.'

'Of course.'

'And shut the door.' She gave a little dance. "And shut! And shut! And shut the door!"'

'Very moving. Thanks.'

'All my own lines.'

'Beautiful, too. You'll go far.'

'Leaves first.'

'Ah, well. Leaves first and then sausages.'

'Can I come?"

'If you like.'

'I like. Love the city traffic on a Saturday afternoon.'

'Now, come on. Bring everything you might need.'

'Keys, purse, fresh knickers. All set. And you, bring your keys. Shout "keys!" as you go out the front door. Then I'll know.' She ran off up the stairs.

'Keys. So that's what that means. Fair enough.' He shuffled through papers. 'Sometimes helps if you go "Keys, keys, keys" when you're looking. Hm, nothing.' He looked around the room. 'Now, where did I have them last? Could it be in the keyhole? No. People don't do that. Think they do, but they don't.' He inspected the higher shelves of the bookcase and sideboard. Somethings jangled in his pocket. 'Ah. Keys. Good.' He strode confidently to the front door. 'Keys!' And closed the door behind him.

'Blimey, there's a strong wind. Still, it shouldn't take a minute. Gloves, safety boots… keys.'

He pushed the leaves down the gently sloping concrete pathway using a stiff broom. Alright, in the summer, but in the colder months, this was like a sheet of wet glass, and Fran was quite right - could easily slip and break a hip. He thought about her hips for a few minutes and found himself at the gate. He had stashed bags there ready. Two or three would do.

A dormouse or vole raised a sleepy head.

'Sorry, fella. Times change. Nothing stays the same. Better get used to it.'

He tidied everything away, got into the car, and pressed the horn quickly twice.

She came down the path warily, eyes left and right - like a bird looking for worms. She opened the door, feigning an Egyptian salute, hands folded neatly.

'You rang, master?'

'Indeed I did, young concubine. Time for your weekly commitment. Here.'

'Oh. Couldn't we go to the bedchamber instead, master? Wrap those silky robes around me and take me to the stars. I like being in the bed with you.'

'You're talking like a courtesan again! Strumpet! Besides, no, we can't. The master needs sausages.'

'Mistress, too.' She handed him a pair of shoes.' Here. You can't drive in those boots.'

Quick change.

Despite Saturday's traffic, they made it across the northern part of the city and parked in their usual space. After leaving the car, she grabbed his arm for support.

'Slippy.'

'Love that coat on you.'

'Me too. It's lovely and warm.'

'As are you. Was it a gift?'

'Of course it was.'

'Who from?'

'Oh, just some mad fella who's crazy about me... You are, aren't you?'

'Have to ask? I must be slipping.'

'It's these wet paving stones.'

They stopped outside Sam's, and Solomon watched the gang of hard hats across the street removing the roof insulation: grey and green four-foot square panels.

'Hi-vis keeps out asbestosis, does it?' she asked.

He nodded. 'True, true. Built about 1900.'

'Employer should know what's what.'

'We'll have a word before we go.'

'Alright.'

'Salty Sam's first!'

That completed. He handed her something.

'Here. Put this on.'

'A mask?'

'Got one too.'

'Fair enough. None of these guys have.'

'No. Can't work in them, some say.'

They edged across the road to the newly erected security gate. A yellow-helmeted man scrutinised them.

'Afternoon, fella.' said Solomon. 'Who's IC here?'

'IC?'

'In charge.'

'Oh. That'll be me, for my sins. Who are you?'

'Saturday. No ID on me. Only stopped for sausages. Great bacon bap of a morning over the road in Sam's. If you're here for long?'

'Right. Thanks. You in the trade?'

'Sausages? No.' The two men grinned. 'Construction, mainly. You know how it is. You end up doing all sorts of things. Put a bath in last week.'

21

'All goes on.'

'Sure does. Those sheets asbestos?'

'Be news to me.'

'What's the boss say?'

'He wouldn't know. Out on the golf course somewhere. I don't know a thing about it. Won't want to either.'

'Place should be checked - basic demolition law. Building Act 1984 Hazardous Substances. You know that. So do I.'

'All I know is, pull it down top to bottom. Six weeks max.'

'Who's doing the skips?'

'Smith's. Be here in a minute.'

'Okay. I know most of their drivers. Mind if I stick around?'

'Whatever gets you through.'

'Cheers.'

'Bye then.'

They re-crossed the road.

'"Bye then," she echoed. You men, you're just like kids, aren't you?'

'Why wouldn't we be? All I've ever learned, since I left school, I've learned from other blokes.'

'And what did they know?'

'Good question. Very little, most of the time. Internet culture has seen those days off. Used to be, half of what you heard was bullshit.'

'Now you can check.'

'Exactly!'

They took off their masks.

22

'You know what I fancy now?'

'What?'

'Pasties.'

'Pernod ou Ricard?'

'That's Pastis, ya great wit. Come on.'

Sam welcomed them back.

'You again, Solly? I'll have to start charging rent.' he said.

Fran smiled. 'Stood outside for two minutes but couldn't resist the sight and smell.' She raised two gloved fingers in a peaceful salute. 'Pasties.'

Sam beamed. 'Ah, now then. I get that way when I'm making 'em. Just a pair?'

'Please.'

Sam brandished a massive pair of platinum-polished tongs and gestured with them. Carefully, he picked two pasties from the glass cabinet and placed them in a paper bag.

'Cornish. Like you m'dear.'

'Ooh arr.' she smiled.

'Talking to the blokes, Solly?'

'Yeah. Skip the lorry on the way. Just want a chat.'

'"Think that's asbestos they're lumping?'

'Looks like it. We'll see.'

'Must've checked.' He handed the paper bag to Fran and took the money. 'Cheers, Fran. Thanks.'

'You'd think they would. Never can tell these days. Weekend work can get a lot done. Do a lot of harm, too.'

'Not good enough. People have to know. Kids and what-have-you.'

'Fine would shut them down for good.'

'For everyone's good.' she chipped in.

They left. 'Cheers Sam.'

'Laters.'

She retook his arm. 'Ooh, I could never work in a shop. Same old thing, day after day.'

'Friendly faces, though.'

'I guess.' She went to the car and waited.

Solomon returned across the road and approached the truck by the passenger window. The driver was smoking.

'Lofty!'

'Hello, Solly. Got you working Saturdays now?'

'No, no. Just passing. Saw the sheeting coming out and thought, "I wonder?" Why a Saturday, I wondered.'

'Best time to do it, if Rovers are away. Imagine any other time.'

'Okay. What's the report say?'

'One minute.' The driver went through a clipboard of papers from the dashboard.

'Insulation, insulation. Not seen.'

'Assessor should have checked.'

'Ah, but who'd do it, Sol? Assessor wouldn't leave his office, and none of these blokes could do it. It wouldn't be a cash job, so there's a paper trail. That's why we get hired. Everyone knows we have an asbestos tank. It's a thousand pounds on the invoice, so the world turns.'

'So it does, so it does.'

'Money for jam. For me. Look at me - not even getting out of the cab.'

'Have to lash it all down, though?'

'Not if I say it's asbestos.'

'I guess not.'

'None of them will mind. It's always the same with the simple blokes. All think they're gonna live forever.'

'True. True. Ah well. Take it easy, Lofts.'

'Always do, fella. Always do.'

On the way home, she cradled the pasties on her lap.

'Well?'

'Yeah, Lofty says the same as me. And he'd know. I've seen it before, and someone has to pay. I'll report it as seen, just passing by. Not much else but rip open any roof, and who knows what you'll find.'

She sighed. 'Good. You did the right thing. Now, get me and my babies home. I'm starving. Pronto!'

'You know what I love about you, Francesca?'

'My pasties?'

'No.'

'What then?'

'Everything.'

'Good. Me too. I mean, I love everything about you, too.'

'So I should hope.'

'Can you drive okay if I do this?'

'No. Stop it. Imagine your parents are sat in the back.'

She gripped her pasty bag again. 'Hm, yes. That works. What's it to be, then? Pasties or bangers.'

'I'll do bangers. Quite fancy them now.'

'Pasties are lovely and warm. Aren't you, my little beauties?'

'They'll microwave up tomorrow.'

'I could have mine now.'

'You could not. Puff pastry all over my fabulous limousine's carpet? No. You must wait.'

'You think more of this car than me.'

'Semantically incorrect. I am always thinking of you. When I'm in the car, I'm thinking of you. The reverse can not be stated to be true with any degree of accuracy.'

'Pig.'

'Yes. But, sow.'

'Hungry now. Take me home, Daddy.'

He did so. They parked outside their house quickly enough, which is not always true. He shepherded her up the now frosted, glinting pathway. It was getting dark, and their breath moved like personal clouds.

'Now, wait and see what I cook for you, my Queen. How are we off for burger buns?'

'Don't know.' she said, keys in the door.

'Must be one or two.'

'And you'll have two! What about a pasty?'

'No. Always some leftovers after children's parties.'

'Maybe. Have to check. If not, home-swirled buttery mash.'

'Bangers and mash. Okay.'

'Shut that door behind you. We're in now.' She placed the pastries and sausages on the kitchen worktop. 'How does Sam know I'm Cornish?'

'Dunno.'

'You must know!'

'It's your sexy accent. Gives you away. One of the things I love about you is your voice.'

'Good answer.'

As it turned out, there were no more buns, so he peeled potatoes while she harvested the pasties.

'Here. Bangers.'

'Thanks.'

'That's that then. Gives us twenty-five minutes.'

'Come on then. Upstairs!'

'Yes, master!'

They rocked and rolled in their clean white bed for an hour until he admitted defeat.

'No more.'

'Oh, go on! Just one more? A quick one?'

'No. It'd be a shame to waste you. There'll be time later. First, though, miss, I need to feed you. Got to keep your strength up.'

'Go on then. I'll have a shower and come down.'

'Could you stay there? I'll bring it up to you.'

'No! No food in the bedroom. House rules.'

'You should have to shower. You were amazing.'

'You inspire me. Besides, I do like being involved.'

'When did you first realise you were any good at this?'

'First time with you. It was like a third person. Yeah? You're the same.'

'How do you mean?'

'I mean, you're not just humping away up there alone, are you? You become a part of it. You give yourself to me. I do, too, and that becomes the third person.'

'And you never got that with anyone else?'

'How dare you! How dare you imply that I've ever been with anyone but you. You're my first. My first.'

'Does it have a name? This third person?'

'Of course it does. It's called love.' She pulled back the covers, revealing her beautiful white skin, bronzed against the brilliant white bedclothes. Not a mark out of place, despite the early evening's activities.

'Mm. Come back to bed.'

'I wish. Unfortunately, there's work to do.' He tucked her back in and kissed her on the nose. 'You know the worst thing about mashed potatoes?'

'Mm?'

'Washing up.'

'Yes, well, you can do that.' She stretched. 'I've done enough to earn my keep.'

He smiled. 'You sure have.'

The telephone rang, so Solomon picked it up.

'Home for wayward girls. Matron speaking… oh… oh really? Yes. Sorry, Sunday Mornings… Yes, she's here somewhere. Probably chained to the sink after yesterday. Hang on.' He found her in the kitchen and put the phone on the table. 'Christy?' She nodded. He backed away.

Women on phones - always the same. Just because you're not the person they want to talk to when, in actual fact, it's the one that pays for the equipment to be on the premises in the first place, they become mildly affronted, as though you've personally interrupted their day, instead of the reverse is true. Christy. He thought. Short and sweet. Neat little figure. Blonde hair, blue eyes. Thug of a son called Jason. Four-year-old. Ah well. So they all go.

He relaxed back on his Sunday sofa. The radio burbled quietly about yesterday's football results. Outside, the sun shone. It was a quiet day.

Francesca appeared and replaced the telephone.

'Alright?' she asked.

'Never better, thanks.'

'Good. That was Christy.'

'She said.'

'Wondered if we could go out for lunch. Thank you for the party.'

'Thank you for the party.'

'That's what I said.'

'So you did. You did, too. Me too?'

'No. Of course not you. What did you do?'

'Brought home the bacon - and sausages. Hunter-gatherer, me.'

'I could have had them delivered.'

'But you didn't.'

'Anyway, it's just the Mums. "Thank you for yesterday." she said.'

'Fine with me. Need the car?'

'No, someone will pick me up. It's The Wellington. Up on the common.'

'Nice boozer. Been there many a time. Big Rovers pub.'

'Another reason you're not going. Don't want you swinging your scarf about and yelling about how someone will get the chicken's head cooked in.'

'Not quite got the lyrics there.'

'I know. Sunday. No swearing. Changed a bit, I expect. There's a brasserie now.'

'Coq au vin.'

'Language! Why's it called The Wellington?'

'Mark of respect. He was one of our first goalkeepers.'

'Really? Never know with you. For all you know, I'd be up there later, saying, "Yes, well, of course, Wellington was one of the first Rovers goalkeepers."'

'Of course. He had the boots.'

'Idiot! Don't care how daft you make me look, do you?'

'Of course not. Don't forget, I've seen you naked.'

'Idiot!'

'You said that.'

'Huh.'

She reappeared minutes later, dabbing her eyes with a tea towel.

'Sad songs on the radio?'

'No, no. Course not. Peeling onions. Steak and kidney pie tonight.'

'Lovely. Of course, if you want to peel onions without bursting into tears, peel them under water.'

'Well, how would I breathe? You horrid man.'

'Just saying.'

'Alright. Off soon. You got everything you need?'

He smiled. 'Got the paper, haven't I? What are you going to wear?'

'Not sure yet. Want to come up and watch?'

He chased her up the stairs.

'Now, I want something that says "Mum".'

'Yours or mine?'

'Something warm and cuddly.'

'Okay. Yours then.'

'My Mum's not warm and cuddly.'

'She is. Knows it, too. You just don't see it. Same as mine, I guess. Could never see us romantically involved.'

'I should think not!' He sat on the bed. 'But you do with mine?'

'Of course. Every man with a beautiful woman has imagined himself with the woman's mother.'

'I'll tell her that. It would make her day.'

'I daresay she already knows. Women do. She's always leaning over closer when she's pouring my gravy.'

'Ha! Is that a euphemism?'

'Not at all. Last Christmas, she wore some underwear with hollies, and ivy patterned all over it. A black thing, flashes of green and red. I could just see it below her loosely-buttoned white blouse.'

'Not that you were looking. Disgusting.'

'Job not to. She's a well-built woman, just like her daughter. "Hello," I thought. "Old man's on a promise this afternoon. In-between the Queen's speech and the Morecambe and Wise Show."'

'Naughty parents. Should never have sex on Christmas Day. Far too many other things to do.'

'Like washing everything up ready for next year. Anyway - we have sex on Christmas Day. Boxing Days too.'

'That is only because you're crazy about me.'

'Remember that first Christmas when I stayed over? Head full of whisky sneaked along the landing to your room...'

'And got into bed with my sister. Yes, I remember. She does, too.'

'Well, how was I to know you'd swapped?'

'I told you. Like you said, you had a head full of Father's best whisky. That's how I knew he liked you. Never usually passes it around. I'll have to warn him - keep that whisky under lock and key, or your wife and daughters could be compromised.'

'Good job, nothing happened.'

'Opinion is divided on the matter. You know what I think. Now. Clothing. NOT something that says I spent much of last night flat on my back with my legs in the air...'

'You had your turns on top. Love you like that. Turn and turn about.'

'Mmm, me too. Oh, don't. You'll get me in the mood.'

'Come here.'

'No! I've got a lift coming. Anyway, they'll all know. Always do. Lots of tittering over salads and Chardonnay.'

'I can imagine. Show me your knickers then.'

She raised her skirt. 'There! Happy now?'

'For now.'

'Like watching me dress, don't you?'

'Of course. Love you in a skirt, with your long, sexy legs. I memorise it. Then, when you're not here, I play it backward in my mind.'

'Ridiculous man.'

'Crazy about you.'

'Aren't I lucky?'

'Come and sit on my lap.'

'No. You'll get an erection. You know I can't resist you when you're like that.'

'Only does it for you. Wouldn't do it for any of your other Mums.'

'Not even mine? How about this?' She held a spotty top-up to her. 'Is this Mumsy?'

'It'll do. Reminds me of Paris.'

'That's right. That's where we bought it. Well, it was duty-free. Okay. That's me. Now, about the pie.'

'Yes?'

'There's a turnip inside to hold the crust up. Lift the lid and take it out before the final countdown.'

'When the alarm goes off.'

'That's right... Doorbell. Here's Lizzie. See you later. Ooh, all of a quiver now, thinking about you. Best grown-up behaviour, Francesca! Keep your genes in your jeans. And you! No sneaking round to my mother's for secret gravy pouring!'

'You're crazy.'

'I know. I love it! See ya!'

He lay back and waited for his erection to abate. What a girl! Slowly, slowly...

At length, he got up and went downstairs. The doorbell rang again. He hadn't heard her yell, "Keys!" but maybe it was just him that had to do that. You never knew. He tightened his robe around him and opened the door. It was Graham.

'Ah! Solomon, Solomon.' he said, expecting someone else. 'Star player. Man of the hour!' He breezed down the hall and into the sitting room. Solomon followed. 'Any tea in the pot?'

'Could be, could be. Come on through.'

He filled the electric kettle in the kitchen, emptied the pot, and found two clean mugs and fresh bags. The alarm sounded.

'Offside!' shouted Graham. 'Never a goal! Oh, pie alarm. Sunday. Right.'

Solomon opened the oven door and put on the oven gloves. On the hob, he lifted the lid and speared the turnip. He placed it in the waste disposal for now. No doubt some neighbour's Guinea pig would be dreaming of the same. Still, there it was.

He replaced the pie, turned the oven temperature up, and reset the alarm for twenty minutes. The kettle boiled. Solomon poured a pot of tea and then sat down.

'All under superb control, Solly. I'm impressed.'

'That's Fran. Never lets me wonder what I should be doing.'

'Good for her! We all need a woman like that behind us. Not just behind either…'

'Yes, yes, Manager. What brings you here anyway?'

'Ah. It was this injury yesterday. League ordered an inquiry - as per bloody usual. Obviously, you must attend.'

'Me? Why me?'

'You administered first-aid.'

'No, I didn't. I just drove him.'

'I know you did, but I've told them you're our first-aider.'

'You lied to the league?'

'Oh, they're used to it, I expect.'

'Well, you'll have to tell them you made a mistake.'

'Me? A manager? Making mistakes? No, no, no. That would never do.'

'Just tell them you were wrong.'

'Me wrong? It was you that drove him off without an assessment.'

'You told me to!'

'So? Would you do that if I told you to dive off the Avon Gorge?'

'Not in shorts, no.'

'Well?'

'Well, what?'

'That is what we must decide, Solomon. What shall we do?'

'What about their side?'

'They didn't have one either.'

'And the ref?'

'Just assumed one of us was. You heard him.'

'Oh dear.'

'Oh dear indeed. Of course, it's the league that suffers.'

'Good.'

'You don't mean that. Think of all the fun we've had over the years. Turf Moor in July. What an outing that was!'

'Those Burnley girls…'

'Alright. Concentrate.'

Solomon nodded. 'Alright. Let's think.'

'Nice tea this. What is it?'

'Hmm? Oh. No idea. Fran takes care of all of that.'

'You've got a good woman there.'

'Some of the time, yes. Okay, how about this?'

'Go on.'

'Out at my place, they're always advertising for first-aiders. There's an afternoon course. I could sign up for it and pass it. Then, when the league asks, I say I'm waiting for the certificate.'

'What about the dates?'

'Dates can always be changed. What about that time Tommy Moss played for us in the Cup when he was actually playing four fields away for another team?'

'Yes, that worked, didn't it?' Graham stood up to leave. 'I think we'll do that then, eh what? Well done, Solly. Man of the match!'

'Always a joy.'

He returned from work the following evening with a big green ring binder.

'What'cha got there?' she asked.

'This first-aid course I have to pass. It's all test questions, tick box answers.'

'Oh, nice. I'm good at those. We'll have a go together later. Yeah?'

'Sweet. What you have been up to?'

'This and that. Spare room mainly. A few of the girls round for coffee. Sharon sends her love.'

'Doesn't she always?'

'Did a bit in the garden. Pricking back, holly and ivy, ready for the big bush, I mean push. Reminded me of Mother.'

'Stop it.'

'Mushrooms too! Off a bit, but if you're up early enough, they could grill up okay.'

'What sort are they?'

'No idea.'

'Leave them then. If the local wildlife won't touch 'em, neither should we.'

'We could get a dog?'

'No. I hate dogs.'

'What about guide dogs?'

'What about them? I'm not blind.'

'Not yet, no.'

'Well, if and when I am, a small child can lead me about.'

'How thrilling.'

'Quite. Anyhoo, it's not a spare room. It will be the nursery.'

'Will be. Will be. At the moment, it's a spare room. A spare room.'

'Come and sit here.'

'What do you want? Dangerous man.'

'Just want to feel you next to me. Big sofa when you're on your own.'

'Alright.' They cosied up together. 'Remember when we bought this place? We said that the spare room would be the nursery.'

'Would be. Would be.'

'Well, what's stopping us? They say if the sex is terrific, a baby's not far away.'

Solomon did a mental calculation. November now. Plus, forty weeks. *"Bébé Juillet."*

'Yes! Why not?'

'You'd have to stop work.'

'I hate work. It represses me.'

'I thought you liked it there.'

'I do. Sometimes. Not often, though. I sometimes sit, twiddling pencils, thinking, "Is this me? Is this really what I wanted to do with my life?'

'What is it you do anyway? I've never been quite sure.'

'Chief pencil-twiddler, me.'

'I'll tell people when they ask.'

'If you must know…'

'I must! I must!'

'I'm an events manager.'

'You manage events?'

'Yes. Sometimes. I could give it up tomorrow. Or you could.'

'I could! I should! Not that I know anything about managing events. But, how hard can it be if a girl can do it?'

'No, no. Silly man. I mean, *you* could give up *your* job. And look after the children. *Your* children. A boy and a girl. Six and four!'

'Odd names.'

'Hmm, we'd probably be living somewhere else in seven years. When you're a millionaire. Alright then - four and two.'

'Sounds like a length of timber. Anywhich-way, how do you know it'd be a boy and a girl? You get to choose?'

'These days, yes.'

'Yes, I could! Virtually work from home anyway.'

'Virtually.'

'Okay. But let's not plan too much. Throw your pills away, and we'll see what happens.' He reached for the green binder. 'Now. First things first. All questions And answers. Yes or no.'

'Yes, it's all questions and answers. Next one!'

'Ridiculous child. Just answer, "Yes" or "No".'

'Beautiful! I love saying yes or no.'

'Yes, you do.'

They waded through the hundred questions, knowing, sometimes using Google. He closed the binder and put it on the bedside table.

'That's that then. Pass or fail.'

'Fail?'

'Fail doesn't matter, really. The binder will show I answered all the questions. Of course, everybody cheats and uses Google. Anybody from the league asks, I'm waiting for the certification. What are we doing in bed?'

'You wanted to see my patella.'

'So I did.' He kissed her. 'Such a beautiful patella too.'

'I've got another one just the same, over here.'

'Impossible!'

She giggled. 'Come on over.'

The factory offices were under half-light. It's not winter light that could wait. Half-light was put on in the afternoons when the low sun shone weakly on the western side of the premises. Saved a penny, here and there.

Solomon sat and waited. Soon, one of the doors opened, and out stepped a suited man.

'Swift?'

'That's me.'

'Oh, hi, Solly. Yes, of course it is. Come on through. They made their way into the room. The man smelled like his office. His name was Chumwell. Friends, if he had any, called him "Chummy." He was head of HR.

'Sit, sit.' said the man. Solomon sat by the desk. The man went round the other side. 'Sorry to interrupt your travails,' he said. 'Only, there's this.' He held up the first-aid binder.

'Problem? Don't tell me I didn't pass? I found it relatively easy.'

'Well, you would. Basic common sense, most of it. Never get anywhere without it. Made me wonder why, is all. Not thinking of leaving us, are you?'

'No, not at all. Like it fine working here. Been here long enough - you ought to know.'

'Often happens, you know. More often than you'd think. Man wants to build up his curriculum vitae - CV. You knew it stood for that, right?'

'Of course.'

'My wife was the same. Always saying, "Is this all you're going to do with your life? Too easily satisfied, that's your trouble." she'd say. "Married you, didn't I?" I'd reply. Where was I?'

'Curricula vitae.'

'Oh yes. The obvious place to start. That, and the twenty-five yards breast-stroke and cycling proficiency, and you're well on your way.'

'I guess. Not that with me, though. The football club I belong to needs a registered first-aider, so I thought I could apply here. Backdate it if you like. To the start of the season.'

The man twiddled a Parker pen between his fingers.

'We paying you enough, Solomon?'

'Well, bound to say no, aren't I? Thinking about babies the other day, as it goes.'

'Babies, eh? Make a difference. It costs a bloody fortune, too. Take my two - both at boarding schools, so I hardly see them. Feel guilty about that sometimes, but wake up on a Saturday morning to an empty house and think, "Thank God!"'

'She still with that new bloke?'

'Far as I know. I suppose so.' The man stroked his own chin, supposing so. 'And what would we get?'

'Pardon me?'

'For this First-Aid certificate. What would the firm get?'

'I dunno. I'd go on a list of first-aiders, I guess.'

'Yes, I suppose so.' Chumwell pushed a box of patellas across the desk.

'Don't smoke these at all, so you?' The company picked and packed cigars here, there, and everywhere.

'No. They will try you the first week. Let you have whatever you want. I preferred cigarettes. Don't touch them either nowadays.'

'Girlfriend doesn't like it, eh? Women. Can't live with' em.'

'No. It's me. Sort of thing a younger person does, I guess.'

'You're probably right. Do you drive?'

'Yeah, can do. Sometimes do. I've been to Wales several times in one of the trucks. I'm licensed up to seven and a half tonnes.'

'Aha. Wouldn't you say no to a few overnights, then? Stay at a Travelodge. There's no need to sleep in the truck. Those cabin beds are as uncomfortable as sleeping on rocks.'

'How far are we talking about?' Solomon knew of the firm's European contracts.

'Sometimes not too far. North and South. Scotland sometimes. It's beautiful up there. Ever been?'

'Not in the football league, are they?'

'One day. Who knows?'

'Alright to take a partner?'

'Unofficially, yes. Officially, what are you asking me for? What I don't know won't kill me. Give yourself a couple of trips until you know the ropes, though. For now, it's just you. Company rules and regs.'

'Okay.'

'Got one this weekend as it happens. Leave Friday, back Tuesday. Manifest here somewhere.' He sorted through drawers on his desk. 'Ah! Here goes. See the foreman, tell him I said so. Okay?'

'Okay. Thanks.'

'That's settled then. I'll notify the wages clerk.' He held out his hand to shake.

'And the first-aider badge?'

'In the post.'

'What do you mean you got promoted? You practically run the place as it is.'

'Mm, I thought that.'

'What do you have to do?'

'Nothing much. A few overnights. Wales and Scotland sometimes. Chummy says it's beautiful up there. I asked if I could take you, and he said, "Yes." Although not at first. Get the hang of it, and we'll see. That's all it was. He saw our first-aid binder and was worried I was thinking of leaving.'

'How odd. Oh well. I don't mind if you don't mind.'

'I don't mind. Oh, and the first-aid course?'

'Yes?'

'We passed.'

'Ha! Clever us.'

'Leave on Friday. I will be back on Tuesday for this trip. Okay?'

'Not me. It's Gilly's christening. Her little one.'

'Didn't know she had a little one.'

'Saucy! Can't get out of it. Besties, you know?'

'I don't have a bestie, me.'

'Yes, you do, silly. It's me. I'm your bestie. Better yet, you get to shag me. I don't let anyone else do that.'

'Cuts both ways.'

She thought about this. 'Yes! I suppose you're right. Good. Let's keep it that way. Go on, then. Undress me and do me on the sofa. I love that!'

Holman spoke to the foreman.

'Yes, Peter?'

'Who's doing the Scotland trip?'

'Jack Blunt, as usual.'

'Who?'

'Sorry. Slang. Let's see.' The foreman read the manifest.

'Here we are. Swift. Solomon. Oh! Nice trip out for him.'

'Good fishing up there this time of year.'

'Smuggling, Holman? In the company vehicle? No other way to get the beasts back over Hadrian's Wall.'

'Oh, throw most of 'em back.' lied Holman. 'Just keep enough for the Barbie. Gamekeepers don't mind that.'

'Aha. So, Solly's taking a trip out in the sunshine. Good for him.'

'Why him, though?'

'Why not? It can't always be you, can it? He's obviously impressed one of the high ups, somewhere along the way.'

'Right.'

But it was not right. Holman was the usual driver and knew exactly what was what. That evening, he collected Raphael, his stepson, and returned to the warehouse in darkness. 'Now remember, any movement, just tap on the gate. And once again, when it's all clear.'

When exported, cigars are weighed, and the weights are recorded on the printed manifest. They were boxed in balsa wood, but a clever smuggler could quickly open the boxes, remove one or two, and replace the lid. This involved a quiet hammering. His stepson waited by the metal gate of the factory with a flint stone. A good night's work could produce about three hundred cigars. And no one was any the wiser.

At length, he brushed the few balsa crumbs from his clothing.

'Bon voyage, Swifty. *Bon voyage.'*

It was a noisy truck, and Solly could hardly hear the radio. He drowned himself in his thoughts until the M6 indicated Carlisle and, beyond that, Gretna Green. He was bound for Langholm on the A7, where there was a superstore. It had been a long drive, the best part of six hours with breaks, and the day darkened. Here and there, the lakes reflected the burgeoning moonlight. There was a flat surface out there. Distant hills to the north. Nothing to the west, east, or south of him. That is reason enough for rumors of the flat Earth to be widespread.

At Gretna crossing, a hi-vis operative told him to leave to switch off the engine and park.

The yardman watched and waited. Then:

'Ticket?'

Solomon reached for his clipboard. Ticket, yes. He had seen one. Ah, here we are.

'Forty-five.' read the man. 'Gate twelve, park on the left as before. He moved on to the truck behind. It was an odd sight, literally dozens of vehicles, all under quiet control.

He did as he had been told and waited. Texted Fran and wrote, "I am in Scotland, the noo." No immediate reply. He settled back and closed his eyes.

He was awakened by a man tapping his metal-topped staff on the window. He checked the time: Seven-ten pm. He opened the window.

'Manifest?'

Solomon handed it down. The yardman sheltered under his umbrella and read it. "Go on up to the tap end - gate forty-seven. Weigh-bridge.' He disappeared again.

Solomon closed the window and put the manifest on the dashboard to dry off. He maneuvered the truck quickly out of its space. The yard lights glimmered with a yellow glow, and the yard was wet with rain. He switched on the wipers, which guffawed to each other as they progressed.

As directed, he drove onto the weighbridge and waited until the red light turned green. An arrow lit up ahead, telling him to park on the left and stop. He did so. A sign ahead read "Fragile Roof - Use Crawling Boards," which meant nothing to Solomon.

He checked his phone, but Fran had not replied, probably at the buffet part of proceedings. He could almost smell the scotch eggs. Ha! Scotch. Funny. He waited.

In time, a yardman appeared with two uniformed officers. Their peaked caps were wet and black.

'Care to come this way, sir?' said one. 'Leave keys in ignition.'

Solomon wasn't sure about this but saw no alternative. He clambered down.

'Overnight bag?'

Solomon nodded and reached behind his seat for it.

'Right. Off we go. Not far.'

They entered a shed of an office. One of the uniforms went behind the desk, and the other stood by the door.

'Problem?' tried Solomon.

'Swift?' queried the officer. 'Good name for a driver.' He shuffled all the papers together. 'You're underweight, Mr. Swift. You're to stay here while we investigate further.'

'Stay here? For how long?'

'Well, not here. We have spaces. First, we need to contact your firm and check weights with them. It's too late tonight, of course. Tomorrow will do.'

'And then what?'

'Provided the weights tally at leaving and arriving, you can proceed.'

'And if not?'

'I wouldn't worry about that if I were you.'

Which made Solomon worry all the more.

He was the only occupant for the night in some dormitory. There was some kind of Faraday cage in place, so he could not use his phone.

The walls were plain, stone grey. Fluorescent tubes lit the room when needed. Redundant for now, they waited quietly for the morning. Little light came from the clouded moon. Tired anyway. He slept.

'First-aid kit? Don't panic. Just a scratch.'

'Oh dear. Top shelf by the oven, Fran.'

'Thanks. Just a small scratch, but you know, blood. Gets everywhere.'

'Whose is it?'

'Jenny's little one - I always think of her as Jenny's wren. Ah! Here we are.'

'Bit of iodine first?'

'Yes. Lizzie's already done that. Always carries some, apparently.'

'Oh yea, she said. Losing those last few pregnancy pounds, she's injecting some new drug.'

'Bizarre. Oh well, better attend. You coming in?'

'Just making tea.'

'Okay.' She threaded her way back to the patient. 'Make way! Make way! First-Aid for the injured!" she sang. The child looked unhappy, but children love plasters, and soon, everybody was leaping and jumping as before. She returned the first-aid kit to the kitchen. Jenny was off on her tea round, but David came in and stood next to her.

'Can just imagine you, done up as a nurse.' he said.

She laughed. 'Never look my best in blue.'

'Shame.' His eyes danced. 'Where's that Solomon of yours? Not seen him today.'

'No. He had to work. Just been promoted, so couldn't get out of it.'

'Promoted, eh? There'll be no living with you soon.'

'No, no. Never forget your friends, do you?'

'Good.' Then, 'Shame.' He wandered away.

Jenny came in. 'At it again is he, the hound dog? I'd know that look anywhere.'

'Good luck to him. Everyone knows who I belong to.'

'Any news on that front? Tiny toes?'

'Not yet, no. Too soon to tell yet. Still at the fun stage.'

'Enjoy it while you can, honey.' Then louder, 'Alright, baby! Mummy's coming.'

Fran stood and thought. "Mummy"? Could she? Would she? She'd heard it said that having carried a child for nine months, you never want to be rid of it. And what about Sol? How is it with fathers? How did they bond? Automatically?

David reappears with the last of the buffet.

'Fancy a nibble.'

'Had plenty, thanks. Try Sharon. Looks like she's wasting away.'

'Not her.'

'Not me either. There's always your wife?'

'Not tonight, Josephine. Gone home already. Terrific migraine, apparently. Of course, they're always "Terrific". Always. Need a lift home later?'

'Thank you, no. I've got my car.'

'You've got the car? What's Solly driving?'

'Company vehicle. Scotland today, that's all.'

'Long drive.'

'Five hours, he reckoned.'

'Five up, five back.'

'Yes.' Something told her she shouldn't tell him too much. 'Mind out.' She edged past him. Conscious that he puffed his chest out so that their bodies touched briefly. She shuddered.

Later, as she emptied the rubbish into the recycling bins on the back patio, he was there again, smoking.

'Disgusting habit, I know.'

'Kill you, one day. Still, whatever.' She concentrated on the job at hand. He flicked the butt away and came up behind her. She turned.

'I'm crazy about you, Francesca. If only you'd give me one small sign?'

She brought her knee up sharply and caught him in the crotch.

'Oomph!' He collapsed onto the decking, grasping for something to hold onto.

'Actions speak louder than words. Okay?' She made her way inside and locked the door. Lizzie appeared in all tea cups and glasses. 'All okay, Fran?'

'Fine, thanks. Washing up stage - again!'

Lizzie peered through the kitchen door glass into the fading light. 'Is that David out there?'

'Mm. Free champagne. Seems to have a strange effect on him. He'll be okay.'

She got home late - nine pm. The night was dark, illuminated in places only by the streetlights. She unlocked the door, went inside, and locked it behind her.

In the sitting room, she drew the curtains and turned the thermostat up a little. It was going to be a cold night. She checked her phone for a message from Solly, but still nothing. He was in a different country, so maybe things were different there: bandwidths, connections, and so on. No need to worry.

The doorbell rang - she'd almost known it would. She unlocked and opened the door, almost hiding behind its great oaken weight.

It was David.

'Hello again. The car's playing up, and my phone's dead. Any chance I could use yours?'

She could smell the alcohol on his breath but felt she could control the situation.

'Sure. Right here. Close the door. It's freezing out.'

The telephone was on a small hall table with an empty vase. Directory and Yellow Pages below. Although, who used them anymore?

'Thanks.'

'Bit out of your way?'

'Dropped Sharon off. Husband drunk - went off without her.'

She closed the door behind him, wondering why later.

He fiddled with the telephone as though he had never seen one before.

'Come here. There's a trick to it.'

In one movement, he grabbed her and pushed her to the floor. She banged her head on the bottom carpeted stairs. He held her down on her back. He pulled her down flat, put his hand up her t-shirt, and caressed a breast. His hands were cold.

'My turn now.' he leered. 'Beautiful, beautiful. Lovely pair of tits, Francesca. Both are the same size. Makes a change. Most women have a larger breast on their heart side. What are you? Thirty-six? Thirty-eight? B? Oh yeah, you're a B, alright. B for busty, B for breast, B for beautiful. Let's get that brassiere off you.'

'No! Don't you dare touch me! I'll never forgive you!'

'You'll be alright once we get going. They say that once you've been raped by a man, you develop a fondness for him.'

'You're going to rape me?' It helped to put it into words - she'd heard that, too.

'Crazy about you, Franny.'

'Don't call me that!'

'Call you what I want now, can't I? Now you've invited me in.'

'I'll scream! I'll scream the house down!'

'Go ahead. Insulation's sufficient, I should say. Solly's a sensible man. He calls you "Franny", doesn't he. Heard him call you that before. Is that his special name for you? Still, he's no use to you up in Scotland, is he? Come on, get your clothes off, and let's look at you.'

'Get off me, you bastard! You're drunk!'

'Yes, call me names. That's exciting. The damsel in distress.'

She tried to get hold of his arms or his hands to keep them off her. 'How much fun can this be!' she wailed, desperate for anything to say. 'How will you live with yourself after this?'

'Doesn't matter, Franny. All that matters is now. There's no yesterday. No tomorrow. Just here and now. I've finally got you where I want you. It'll grow on you. Oh my! Feel how I've grown on you already! We'll travel, I've got money. We'll see the world. I'll make you love me. Let's have those knickers off.' He put his hands up her skirt. 'Love you in a skirt. Long, sexy legs. Beautiful. Skin like a peach. Never see the sun. Smooth as silk.'

Her knee was still tender after the last time, so she used the other, with some success.

'Oomph!'

On the table was the Waterford vase, a present from her Mother. She grabbed it quickly with one hand and smashed it on the back of his head. It splintered, glass everywhere! He made no further noise.

With her remaining strength, she pushed him off her. He lay unconscious. Blood seeped from the wound she had given him. Maybe she'd found an artery?

She crawled to the phone, pulling her skirt back down as she did so. The last number redial was Lizzie.

'Lizzie? It's Fran. Can you come round?'

'Oh! Bit pissed, honey. That cheap champagne! Rodney's all over me!'

'I know. I'm on the floor here.'

'What's up?'

'It's David. He tried to rape me. I think I've killed him.'

Pots of tea were made and drunk. Lizzie sat with Fran on the sofa. The ambulance siren faded away. A WPC perched on the armchair, taking notes.

'You shouldn't be alone tonight. Is there someone?'

'Her other half is away on business. I will be back Tuesday, but I'll stay with her for now. That okay, honey?'

Fran nodded. 'Yes, of course. Thanks, Liz.'

'No problem.'

'So,' said the policewoman. 'You definitely did nothing to encourage the man.'

Lizzie was affronted. 'Why is that a question? A woman must make herself plain and unattractive for her own safety? Ridiculous!'

"Sorry. Have to ask. Just the routine. Once all the facts are gathered, there's little more we can do.'

'Thanks. I feel so much safer now!' said Lizzie.

'Just telling you how things are. You invite a drunken man into your own home…'

'And you expect to be raped? What nonsense!'

'It does happen. The defendant's solicitor will suggest contributory negligence. There is precedent. Provided…'

'Provided what?'

52

'I'll leave you alone now. We'll ring if there's anything further.' She gathered up a colleague and left the house.

'Provided he's still alive, she meant!' said Fran. 'Oh my God, Lizzie. I've killed him!' Her friend wrapped her arms around her. 'If you have, you have. Don't you think he deserved it? Do you want to live in a world where men and women do this to each other? Why, we might never leave the house again. Now, where will you sleep? Don't worry. I'll be here for you.'

'I want my big double bed. Feel safe there.'

'Of course.'

He stood before the officer's desk. There were no chairs.

'To the best of your knowledge,' said the uniformed man. 'Did anyone have access to your vehicle - once you had signed it out?'

Solomon thought. 'No, no. Not at all. It was all sealed up - as it should be.'

'You made no personal check of the contents?'

'No. Not required to. I was handed the manifest and the keys.'

'You made a stop on the M6 - a scheduled break. Correct?'

'Yes.'

'Did you leave the vehicle then?'

'No. Expressly forbidden to. We have a camping toilet in the cab.'

'I see. What would you say if I told you that every box on board had been opened and several cigars removed?'

Solomon frowned. 'Not sure. Is that what you're saying?'

'How about it?'

'Alright. When?'

'You tell me.'

'And then what? What would I do with them? That would amount to a small sackful of cigars, I imagine.'

'Would it, sir? Well, could always leave them at a prearranged place.'

'Wait, though! There's CCTV in all the services. You can always check.'

'Already have, sir. We knew about the CCTV. More to the point, so did you.'

'Oh.' Solomon thought. 'What about our usual driver?'

The officer consulted his notes. 'A Mr. Holman. Can't throw any light on the subject. Comes up every two weeks or so. Never a problem with us.'

'Well, I don't know what else I can say.'

'No sir. I imagine not. We'll keep you here for a while as we investigate. You'll be quite comfortable. Gets pretty cold up here this time of year, but there are plenty of blankets. Whisky in your porridge?'

She was up at first light. A cold, clear day. Some blue sky. She watered their window box on the bedroom window sill. She went downstairs, stepping over the bloodstains, which made her retch. In the living room, Lizzie snored her head off on the sofa. Fran smiled. How on Earth did Rodney put up with it? There was no news from anybody and no messages on her phone. She took her clothes, some matches, and some old newspapers for Tinder and went out into the back garden.

The policewoman rang the bell, and Lizzie answered it. She was the same one as the day before. They entered the sitting room, and Lizzie showed her to the armchair.

Francesca came in from the garden.

'Brrr. Nippy out.' she said. 'Shall I make some tea?'

'No thanks. Come and sit with your friend.'

Fran didn't like the sound of that.

The WPC held out her hand, flat. 'How did you sleep?' she asked solicitously.

'Badly.'

'Okay. First of all, the man's not too bad.'

'Hah!' said Lizzie.

'I meant physically. Made it through the night. He is still unconscious, but doctors are monitoring his progress. At least he's alive.'

'Thank God.'

'Bastard.' said Lizzie.

'One hell of a blow you caught him.' said the officer.

'You can tell by all the blood.' said Lizzie. 'I'll have to get the Vax over it later.'

'No.' said Francesca. 'I want it out of here. Gone. All the blood and everything.'

'Have to wait for forensics first, I'm afraid. They'll be finished today.'

'What happens now?' asked Lizzie.

'Depends on his reaction.'

'If he lives.'

The officer gave Lizzie a hard stare. As if to say, "You're not helping much." 'Quite. Technically, in the eyes of the law, you assaulted him. He's entitled to a lawyer. Usually, they are the first line of defense. Counter-claim.'

'Absolute crap!' said Lizzie, unable to contain herself.

'I agree with you. Still, it'll depend on their approach. Whether they want to press charges or not.'

'Never mind them!' said Fran. '*I* want to press charges. Attempted rape. The bastard had half my clothes off me. In my own home! I'm not having someone coming into my home and attacking me. No way!'

'As I say, technically, it's an assault case. What you have to do is prove otherwise.'

'Prove?' said Fran, aghast.

'Think of it like this: You're in a court of law. You are asked whether you invited him in. Whether you were both at a party with alcoholic drinks earlier that afternoon. You can see the way the case could turn.'

'I refuse to see myself as a case! Surely the law is for people's protection?'

'So it is. But there are always complicated cases. I've seen it before a hundred times. Still, if you want to press charges, there are a few things we need to do first.'

'Like what?'

'The clothes you were wearing. We'll need all of those.'

'That's out.'

'Oh? Why?'

'Because, first thing this morning, I gathered them all up, took them out into the back garden, poured petrol over them, and set fire to them! My favourite skirt too!' She burst into tears. Lizzie wrapped her arms around her friend and let her cry.

The WPC looked out of the window at the back garden. Smoke was still rising. 'Okay. Fair enough. I'll get them picked up anyway. Never know; it might establish something. Have you heard from your partner yet?'

Francesca shook her head. 'Not yet, no.'

'Sometimes, in those places, they prohibit phones. Or the signal's terrible. Had an old girlfriend up there once who I could never get hold of. It could just be that. Phone his work. They should know what's what.'

'Okay. Thanks.'

Lizzie sprang up. 'Time for tea? Feel sure we've all earned one.'

'Why not?'

'Lousy job you have to do,' said Lizzie.

'I know. Never get used to it. Some men are such bastards. Particularly with a drink inside them.'

Solomon's door opened.

'Free to go, pal.'

'Really?'

'Get all your stuff together.'

'What happens next?'

'Not much. We'll report to both sides, and they'll make inquiries. Seems to me that someone at your end was light-fingered. Could have been at it for years. As long as the weights are the same at both ends, who's to know? Not for me to say, of course.'

'But how is it that you haven't noticed before?'

'Who knows? You're a new face. Probably pulled you just because of that. Things could have been different if we had had a salmon in it. All goes on. Just have to make the overall weight up. That's easy. Come on, off you go. Jobs to do.'

'My phone's gone flat.'

'Let's have a look? Apple. No good. We're all on Android here.'

'Is there a phone I can use?'

'Not here, no. Ask at your destination. See ya. Have a good day.'

Forensics called later on and took away a bag of ashes. Lizzie was concerned.

'You gonna be okay, honey? Rodney will be wondering what's become of me. Always said I'd leave him one day but don't want him getting the wrong idea.'

'I'll be fine, Liz. Thanks. You've been a rock.'

'Still got my number on redial. Anything you want, just call. Night or day. Okay, my love?'

Fran smiled and said okay. She waved her friend off and phoned Solomon's work.

'Mr. Chumwell?' said the receptionist. 'He's on annual leave this week. Anyone else that could help you?'

Fran didn't know. 'I'm trying to find the whereabouts of my partner. Solomon Swift. He's on a Scottish delivery, and I can't reach him.'

'Scotland? That's usually Pete Holman's job. Why the change?'

'That's why I wanted to speak to Mr. Chumwell.'

'Well, I'll ask around the despatch office. Do we have your number?'

They should have, but Fran gave it again anyway. She was tired now. Needed her bed.

In her dreams, the bastard came visiting. Quickly slipping between her sheets and holding her head back. A terrifying, vigorous dream. She woke with noisy, heartfelt sobs, her arms and legs thrashing in the darkness. Shakily, she went downstairs in the eerie silence.

'Oh, Solly, my love. Where are you?'

The only drink in the house was three-quarters of Cinzano from Christmas. Holly and ivy intermingled on the red, silver, and blue label. She curled up on their three-seater sofa, tucked her quilt around her, and drank. And slept.

On the wild road to Langholm, Solomon spied a hitchhiker. He looked cold and wet, but he was using a mobile phone. He slowed and stopped.

'Hop in!'

'Thanks. The man climbed up. 'Filthy day for it.'

'Must admit, I only stopped because I saw you on the phone. Problem with mine.'

The man handed it over.

'Help yourself.'

'Thanks.'

The man produced a pistol, a Colt forty-five. 'Leave the keys in the ignition and get out!' He grabbed his mobile phone. 'Go on, go on!'

Solomon got down onto the hard road.

'Firm never told you not to pick up hitchhikers? Feckin' eejit!' He roared off, leaving Solomon in a windswept silence. He looked around at the reeds, the weeds, and the overgrown lakes. There was the fragrant scent of heather from the heath but no signs of motion. The whole place was a wilderness. Surely there should be wildlife? Birds even? But no. Not a thing in sight. The road stretched like a black ribbon ahead of him and behind him. Solomon imagined his highwayman with the heating turned up full. He gathered his coat around him at the scruff of his neck and continued north, one careful step at a time. The surface was slippery, but he tried to concentrate on the present and let the future take care of itself. Whatever.

A car approached from the north, heading south. Having no alternative, Solomon held up his thumb.

Luckily, it was a police car.

Solomon slipped between the two uniformed officers in the back and explained his situation.

He was glad when the car stopped, turned around, and returned the way they had come at sixty to seventy mph - an easy match for the truck's top speed, a regulated fifty.

'Can't get far.' observed one. 'And as you can see, there's nowhere to pull off. Got your piece, Jim?'

'Yep. All loaded and ready to go.'

'Good. Let's see if we can make one of the bastards' days.'

They caught the truck, which pulled up at the side of the road.

'You stay in the vehicle, sir. No matter what happens.'

'Spare shooter here, Carts. Safety's off.'

'Thanks, Jimmy.' To Solomon. 'Used one of these before?'

Solomon thought back to Company hunt weekends with rifles on the Sussex downs. Grouse mainly, a few pheasants. This gun looked like a child's toy.

He nodded, then shook his head.

'Alright. Just squeeze. Always aim for a leg shot. Don't shoot to kill. Just one man was there? Absolutely sure?'

'I only saw one. He was on his own when I picked him up.'

'Generally are. Losers! Okay. C'mon Jim.'

The two officers covered each other as they approached the truck's rear. There were two large blasts. Solomon thought someone had shot the tires, but, having peered cautiously through the rear side window, he saw the two policemen, unmoving on the asphalt.

Solomon could hear the thief's slow footsteps approaching the squad car.

He swallowed hard. Come on, Solomon. Do this! One clear shot.

And yes - he shot to kill.

The criminal lay flat on his back. Blood seeping from a chest wound. Even Solomon had to admit that the man was dead. He was deader than anyone he had ever seen. He exited the car and made for the first of the two officers.

The officer, whose name wasn't Jim, wore a chest radio. 'Three-Six to base. Request backup. Possible fatality - both officers down. Perp down and killed. Urgent please. Oh, shit. Hurry, please. Three-six out.'

'Are you okay?' asked Solomon.

'Don't know yet. Know any first-aid?'

'A little.' said Solomon.

'Bastard got me in the shoulder. Knocked me out at first, but I'll survive. Needs a tourniquet. High as you can. Christ, on a bike, I'll probably freeze before help arrives. Blankets in the boot of the squad car.'

'Okay.' Solomon was as fast as he could be and soon had the man wrapped up and his wound dressed - after a fashion.'

'You didn't tell them where you were.'

'They'll know. All clever stuff these days.'

It looked like rain.

'Here.' said Solomon. 'Put your cloak over your head. I'm sure they won't be long.' 'Ouch!' He sat up a little more and rested on an elbow. 'Poor Jimmer. Always said they'd get him one day.'

The dead officer's uniform blew about him in the gathering breeze.

'Won't be long.'

'I'm sorry. I never should have stopped.'

'If wishes were ponies. Had a gun, didn't he? You'd have stopped - one way or the other.'

'Happens a lot, does it? This kind of crime?

Carter shrugged. 'Ouch! A fair bit, yes. It's all they know. Unwatched out here. Could do anything.'

'Just one man.'

'Nah, there's a gang of them. Occasionally, I get to pick one off. Like you! Today! Not that anyone will ever know, but you're a hero now.'

'Don't feel like one.' said Solomon.

Francesca had locked the door properly, but the WPC was good with locks and let herself in.

Her third visit to the house. Perhaps it is time we got to know her a little better.

Her name was Wendy. Tall and dark. Her hair was swept back in a uniform bun. There was a slight trace of make-up on her face, but nothing too excessive. Also, she had the bluest eyes.

She entered the sitting room and saw Fran tucked up under the covers. She picked up the empty bottle.

'Christmas came early, I see.' Fran opened her eyes. 'Come on, sleepy head. Let's get you up to your bed, where you belong.'

They made it to the bedroom, and Wendy ensured she was comfortable. 'Tea,' she suggested. 'I'm Wendy, by the way.'

'Good to see you.' Fran burrowed into the bedclothes. 'Tired.'

'Bound to be. Sleep, - nature's remedy.'

'Bit cold.'

'Sofa sleep. Always seems like a good idea, but there's nothing like your bed. Don't worry. You'll warm through.'

'Freezing.'

'Need a little cuddle?'

Francesca opened a weary eye. 'Are you allowed to?'

'Sure. Free country, last time I checked.'

'Oh. Okay.'

'Hold on then. Have to take the uniform off first. Black picks up everything.' She took off her tight jacket and skirt and folded them neatly on the bedside chair. She kicked off her shoes and got into the bed. 'Alright?'

'Mm. Yes. Lovely. Thanks. You've still got your tie on.'

'Man thing. Let's get rid of it.' She pulled the tie by the thicker end, and the Windsor knot became undone. She let the tie fall to the floor. 'Bat for the other side, you must know.'

'Takes all sorts.'

'Sure does. Bet you never thought you'd be curled up in bed with a half-naked lesbian policeman this morning, did you?

'Let's not talk about the past.'

'Sorry.'

'Oh!'

'What is it?'

'You've got grips in your hair. My mother used to do that.'

'Mine too.'

There was a banging at the window.

'Window cleaner.' said Fran. 'Don't worry. He uses an extending brush. He can't see anything.'

Wendy laughed. 'Nothing to see. Not yet, anyway.'

Fran laughed, too. Then:

'Wendy?'

'Yes?'

'Unbutton your blouse?'

'Okay. Hold on.'

'Look so official with it on.'

Wendy smiled. Her hair crackled static as she removed her shirt. Brassiere next. Pants and tights. Francesca gazed at her while she undressed.

'Beautiful.' she said.

'That's alright then - you are too. From what I can see.'

'Want me naked too?'

'Best way. Then we can do anything we want.'

Wendy held her friend close and eased her out of her nightdress.

They listened to the window cleaner banging away. They were quiet for a few seconds.

'Just a few minutes, and that's the end of my shift. For the rest of the day, I'm all yours.'

Francesca sighed contentedly. Light traffic rumbled by outside. It was quiet and peaceful. Wendy's watch ticked quietly.

'Alright?'

'Me? Mm, yes. You're lovely and warm.'

'Healthy living. Have you ever done anything like this before?'

'Like what?'

'This.' Wendy's hand wandered over her. All her peaks and curves.

'Oh. No. Sorry. Needed someone.'

'Only natural.'

'No. Always fancied men - since I was about fourteen. Couldn't wait to have one.'

'Shame.' They both giggled.

'Woke up one morning with my, well, with my full figure. Wondered what to do next. All the girls in my class were the

64

same. Finished school in June as stick-insects and returned in September as a young women. Drove the boys mad.'

'I'll bet. You're beautiful.'

'How about you?'

'Me? Different really. Men always seemed so rough - and hairy! Women were sweet. Softer. One of my teachers saw how awkward I was around boys and asked me to help her clean board rubbers after school one afternoon. What we did then, and there would have made the Sunday papers.'

They lay in the relative calm. Two people alone together.

'Do you use anything?'

'Mm? Oh. No. Solly disapproves. Always says, "If you want a cock, that's what I'm here for."'

'Romantic.'

'Mm. It's okay. He's my fella.'

'Do you think he'd mind? Me being here?'

'Not sure. My mind's a blur after last night. Maybe he'd be pleased that someone was here for me. When I needed somebody.'

'Sure. Fingers first, then. One…'

'Aah.'

'Then the second.'

'Oooh. That's nice. Kiss me while you're doing that.'

Wendy shifted her position. 'Oh, I'll kiss you alright.' She burrowed beneath the bedclothes. Presently, Fran felt her tongue on her - in her. Wendy's about turn had presented her nether regions before Francesca's eyes.

She licked her lips.

Later, as the Saturday sunset, they chatted amicably as they made love.

'Do you shave under your arms?' asked Fran.

'All the time.'

'Beautiful. You have lovely skin.'

'So do you.'

'Yours is so supple, so strong. Olive tones.'

'Get that a lot. Mother's from Greece.'

'Kalamata.'

'If you like.'

'Wendy?'

'Yes?'

'Would you kiss me? Not like before. Up here. Mouth to mouth. Like lovers do.'

'Love to.'

Francesca tasted like Cinzano.

'Crumwell.'

'Trying for you now… No reply, I'm afraid.' said the receptionist.

Probably out the back having a fag, thought Solomon.

'Could anyone else help?'

He couldn't think of anyone.

'Can I leave him a message?'

'Yes, I should think so. Hang on, I'll get a pencil… Right, carry on.'

'Can I just say, Please contact Francesca and tell her I've got no phone, but I'll be home on Tuesday as planned.'

'As planned… Right, you are. Thanks.'

Solomon replaces the telephone on its ancient-looking handset. Smelled of Bakelite.

The policeman placed a mug of tea on the counter.

'Get that down you. Good for shock.'

Solomon grasped the mug gratefully. 'Thanks.' He sipped the hot tea.

'Get through alright?'

'Not really. Left a message. That'll do. What's next, then? Any more statements?'

'No. You've said everything. Carter's tucked up in his hospital bed. Chances are he'll be flirting with nurses before you can look around. Gotta phone his wife later - she'll be livid. As for poor Jim - he always was a glutton for punishment. Full honours for the funeral, I guess.' He looked at his shoes. 'Better polish up best boots.'

'What about the murdered man?'

'The killer? What about him? Piece of shit. Shouldn't think he'll be missed. Believe you me, pal. I don't know how things are down in England, but here? Won't even make the evening news.'

'But, but, what about me? I killed a man!'

'Prove it. There's nothing there anymore. Everything tidied up.' The officer shook his head. 'Think of it like this - like waste disposal. Go on and enjoy your life. A split second later, it could have been you. Be grateful for the things you should be grateful for. We're all a long time dead.'

'But what about justice? Law enforcement?'

'What about them? Look at it like this: You thought you were doing the right thing. It was him or you. Correct?'

'Well… yes. I guess.'

'Never gonna brag about it, are you?'

Loaded question.

'Well, no.'

'Or tell your wife?'

'She's not my wife. Not yet.'

'Gonna tell her?'

'I don't think so.'

'Think about it. Come on, then. You have to get your truck to its destination. We'll follow on behind. You're a prime target now, so we'd better keep an eye on you.'

'A target?'

'Figure of speech.'

'How far is it?'

'Ten miles, give or take.'

'Okay.'

Wendy gave her the present.

'Got you a gift.'

Fran opened the bag. 'Levi's! Wow! Thanks.'

'As blue as your eyes.' They smiled at each other. 'Kind of a parting gift, really.'

'Oh?'

'Husband will be back home soon.'

'He's not my husband. Not yet, anyway.'

'You know what I mean. Snap him up, Fran. You're clearly crazy about him - no matter what might have happened.'

'What about us?'

Wendy shook her head. 'There's no us. I was there when you needed me; I'm glad about that. Time we moved on.' She stood up. 'Breakfast in bed? Bacon, eggs. Tea and a slice?'

'Lovely.'

'You're lovely. I shall miss you. Little did you know it, but you were there for me too.'

'I'm glad. Sorry to see you go.'

Wendy shrugged. 'Life goes on.'

'Such is life. We're forever saying goodbyes.'

'Or wishing we could.'

'Well, yes. From time to time. Take us for instance.'

'Thought there wasn't an us.'

'Say there was? On the one hand, we have all of these happy memories…'

'And on the other?'

'Who knows? That's the difficult part of relationships. It's like trying to bake the perfect cake.'

'A cake? How so?'

'You try to stick to the ingredients - the recipe. But any new, unknown thing makes a mess of it all.'

Fran chuckled at something in her mind. Then, 'I will miss you.'

'Could you always come with me?'

'Always? No, no, dear thing. That can never be. We may have made the perfect cake, but that was then, and this is now. Besides, you hardly know anything about me.'

'Ah, well. No time to miss you anyway. Going to Colchester next week - for a month or so. Firearms training.'

'Firearms?'

'Training. This could lead to a promotion. One never knows.'

'Why Colchester?'

'Army town. Barracks, I guess. Empty spaces. Who knows? A few weeks away in any case.'

'Keep in touch? Write?'

'I'll message you. Easily deleted afterwards.'

'Good plan. It mustn't be caught. Ha ha! Sound like a criminal.'

'Don't worry. Good policewoman, me. I'll make sure there's no evidence.

'Where will you stay?'

'In the wilds of Essex. Old barracks up there. Dormitory. All girls together.'

'Sounds like fun. All Essex girls.'

'Could be. Hard work, too.'

'What could you be promoted to?'

'Sergeant, at first. Then I could go anywhere. A colleague of mine ended up in Gibraltar. Sends postcards every now and then. Apes and grapes.'

'We have a station over there? Or precinct. What d'you call them?'

'Small one, yes. Still, size isn't everything.'

'No.'

'These sheets could do with a good wash.'

'So could you, my dear. So could you.'

'It's alright, I can do it. You'd better get off. Got people coming in a bit.'

'People?' said Wendy suspiciously.

'My friend Lizzie. You met her earlier.'

'Oh yes.'

Near the river Esk at Longtown, Solomon had a reasonably good night's sleep at the local hotel and then continued his morning journey.

Sunday, and the sun shone weakly. Always in his mind was the knowledge that he had killed a man, but it didn't seem that anybody else thought of it as a crime. All authorities had been informed, but further action was not envisaged, so Solomon had decided that the best thing for him to do was to complete his journey.

The warehouse supervisor did not seem at all surprised to see him. Here and there, men in overalls toiled away at their various activities, and pages were turned and discarded neatly. Commerce thrived. The truck was parked, and the supervisor approached the cab, hand and arm extended.

'Keys?'

Solomon was getting used to this. Still…

'What do you want my keys for?'

'Listen, friend - so you'll know next time. When the vehicles are being unloaded, the last thing we want is that they should move.' He jangled the keys that Solomon had handed him. 'Easiest way. Besides, I dare to say you'll want a hot cup.'

He nodded toward the tea counter a few yards away. Solomon agreed.

'That's the spirit. A quick gasp of tea, and we'll have you on your way. Back to England tonight?'

' Hopefully.'

'Speedy Carpets?' said the man. It sounded so on the van. Lizzie nodded and let the two of them in.

'My friend's house, but don't worry,' she said. 'I know what's needed. It's just the hallway. I've taken the old carpet out and bunged it in the car boot - forgot it was a Sunday and the recyclers aren't open yet.'

'We'll take it if you like? Got a few to get rid of. Of course, it all goes to landfill.'

'Is that right? No, no. No need. Going that way later, anyway. Garden stuff. Same every Sunday.'

'Lady said online she didn't care about the pattern. Anything would do.'

'That's right. Anything at all as long as it's speedy.'

'Got kids, has she?'

Solomon turned the key in his own front door. Home at last.

After miles and miles of lanes and cones and flashing lights and signs, he was relieved to be back.

At least, he thought he was back. A strange sight met his eyes:

Here and there, Piglet frolicked with Roo while Kanga looked on with a benign smile. Rabbit, wearing glasses, was reading a book. Eeyore wandered sulkily back to his new house behind the old oak tree. Overhead, Winnie the Pooh, supported by half a dozen helium-filled balloons, surveyed the neighborly scene, clutching a pot of honey. It was a blustery day.

She stood at the sitting room door. 'It was all they had.'

He took off his coat and hung it on its peg. 'Okay.'

He took off his coat and hung it on its peg. 'Okay.' He closed the front door and followed her in. She sat at one end of the sofa, which left room for him on the other side. He stretched his aching muscles.

'Long drive.'

'I'll sleep down here tonight. Got a bit of a headache.'

He shook his head.

'No, no. That's okay. You go on, and I'll grab a quilt from under the stairs. I know you love your bed. Once my phone is recharged - blasted- you'll be able to call if you want anything.'

'Thanks.' She gathered up her quilt from beside her and headed out. 'Goodnight.'

'Goodnight.'

'Glad your home.'

'Me too.'

He gave her a minute while she shuffled up the stairs.

Then, he removed his shoes and stole across the sitting room and out into the hall. He reasoned that the door to the cupboard under the stairs was difficult to move over the new Disney carpet, but it would be okay in time.

He found a continental quilt left from their camping excursions all over Dorset and, three or four times - the ferry to France. After closing the door, he crept back with the duvet into the sitting room.

It wasn't too dark yet, and the trip hadn't taken too long - even with the compulsory breaks. Returning the truck to the works was effortless, too. All you had to do was place the keys in the Key Bin.

He left the curtains, pulled back, and lay on the sofa - his head at her end. He could still smell the scent of her.

He wrapped the quilt around himself and fell asleep.

She felt guilty about sleeping alone, but for some reason, she didn't want him near her for now. Maybe that would pass - she hoped so. He must be exhausted from being stuck in the truck for the best part of four days. Was that right? Let's see: Friday, Saturday, Sunday. It was Sunday night now - he was early. She vaguely wondered why. Her hero, Solomon, was probably better at the job than his predecessor. She expected that was so. He always seemed to be better than anyone else - her hero. He was probably asleep by now, and, whatever the way, they could talk tomorrow. She couldn't help how she felt. Tomorrow, they would both be less tired. News from the hospital hadn't cheered her, but she tried not to think about it. She thought about her new carpet - dear Lizzie. She closed her eyes and told herself to sleep well.

Monday morning.

Solomon awoke without opening his eyes. In his mind, he replayed the events of the previous four days. He shivered and wished he had a time machine.

He opened his eyes and saw that the morning light had filled the room. He reached for his phone from the coffee table and saw it had been safely recalled to life. There were no messages from anyone. It was ten twenty-eight am.

He assumed that Fran had gone off to work without waking him. Sobeit. He stood up slowly and stretched his legs. Grabbing the remote control from the coffee table, he turned on the radio. It crackled. Fran had it tuned to Greatest Hits FM again; bless her. He selected his preset and found the Radio Five live news "Headlines at the top of the hour!" He didn't expect to hear anything about what had happened up in Scotland, but at the same time, he wouldn't want to be the last to know.

He wandered over to the rear window and looked out. Somebody had been lighting fires on his lawn.

He opened the French windows and padded out onto the slabbed area - one day, they would make this into a conservatory.

The lawn edged the patio - their lawn! His and hers. He remembered leveling the ground, raking away all weekend. Francesca's delight at every stone she found and hurled away to the rocky area at the end of the garden. He remembered the seeding: Scotts Turf Builder. They liked the sound of that.

So, why - in this corner, nearest the house, had somebody lit a fire? He looked at the remains. Newspaper folded into paper logs - something Fran had learned at Girl Guides.

Okay, so what had she been burning? Barbecue? In November? Unlikely.

What then?

He didn't know. It seemed that something must have happened. She had been cagey the night before. Not like her at all. So, who could he ask?

He returned to the house, across the sitting room, onto the Pigletty carpet, picked up the telephone, and pressed LR.

Fran reassured herself at her office with comparatively safe and familiar surroundings. She didn't have much to do. In her tidy-minded way, they were all up to speed with who would say what to whom. Occasionally, her email would beep, but everything was under control. Her control. The photocopier needed paper again, and Shona had called in sick – again, but everything else was ordered and sorted.

Her mind wandered. She looked out of the grey, rain-streaked windows to the buildings opposite. All of us doing the same old thing every day. There was no alternative.

Unless her rational mind queried, unless we break free of society's conventions and do whatever we want to do?

Like what? She wondered. Force your way into a woman's house and defile her?

She was doing it again - dwelling on something that belonged in the past. Something that she should - and would, move on from.

But what if he dies?

What if he does? That was the answer. Good riddance to bad rubbish. She wouldn't want her friends to be attacked like she had been. Perish the thought. Lizzie, for instance. Lizzie had been half-cut when Fran had telephoned her. If the bastard had picked her instead, she doubted there would have been much resistance.

Yes, but the bastard had picked her because she'd told him Solomon was away in Scotland...

'Post!' The boy woke her from her reverie.

'Late again, fella.'

'Better I should come late than not at all.' came the retort.

'Yeah? Who says so?'

He disappeared with a cheery wave.

Okay. Post.

'Lizzie.'

'Hello, Solomon.' She pointed downwards. 'Sorry about the carpet.'

'Not a problem. You get used to it. Come in.'

She stepped in. He closed the door and took her coat. Although she knew the way, he showed her down the hall to the sitting room.

'You do it too.' he said.

She turned in the doorway. 'Do what?'

'Walk so as you don't step on their faces. I've been doing it all morning. Some kind of childhood subconscious thing, I guess.'

'There's no Wol.'

'What?'

'No Wol. The owl. The name was Wol, wasn't it?'

Solomon thought for a moment. 'Yes, I believe it was.'

On the coffee table, a cafetière was cooling. He sat beside her and poured two cups.

'Thanks. You should put in a complaint.'

'I could. So could Fran. It was her idea.'

'Of course.'

'Elizabeth,' (So she knew he was serious. No one ever called her Elizabeth, except her mother. Lizzie hated it.) 'It's just that, I go away for three days and come back to find she's in an odd mood. She hardly said a word to me; she wanted to sleep here. I sent her to bed because she loves it up there. Woke up this morning to find she'd gone off to work. No notes, no messages, no nothing. Made me wonder - have I missed something?'

'I don't know. I don't think so.'

'And you'd know. That's what I thought. Any idea why she's been lighting fires on the back lawn?'

Even though she was wearing full make-up, Solomon said she blanched.

'No, none at all. It could have been something that had gone off. I do that sometimes. Just don't want it in the food waste, attracting rats and gulls. Far easier to burn it.'

'No. Fran's too green for anything like that. And why there? We've spent months on that lawn. And why the new carpet? Alright, the old one was worn and probably needed to be replaced, and maybe she thought she'd do it while I was away as a kind of surprise, but it didn't seem like that, judging by the look on her face. "It was all they had," she said. What did she mean by that?'

'I don't know, Sol. I wasn't here. There was a sign on the van, but who reads it? Something carpets.'

'No doubt.'

'It'll be on her internet history?'

'No good. Separate pads - golden rule. I don't know what's on hers, and she doesn't know what's on mine. Well, every couple has to have some secrets, right?'

'Is that why you called me?'

'Of course. You're her bestie. And you were on the last-number redial. Knew you would be. Oh, that reminds me. The vase has gone too.'

'Vase? What vase.'

'Waterford vase. Expensive. Gift from her mother. It lives on the telephone table. Not there now. Hardly ever use it in any case. Might pick up some cheap flowers from the supermarket sometimes. Always makes her laugh. Sometimes, anyway.'

'Perhaps she broke it? Or the carpet fitters?'

'Waterford doesn't break easily.'

'Well, perhaps she got fed up with it.' reasoned Lizzie. 'Carpet's gone. Why not the vase, too?'

'Looked the price up on the internet when we got it. Over two hundred pounds. Not the sort of thing you'd just throw away.'

'Well, maybe she sold it. The best thing is to ask her.' Lizzie spilled coffee down her blouse. 'Oh! Nuts! Doesn't matter. Okay, can I just put it on a quick wash in your machine? Gotta be quick with coffee.'

'Sure. Go ahead.'

'Thanks.'

She disappeared out into the kitchen and reappeared wearing his bathrobe.

'Alright, if I slip into this?' she asked. 'Don't want me sitting there half-dressed, do you?'

'Not half-dressed, no. Sorry. Joke.'

She gave a little laugh and sat down again. 'Mmm, smells like you - Brut and Old spice. Where were we?'

He shrugged. 'Just saying that nothing has happened in the last three days that we are aware of. I wonder if it's her time?'

'Could be that, could be that. What with the two of you trying for a baby. Estragon levels all over the place.'

'Maybe.'

'Maybe it is right. I'm sure it's that. I was the same.'

'But we've only just started trying.'

'Only takes one.'

'True. Trying to remember when her last one was now. I can always tell. A moody lot, you girls.'

'But we're not girls anymore. We're women.'

'The pair of you.'

'What?'

'What do you mean, "What?"? I mean, you are now women and not girls.'

'Oh. I thought you meant…'

'What?'

'Oh, you know. Here's me sitting next to you in my prettiest brassiere, and you're saying things like, "The pair of you." What's a girl to think?'

'You're not a girl anymore. You're a woman.'

'That's right. I am, aren't I? A full-figured, vibrant, sexy woman.' She took off his robe. 'In her prettiest brassiere.'

He nodded. 'Yes, that is pretty.'

Kissing's okay, she thought. A little kissing would take his mind off things.

'Kissing's okay.' she said softly. 'As long as I don't get lipstick over everything.'

'Everything?'

'Everything…'

'Hi, bestie….. yes, not too bad. Thought I'd better come in….. No, nothing at all, thanks. Can always pop across the road if there's anything….. No. Got a bit to do but nothing too strenuous….. "Drinkies"? It's funny to hear you call them that….. Yes, that'd be nice….. Oh, about four o'clock, I should think. Where are we heading?….. Belisaro's? Fine….. Okay. See you at four. Bye!'

'There now.' said Lizzie. 'Now we know she's at work. We can do anything we want.'

'Only one thing I want to do,' he said huskily.

'I know. Hold on. I need to get ready. Just unhook me. Off to the floor with you, pretty bra. Mama has other fish to fry. Don't worry. I'll pick you up later.' To Solomon: 'Smashing pair of tits, eh? Go on, then. Cop a feel. I bet you've always wanted to.' He took her in his hands. 'Can tell sometimes. That barbecue at mine a few summers ago. I was washing up, and you came up behind me. I was only in my swimsuit. All the rest were playing badminton on the lawn. "Go on then!" I thought. "Now's your chance! Never get a better one! We're all pissed anyway." And now look at us!'

'God, Lizzie. Your breasts are fabulous.'

'I know. Always have been, even at school. All the boys wanted to see or to feel. I used to charge them. In the girls' toilets at break times, they all knew which cubicle I was in. All knew my number. Never anything dirty, though. All too young back then. Didn't know what went where. Don't have that problem anymore, do we? Go on, get my jeans off. Take it all off. Then you can see everything.'

'You sure this is what you want to do?'

'I am naked, Sol. What do you think? I can feel that your friend wants to play. Hey, it's okay. Our other halves aren't here and will never know about this. Call it a one-off. But make sure you enjoy it. I'm certainly going to. That's it, that's it. Oh my! She said you were huge. Slide your robe under me. That way, it'll all be soaked up if I leak everywhere.'

'Do you think you will?'

'Frankly, my lover, I'd be terribly disappointed if I didn't.'

At the hospital, the doctors compared notes.

'Lost a lot of blood, I see.'

'Almost too much.'

'We'll see. Still picking glass splinters out of the wound. Is that the wife over there?'

'Think so, yes. Having a word?'

'Best to, I think.'

The doctor made his way across the ward to the woman.

'I'm awfully sorry…' he began.

Jessica, David's wife, shrieked.

'Sorry.' continued the doctor. 'I was only going to say that you can't wait here. Let me take you through to the waiting area.'

They walked slowly, his hand supporting her at her elbow. She seemed a little unsteady. Shock or drink? He couldn't tell. It didn't much matter.

'Will he be alright?' she asked. 'What happened?'

'What happened, I couldn't tell you. You'll have to ask the police. It's useless for me to speculate. As to your first question, it's too soon to say. I don't want to discourage you, but what's needed now is time.'

'Time, the great healer.' she quoted.

'Quite. Come see us all tomorrow, and we'll see where we are. Is there someone with you?'

'No. I don't have anyone. It's just him and me!' She burst into tears.

'There must be a friend you can call?' he suggested.

She thought. Friends. Yes.

'Thank you, doctor.'

'This never happened. Right? Right?'

'Right.'

Belisaro's was the latest hot spot. Previously a disregarded boozer, with blackboards displaying food and drink recipes in colored chalk and Italian Renaissance music playing softly in the background, it had become the place to be and be seen.

Fran sat at a two-seater table and waited. She looked at the time on her phone. A little after four, but Lizzie was always late for everything.

The table was old. Not quite the antique it pretended to be, its edging was a clover leaf pattern around the circular top. A waiter approached.

'Can I get you something?' Drinking at the bar was not encouraged.

'Not just yet.' said Fran. 'I'm waiting for a friend.'

The waiter bowed slightly and mooched off elsewhere.

Lizzie appeared, laden down with shopping bags - as usual. She went through the developing crowd and got to the table, where she unburdened herself.

'Sorry. Sorry. Crowds and queues everywhere - it can't be Christmas yet. I thought everybody shopped online these days? Anyhoo, sorry again. How are you? Everything okay?'

'Yes. Not too bad. Made it through the day.'

'Good, good. Best way. Try to get back to normal.'

The waiter reappeared. 'Can I get you something?'

'Ah! Yes, please. We'll have a bottle of Prosecco. And two glasses.'

He nodded curtly and disappeared into the fray.

'Alcohol?' asked Fran. 'At four in the afternoon?'

'Be good for you, honey. Get a little fizz up your nose, why not?'

'Meant to say when we spoke earlier. I phoned the hospital.'

'Okay.'

'Just to see if there was any change.'

'Aha.'

'Said there was no change. It's too soon to tell. Wondered who I was, if you please!'

'Harsh.' agreed Lizzie. 'Still, I don't suppose they have to tell everyone who rings in how each and every patient is, do they?'

'I suppose not.'

They were quiet for a few moments. The waiter brought their order and departed without a word.

'Don't teach them much English.' said Lizzie. "Can I get you something?" is all he knows. How do places like this catch on?'

'It'll be somewhere else in a month or so. So it goes.'

'So it does. Nice waiter, though. I'll bet I could teach him some dirty words.'

Fran smiled. 'You're terrible, you are.' she said. 'One of these days, you'll get caught.'

Lizzie leaned back, took a large swig, and swallowed it. 'Oh, no. Not me, honey. They'll never catch me.'

Solomon went for a walk. The girls had said "Drinkies," which meant an all-afternoon, early evening session. Probably a taxi home, too.

He walked his usual route. From his home, out along the city streets, and around the block. His favourite walk. He looked at his watch. Four thirty-five and nearly dark already. Roll on the spring.

He found himself gathering his thoughts. This afternoon with Lizzie - of course. Never to be repeated, afternoon fun. Lovely.

The events of the Scotland trip, too - beginning to fade. It all seemed like a bad dream now.

He turned the corner. This street had a park on the opposite side. Its green spaces are lit with autumnal light. Winter soon.

This site had been planted with horse chestnut trees. Imported at great expense from Norway a couple of years ago. If he remembered correctly. The road had been closed for two days.

Of course, children didn't play with conkers anymore - they weren't allowed them in schools and probably had enough battery-controlled equipment in their homes to occupy their thoughts. Maybe all that would change one day, but for now, the street was littered with fruits or nuts, making it slippery. Alright, he could gently kick them aside for him, but it was a different story for other street-users. Maybe the council should detail someone to sweep the pavements every day.

One day, yeah.

He turned the next corner. There is nothing here but parked cars in front of terraced houses. Here and there, a net curtain fluttered. People with nothing else to do but watch other people.

He was filled with a sudden fatalism. Where will it all end? He thought. What does it all mean? If anything? Having no answers, he thought about Lizzie's breasts instead. Ah!

Men and breasts. What was the attraction? Was it simply that it was something that man had been forbidden from? Knowing man, that was usually the way. Tell a man he couldn't have something, and he would do everything in his power or control to get it, take it, own it, and possess it.

Women weren't quite the same. Although, given the daily shouts for equality from all sides, Solomon guessed that a man's appendage would be as widely seen as a woman's uncovered boobs in fifty years.

And then what? Eh?

He turned the final corner.

David's car was parked halfway along. 'Hello.' he thought. 'Looks like I have visitors.'

David wasn't a friend - just the husband of one of Fran's friends. It's funny how they all came to be together. The women were all friends - had been for years, through school, work, or college. As they accumulated husbands or lovers, the men were welcomed into the group without hesitation or judgment. Odd really.

He made it to his gate, but there was no sign of David. Maybe he was visiting somebody else? He turned the key in his front door and was again greeted by the Pigletty carpet. Where was Wol? He smiled.

Turning to the telephone, he dialed a number from memory. A female voice answered.

'Hello?'

'Jessie? It's Solomon. How are you?'

'Solomon? What do you mean, "How's you"? How do you think I am?'

'Okay.' He knew that Jessica was a lush - they all knew. Evidently, she had started early today. 'Just wanted a quick word with David.'

'David?' she said tremulously.

'David. Yes. Is he there?'

'No, of course he isn't!'

'Oh. Okay. His car's parked just along from me, but there's no sign of him. Just wondered. He'll turn up. Thanks. Sorry.'

He could hear her loud sobs as he disconnected. Hell, he'd have to go round there now.

Despite the cold, he opened the front door and waited to see if his friend would attend. He knew it was David's car - he recognised the number plate. David had purchased a personalized thing for himself at a cost of two thousand pounds. Solomon remembered David turning up at the cricket match with it, grinning from ear to ear.

What then? If David was visiting somebody else, he wouldn't be all night about it. It could be a client; it could just be that. And Jessie's tears didn't count for much. Every chance, she'd been curled up on the sofa with a black and white movie and a bottle of Martini.

He'd give it an hour.

But an hour later, there were no further developments. Solomon put on his shoes and walked down the Pigletty carpet to the front door. He opened it. An icy blast whipped in. He pulled on a coat and hat and walked the short way to where David's car was parked.

Still was. Must be one hell of a client.

Maybe not, though. It may have been stolen and abandoned here. Just a coincidence?

He looked at the houses all about. Tried every door of the car, but they were all locked. Made an abandonment seem unlikely. What thief or joyrider would stop and lock the doors?

What then?

He returned to the house with the Pigletty carpet and stood by the telephone. Either David would be back wondering where his car was. Or…

Or, he was "entertaining "another sort of client. A near-neighbor of Solomon's?

Or…

Or Jessica would be flat-out drunk on the sofa and wouldn't answer the telephone. Or…

There weren't any more Or's. Fran and Lizzie wouldn't return soon, so that was no help. Why not just pop around? Could say he was just passing…

Jessica opened the door and fell into Solomon's arms.

'Easy there. Steady. Come on. Let's get you inside. It's freezing out here.'

They stepped into the house. Her eyes were black with mascara tears.

'Jess.' he said. 'Can I get you something? Coffee?'

She nodded. 'Please.'

He went to the kitchen. It was a bigger and, therefore, better house than his. David had done well. Great place great car, good job, trophy wife. Solomon thought about this as he poured her coffee. Yes, she would have been presentable ten years ago. Not much to look at at the moment, but it was clear she was upset about something. There was no sign of David, but her appearance didn't suggest a movie show. Maybe a bust-up?

He returned to the living room, where she sat on the sofa with tissues.

'Here you go. Nice and strong.'

'Thank you.' she said. 'Ooh, that is strong.'

'Do you good.' he tried.

She sipped her coffee. 'Hot.'

'Yeah. Sorry. Not used to the machine. Should make them all the same, shouldn't they?'

She nodded. Then, thoughtfully: 'Did you say David's car is round at yours?'

'Yes. Know it anywhere. From the license plate.'

'Oh. That. Ridiculous.'

'Just assumed he'd come round to see me. Had a second look, but there was no sign of him. You sounded upset on the phone, so I thought I'd come round and see if you were okay. Fran and Lizzie are out for "Drinkies," so all I had planned was a quiet evening.'

'"Drinkies,"' she said, smiling.

'Thought, maybe he has a client round there. Do you have a mobile for him?'

The tears started again. He took the cup from her while she reached for the tissues and sobbed.

After a while, she looked at him. 'You don't know, do you?'

'Know what?' So, he was right. A bust-up.

But, no.

'David's in hospital.' she said. 'Badly beaten up. We don't know by whom. He's not conscious, lost a lot of blood. Who knows what happened?' She thought for a moment. 'Why is his car round at yours?'

He shook his head. 'Couldn't tell you. I've been away in Scotland for the last three days. Don't know what's been going on.'

'Three days. That's right. You weren't at Gilly's christening party, were you?'

'No.'

'Well, I say Gilly's. It wasn't hers; it was her child's. Can't think of the name now. Doesn't really matter.' She thought. 'Fact is, I was at the party. So was David. Must admit I got a bit slewed, and he called a taxi to bring me home.'

'Okay.'

'Where does that leave him though? That's the last I saw of him. Next thing I know, the police are calling me, saying he's been "Injured in an attack." And now you say that his car is parked around at yours. What would be the reason for that, do you think?'

'He's not parked outside of mine. Just nearby.'

'Well, he would be, wouldn't he? He wouldn't park right outside. Too obvious for the cheating sod! Did he know you were away?'

'What are you saying?'

'Oh, don't mind me. Just thinking aloud. I know David. This is exactly the sort of thing that he would do.'

'Do what? What are you talking about?'

'Oh, don't tell me - Fran's not the type. Wouldn't do anything to jeopardize the relationship the two of you have. Perfect couple, aren't you?'

'Look, listen, let's not go jumping to conclusions. Maybe he was a bit drunk and parked there. Maybe wanted a lift home. From me. Or Fran. Nothing to suggest anything else went on.'

'No?'

'No.'

'Nothing untoward at home? Bedroom not smelling of something it shouldn't? More glasses in the dishwasher than the usual one? Those kinds of things? Anything?'

Of course, Solomon was thinking about the Waterford vase and the Pigletty carpet. And the lawn...

'Believe you me, Solomon. These things happen all the time. Sometimes without people even noticing.' She inched closer to him. 'Could even happen between the two of us.' She untied her dressing gown, revealing her naked breasts. 'Nice, huh? David says they're my best feature. Don't like them myself; they are all fat and pink. Don't like the way they hang.' She stood up and let the gown drop to the floor. Beneath it, she was naked. She made for his lap and settled down. 'What do you think, Solly? Do you think my teeth are nice? Say "Yes," and I'll let you make love me - right here! Right now. Oooh, right now!'

He kissed her.

Kissing's okay. It didn't mean anything...

'Good news!' said Lizzie. 'Guess what? He lives upstairs. What a bit of luck.'

'How's that lucky?' asked Fran.

'Well, don't you see, silly? This means I don't have to go back to his place. His place is here.' She drained the last glass of Prosecco. They'd both had half the bottle each. 'Come on. He's nearly finished his shift. Could you bring the bags up?'

'Me?'

'Of course you. I'm not going to leave you sitting here like a wallflower. What kind of bestie would do that?'

'But, what will I be doing while you and him are... you know?'

'Sure, we'll think of something, honey. Come on.'

She flitted off to a side door. In her work shoes, Fran followed behind and climbed bare wooden stairs. By the time she got up there, Lizzie and the waiter were both naked - sprawled on a single bed in a sparsely-furnished bare room and giggling at each other.

'Thanks, honey.' said Lizzie. 'Brun says you can sit on the chair and watch.' She indicated an upright chair by the door. Fran sat on it, placing the shopping bags behind her against the wall.

'What am I watching?' she asked. She was aware of a feeling of revulsion that reminded her of Friday night.

'Not sure yet.' said Lizzie. 'Don't actually have to watch. Just make it look as though you are. Like those old X movies, we used to sneak into. You remember?'

Fran supposed that she did. 'That his name then? Brun?'

'Think so, Yeah. Like I said, they don't know much English. He knows a new word now.' She pointed with an index finger. 'Upstairs! Oh! Easy, tiger. Not quite ready for you yet.'

He muttered in her ear, casting glances in Fran's direction.

'Oh, I think I see. Alright. Fran, he wants you to join us.'

'Me?'

Lizzie to Brun: 'My friend?'

He got up out of the bed and came across to her.

'You. Superb!' he said in his faltering English.

Fran blushed. 'Why, thank you, kind sir. You're not so bad yourself.'

'Solid, isn't he, Fran?' said Lizzie from the bed. 'Imagine him pumping away inside you. Go on, then. Take your clothes off.'

'I'm not sure.'

'Go on, go on. This could be the best day of your life.'

'Well, yes. It could be…'

Brun grabbed the hem of her sensible office top. 'Off?'

Well, at least he asked, she thought. Aware that the alcohol was doing the job that made it famous. She crossed her arms, grabbed the garment, and it was off, over her head. He was on her like a flash: undoing her bra skilfully and throwing it away. He led her to the bed and began unbuttoning her jeans.

'What's this?' cried Lizzie. 'Another one for the party?'

'Move over then. Let me get in.'

'Got your Little Misses pants on, I see. Who are you today?'

'Little Miss Amorous.'

'Little Miss Dangerous, more like. I'll have to watch you.'

'What? You watch me? I thought it was the other way about.'

'One thing at a time, honey. Don't get too far ahead of yourself. Ever done anything like this before?'

Fran smiled. 'Once or twice.'

The waiter was on top of her, snuffling and grunting in her ear. She felt a kiss. But that couldn't have been Brun. She opened her eyes. It was Lizzie. 'Hold tight, honey.' she said. 'This may be a bumpy ride.'

Later, - much later, they left him sleeping. 'Why do men always snore?' They crept down the stairs and out through a side door.

'Oh, good! I've got my car. Nearly forgot about that. How about you?'

'For work, I always use public transport. Always come on the bus.'

'Come on the bus, do you? Dirty little minx. Tell you what then, you come back to mine. Solomon might guess we'd be out of our trees. I'll message him. Hang on.'

'You message him? What about me?' Lizzie put her hand between Fran's legs. 'You've done enough for one evening, my sweet. Hang on - gone straight to messages. Sshh.' In a louder voice: 'Hi there! It's us! Bit bladdered, as usual, so we're going back to mine. Rodney's away till Friday, so I may as well have a sleepover. It's Lizzie speaking, by the way. Fran says, "Hi." Night, night!' She disconnected. 'There. That should do it. Now, back to mine. I'll rustle up some hot cocoa, and we can curl up together and forget about the world for a while. Are you working tomorrow?'

'No.' said Fran. 'Don't have to.'

'That's settled then. Wagon roll!'

Jessica opened her eyes, safe in her own bed. Solomon had kissed her awake.

'Oh, morning.' she said.

'Good morning to you. How ya doing?'

'Yes. Not too bad. Wonderful, what a good night's sleep can do.'

Next to the bed was a unit that held cotton balls and cleanser.

'Here. Hold still.' he said. And began cleaning her eyes. 'Horrible black stuff, mascara. Keep still, and I'll wash your face.'

She gazed up at him. 'Lordy, what did we get up to last night?' she asked.

'Nothing they could hang you for.' He replied. 'Fun, wasn't it?'

'Well, I can hardly remember, as it happens.'

'Want me to remind you?'

'Could do, I suppose.'

'Let's get you clean first. Nearly there. There! Look about ten years younger now.'

'Great. Thanks. I needed that.'

'What's the plan then? Got to phone the hospital, I guess.'

'Yes. And we'd better go and get the car.'

'Where does it go?'

'In the double garage. Next to mine. What's the time?'

'A little after six.'

'Six in the morning? A little early for me.'

'I'll do you some tea and toast.'

'Mm, no. Coffee. After a hard night. And it was a hard night, wasn't it?'

'Sure was. You were incredible.'

'Ha! So were you. Have to say that, don't we?'

'Say what you like. One thing is for sure. I'll never look at you again and wonder what you look like naked.'

'I could say the same. Never dreamed it would be like this, but there you go. Goes to show, you never can tell.'

'And you were fantastic.' He kissed her.

She giggled. 'Why? Didn't you think I'd be any good? Heavenly body like mine?'

'Have to remind myself.' He ran his hands over her.

'Oh, don't. You'll get me at it again.'

'"Don't"? Really? Tell me to stop, and I will.'

She giggled some more. 'Don't you bloody dare. You stay right there. Oh, a little higher. That's it. Just there. Wonderful. Uh-oh. I don't think this is going to take long. Ooh, early-morning sex. Nothing like it, is there? Nighttimes are great, but one or the other is generally stoned. Early mornings, you can see for yourself what you've got. Makes me feel sexy. Makes me perform!'

'Could say that. Wonderful performer you are, too.' He kissed her. 'Although, I like to think I played my part too.'

'Mm. And what a large part it is! Come on.' She slapped his backside. 'Tea and toast. I'll phone the hospital.'

'Bit early for them, isn't it?'

94

'Maybe you're right. Better give them an hour or so.' She looked into his eyes, her pupils dilating. 'And you, my love…'

'Yes?'

'You can have an hour too.'

Fran woke at night but, when she was with her friends, the bastard couldn't get to her. She curled up around her friend and hugged her waist.

She thought about the past few days. What was today? Tuesday, early. That meant she had slept with two women in the past four days!

And how different they were: Wendy was as big and strong as a girl. Fran had loved her. Her gentleness and assuredness. Her drive and self-control. Lizzie though…

Lizzie was soft, sweet, and sexy. Fran squeezed her lovingly and sought out her breast with her hand. They both slept naked on the black satin sheets. Lizzie sighed in her sleep.

'Lovely breasts, Lizzie. Nearly as nice as mine.'

They slept.

Solomon dropped Jessica at David's car and drove himself to work after ensuring she started it okay. A pile of papers hadn't been touched while he was away. Because of that, he was three or four days behind schedule. He set to work.

His first interruption was the driver, Pete Tolman.

'Hi, Solomon! Dude!'

'Pete.'

'How's things. All okay?' How are things?

'Not really. Nobody's done a stroke while I was away, so I'm all behind now.'

'Right. Right. Like a cow's tail!' joked Tolman.

'What?'

'You know, the old joke? I'm all behind like a cow's tail.'

'Was there something, Peter?'

'No, no. Nothing.'

'Good.'

'Just wondered how it went up in Scotland.'

'Scotland? They are a lovely part of the world, so they say. Can't really agree. Hardly saw anything but mud and weeds. That and the constant drone of the windscreen wipers and FM radio has made me decide I won't be going again.'

'Came back a little early too.'

'That a problem? All work completed. Decided to get back.'

'Doesn't matter.' said Tolman. 'Normally, there's time enough for fishing. I generally drop Chummy one or two salmon, - especially with Christmas coming. It'll be alright.'

'I'm pleased.'

'Another trip this weekend, as it goes.'

'Well, I'm not going. I'd be pleased if I never saw that God-forsaken landscape again. You go. Fish a little. Enjoy yourself. Go in peace.'

'Thanks.'

The two lovers slept. The morning sunshine filled the room, but they saw nothing but their dreams and each other. Occasionally, they would wake and kiss, not sure who woke who. They were both blissfully happy. Until they heard the front door open and close.

'Lizzie!' called Rodney's voice. 'You in?'

They froze. 'What the hell's he doing here?' whispered Lizzie. 'He's supposed to be gone until Friday.'

'What shall we do?' asked Fran, a little concerned.

'Nothing.' said Lizzie, and lay back with her arms behind her head. 'He'll need a drink after the drive - always does. He's recorded football off the TV. He'll be asleep before too long.'

'And then what?' asked Fran, a trifle indignantly. 'I'm not shinning down any drainpipes in full view of the neighbourhood.'

'Sshh. Don't make me laugh. Don't worry, You won't have to. I'll think of something.'

They heard Rodney's voice again. Bizarrely:

'It's alright, she's out. Probably off with friends somewhere.'

They were coming up the stairs. The bedroom door was flung open...

The blonde was a stunner. They all had to admit that. All boobs and make-up. A pencil-thin waist. Legs up to her armpits. Bottle-tanned. Rodney took stock of the situation.

'Ah. Yes, this is awkward. It could be, anyway. I don't suppose we're all up for a foursome?'

As it turned out, they were. The blonde's name was Hilary. She undressed quickly like she'd done it a thousand times, which could have been the case. She squeezed in between Fran and Lizzie - who immediately took a shine to her. The two of them were soon locked in a seemingly endless embrace.

Rodney took Fran's hand and led her across the landing to the spare room. Here, the bed was made up, ready for visitors. Fran got in and pulled the covers over her. Rodney smiled.

'Never would have had you down for anything like this.' He said. 'Good for you.' He stood at the side of the bed. 'My close friends call me Rod.'

She giggled. 'I can see why.'

Solomon opened the front door with the key Jessica had given him.

'Hi, Jess!' he called. It's me.' He thought. 'Solomon.'

He trudged down the hall, all the day's cares on his shoulders. She was pleased to see him sitting on the sofa, sipping tea. 'Hi.'

'Hello.' he said. 'Good day? By that I mean, any news?'

She shook her head, strawberry-blonde hair loose about her face.

'No. Nothing.'

'Want to go over there? I'll take you.'

'No. No thanks. No point. They'll ring if there's any change. How was work?'

'He shrugged. 'Work is work.'

'Have you eaten?'

'Many times. Sorry. Joke. Uh, no. I had a sandwich at lunchtime, but it was tuna, and I had promised not to eat it anymore. Those things are huge, I never realized. No wonder they get mistaken for dolphins.'

'I'll make you something.'

'Oh yeah? Like what?' He came and sat beside her.

'I'll think of something.'

'I already have.' he said with a mischievous leer. 'Shower first, though. Golden rule after work. The place is okay to work from, but it does stink of tobacco. Have to get rid. Fran hates it.'

'Been in touch today?'

'I texted her earlier. "Delivered", but no reply. Just told her I was staying here to look after you for a while. She'll know why.'

'"Looking after me"? One way of putting it.'

'There are other ways…'

Fran's name seemed to hang in the air while they gathered their thoughts.

98

She was first.

'I've been thinking.'

'Go on?'

'I've been thinking there really isn't any reason for David's car to be round at yours.'

'I know. We've said.'

'Sooo…'

'What?'

'Suppose he attacked her? After all, he was drunk.'

'Car's parked okay.'

'Oh! You men and cars. What's the matter? We women aren't enough for you?'

'No. I mean, yes. Oh, I don't know what I mean. Okay, he was drunk. You know him best. Do you think he would have, I dunno, made a pass at her?'

'I'm afraid so. That's exactly the kind of thing he'd do. Sometimes, he'll come home, gather me in his arms, and… force me. I hate that. Almost made me cry, "Rape!" And it would explain the wound. The vase.'

'Yes, I've thought about the vase. The times we've edged past it, her and me. Treasured possession.'

'May have been one of the fitters?'

'That broke it? Yes, it may have been. But, as I say, it would take a lot more force than a three-foot fall onto a deep-pile caret to break it.'

'Deep-pile? In the hallway? Maybe that's why she changed it? Sorry. Go on.'

'Thank you. May have had a fault in it, of course.'

'Tell you what?' she said, putting her teacup on the coffee table and smoothing her chinos down flat.

'What?'

She stood up. 'Let's go round there.'

'What for?'

'To look for clues.'

'Clues?'

'Sure. Why not? She won't be there if she's out and about with Lizzie. Has she called you today?

'No. Another golden rule - no phone calls at work.'

'So many rules. It's a wonder you got anything done. Anyway, what about it?'

'What?'

She shook her head. 'So many "What" s. Try to keep up. If she's there, we'll know. If she's not, we'll sneak in and see if there's any evidence.'

'Evidence? For what?'

'Well, you know - bloodstains, shards of glass, and the like. Those kinds of things.'

'Alright, Mrs. Poirot. Don't suppose it would do any harm.'

'Might explain the fire on the lawn. What could she possibly have been burning?'

Belisaro's was buzzing, as usual. Fran didn't feel like drinking.

'Still a bit rough from that Prosecco.' she said. 'I'll just have a gin and it.'

'Me too.' said Lizzie to the waiter - a different one. His name was Gustav - and he was gay, Lizzie had already discovered. 'Let you in on a secret.' she said. 'They lace it with vodka.'

Fran nodded and smiled. 'That explains it.'

'Anyway, what's the plan for this evening? Want to go home?'

'Home.' She thought. 'No. Not just yet. Need to think.' She raised her gin. 'This often helps, in moderation.'

'Quite welcome at ours. Fine with me. And Big Rod, too, I shouldn't wonder. Don't panic - he's no good the second time around. Tries too hard. It is all over too quickly. And he's relatively small compared to… other men I've known.'

'I'll take your word for it.'

'Do so. Anyhoo, we haven't eaten yet. There's a great Chinese around here. And he runs a great takeaway, too.'

They drove past the house slowly.

'What are you doing?' asked Solomon. 'You've gone straight past the house. It's back there.'

'I know. Don't want to park outside, do we? What did you think anyway? Any lights on?'

'No. Didn't see any. Might be asleep in bed, of course.'

'At six-thirty? Anyway, if she is - what are we doing wrong? It is your house, and she knows you're looking after me.'

'"Looking after"? Could call it that.'

They drove around the corner and parked. There was a scrunching beneath the wheels.

'What's that? Squirrels?'

'No.' he said. 'Conkers. Get everywhere.'

'No, no. Over there, in the park.'

'Yes, could be.' he supposed. 'I guess that's where I'd be if I was a squirrel.'

'But you're not, are you? Come on.'

They got out.

'Brrr.' she said. 'It's freezing!'

'Sshhh. Come on.' They crept down the street to his house, which was in darkness.

'Car said it was nought degrees. Surprised it started. Obviously, he didn't want to come.'

'Sshhh. No nightlight.'

'What?'

'Nightlight. She always sleeps with the nightlight on. Makes a faint glow, but no, not tonight.'

'Must be out then.'

'Soon, see.'

He went up the path with her, close behind, and turned the key in the front door.

'Aw,' she said. 'Nice carpet.'

'Think so? Come in. Better take our trainers off.'

'Okay. Yes, I think it's cute. Kids'll love it.'

'If we last that long. Now, I'll just go up and check the bedroom. You hang on here.'

'Okay.'

'Sshh. Hard consonant. Should avoid those. Try "Alright".'

'Alright.'

'Better. No T.'

'I said I'd make you something later.'

'Sshhh! Don't laugh. You'll set me off.'

'Well, honestly. Look at the pair of us. What on Earth do we think we're doing?'

'We know what we're doing. Let's get on with it.' He crept up the stairs.

There was nobody in the bed. Nobody is on the sofa either. It seemed they were alone.

'Alright.' he said. 'What do you want to do?'

She got down on her hands and knees.

'Sorry, Piglet. Sorry, Roo. Playing hide and go seek!'

She made her way back down the hallway towards the front door.

'What are you doing, crawling about down there?'

'Searching.' she said.

'What for? Truffles? You've got eyes, haven't you - to see things.'

'I also have a nose.' she said by way of explanation. 'Not truffles. Bleach. Or some kind of cleansing product. Have a look under the sink.'

'Why?'

'Because that's where I keep mine.'

'Oh, okay.'

'Alright! Not okay!'

'It's alright - okay. Now that we know no one's in, we can make more noise.' He rummaged under the sink. 'How's this? Cif cleaner.'

'Bring it. Let me smell.' He took it over to her. She stood up and sniffed it experimentally. 'Yes. That's the same stuff. The skirting stinks of it. Smells the same anyway. Still wet around the nozzle. I would have wiped that clean.'

'Maybe in a hurry?'

'Yes. Maybe.'

'What would she be cleaning anyway? Not glass?'

'No. Of course not glass.'

'What then?'

'Blood, of course! Get down there and look closer.'

He got down on his hands and knees. The skirting board was a three-inch standard bullnose painted once by the house builder. Solomon had emulsioned the walls himself a few years ago. Hadn't done such a great job of cutting in, now he came to look closer.

He fancied that the emulsion had suffered a bit where the wall had been recently cleaned. "Honeydew Melon," it had been called. Daft has an idiotic job to do: naming paints. He remembered a colour chart with "Easter Eggs" in purple when it should obviously have been brown.

'Well?' she asked.

He stood. 'Definitely, been rubbed with something. May not have been recently, though.'

'It's the only piece that's like it.' said Jess. 'Must have been trying to clean something off.'

'Doesn't prove anything, of course. She's always cleaning and tidying.'

'So I see. Why there, though? New carpet arriving… Why clean just there?'

'Just there?'

'Yes. Just that length from the stair carpet to the front wall. Why not all of it? I mean, I would. Wouldn't you?'

'Maybe ran out of time.'

'Yes, maybe. I'm trying to put myself in her mind. What would I do?'

'You're not her. She's not you.'

'I know. Here, you know her best. What do you think?'

'I'm thinking I want you in my bed now.'

The Cantonese takeaway on Pigsty Hill wasn't much to write home about. Just a long service counter with, opposite, a long, basic wooden bench for customers to sit and eat their meals - chips mainly. Students mainly. Still, it was all money.

Alf, the owner and chief chef, had migrated from Shanghai thirty years ago and now considered himself a local. He worked tirelessly behind the counter, generally cooking and sieving chips in the large open oven in front of him - "To keep customers away from me!" he used to joke.

He knew Lizzie of old. I made a new friend this evening.

'Alfie!'

'Hello, ladies. Nice to see you. Wouldn't want to be you.'

'He always says that.' said Lizzie to Fran. 'What's good tonight, Alfie? Anything without any cats in it?'

'You make a joke, I ban you from premises!'

'Yeah, he always says that too. I'm gonna try the sweet and sour pork. No, - chicken.'

'We have plenty of chicken.'

'No. I mean, I'll have sweet and sour chicken. That's all.'

'No rice?'

'Well, of course, rice.'

'Not all then.' said Alf with a smile.

'I'll just have a spring roll.' said Fran.

'Vegetarian?'

'Me? No.'

'No. Not you. Spring roll.'

'Oh. I see. Yes. Please.'

'Ah. Love this place.' said Lizzie.

'Seems nice.' said Fran.

Attached to the counter was a vertical broomstick containing three kitchen rolls of paper. "Saves paying window cleaner to do both sides!" Alf explained to anyone who asked.

'What was that about cats?' asked Fran.

'Oh. Place roundabout here. Cat's collar in the chow mein. Bell and everything!'

'Mmmmm. It is a lovely, big, warm, soft white bed. With a lovely, great big, warm, not-so-soft white man.'

'Happy now?'

'Mm, delirious.'

'What'cha doing? Taking photos?'

She laughed. An easy, contented laugh. Comes from deep down inside. 'No, no need to, is there? No. I'm checking Lizzie. I've got her on Location tracking. Well, she asked me to. Forever waking up in places she couldn't remember. Aha. Yes, she's in the city. Doesn't mean that Fran's with her, but we might assume so.'

'Give her a call.'

'Mm? Yes, could do, couldn't we?'

She pressed a memory number.

'Try to sound a little drunk.' suggested Solomon.

'Hi, Lizzie? It's Jess….. Oh, not bad….. No. No news….. Say they just have to wait for him to, what's it called, pull-through. How are you?..... Yes, I know….. Got you on track, or whatever it's called….. Yes, he's here. At my place, I mean. Showering after work. Sends his love….. No, not to you, silly….. She with you?..... Okay. I mean, alright. I'll see you soon, yeah? Okay. Bye.'

She replaced her phone on the bedside unit. 'Yeah, she's with Fran. Looks like we've got all night.'

'Can I tell you something? Seriously?'

'Oh dear. What?'

'You're a lot more fun when you're sober.'

'Aw. Thanks. Come on. Get up. Time to resume the search.'

'Couldn't we just…'

'No. Not till later. Come on.'

They dressed easily, both reminding each other of their other halves. Solomon was remembering the last time he had watched Francesca dress herself. Seemed like a lifetime ago.

And what was she doing, cleaning the skirting board?

They went back downstairs.

'Now.' said Jess. 'The thing to do is shift that hall table.'

'What for?' asked Solomon.

'Well, say we're right, and she ran out of time. Perhaps she didn't clean behind the table. Let's have a look. You take that end.'

Taking an end each, they moved the table to the center of the hall.

'Fitters would have moved this.' he said. 'Maybe into the kitchen.'

'Of course.' she said. 'But would they have cleaned the skirting board?'

She was down on her hands and knees again. He looked lovingly at her backside and tried to concentrate.

'Ouch!'

'What's wrong?'

'Cut myself. Just a sliver. Another one along here, too.' She sucked her finger. 'Ooooh.'

'Gone in?'

'No. Doesn't matter. Just a scratch. Well.' she got to her feet. 'There we are then.'

'Where?'

'Well...' She thought for a moment. 'Yes, see what you mean. Proves nothing except that the vase was smashed, smashed mark you, here by something. Something hard.'

'Like your husband's head?'

'No need to call him that. Not when I'm still wet from you.' She affectionately brushed his cheek. 'Next thing is, what was on the fire?'

'Shouldn't eat in the car,' said Lizzie. 'Hate me in the morning.'

'We're the same.' said Fran. 'Although, no - we're different. We always eat in the car so we don't stink the house out.'

'Aha. Takes all sorts. Here - paper towel. Pinched some on the way out while Alf was on the till.'

'Thanks. Ugh, horrible, messy things.'

'All over now. So, what do you want to do? Where can I take you, my princess? Ready to go home?'

'What about the others?'

'Oh, Rodney will sleep for hours if he pronged you.' She glanced at her friend. 'I take it he did?' Fran nodded. 'That's him then, as for Hilary. She's probably in someone else's bed by now. Leaving us free to be in ours. What do you say, honey?'

'Sounds like a plan.' said Fran.

Lizzie parked outside, and they scurried up the path and into her house, both shivering coldly.

'Tell you what.'

'What?'

'Shower. Come on up.' She skipped up the stairs, two at a time. Francesca followed close behind. At the top of the stairs, a door led to the "wet room." 'Decided to call it that after Rodney took the bath out. We've got a walk-in shower now. Go in, I'll switch it on from just here.'

Fran disrobed and, uncertainly, waited for the water to flow., It steamed. 'Oh! Lovely!' She went in. The heat was welcome but almost overbearing. It relaxed her.

'Okay?' called Lizzie.

'Yes! Wonderful.'

'Good.' Shortly, the door was swung open, and Lizzie got in too. 'Move up, move up. Thought I'd join you.'

He lay on top of her, taking his weight through his upper arms, on his elbows either side. Like a gentleman should.

'Oh. It's no good.' he said. 'I can't get enough of you.'

'I think you've had everything I've got.' said Jessica, radiantly smiling. 'Probably won't be able to walk for weeks! Mmm, love this bed.'

He shifted slightly. 'Tell me something?'

'Yes.' she said. 'You are the biggest and best I've ever had.'

'No, not that. Goes without saying. Something else.'

'What then?'

'Do you color your hair?'

'No, of course not. Natural blonde, me. Well, you know that now. Collars and cuffs all match.'

'Hm.'

'Why? What are you thinking?'

Solomon picked at something from the pillow.

'I'm thinking, who do I know with black hair?'

He woke, as usual, at six a.m. Not wishing to disturb her, he left a note on the bedside table. He showered and shaved, broke his fast, and left the house. It was a glum day, overcast and cold. He had booked a taxi which would take him to Jessica's. She'd be okay; her car was parked on the conkers.

The cab turned up on time.

'Morning Drive.' Solomon said as he got in the back.

'Good morning to you, sir. Brass monkeys again this morning, I see.'

'You're not wrong.'

'Feel it in your bones, can't you? Still, Christmas in the Maldives for me. Couple more weeks, and I'm off.'

'Good for you. Expensive trip though?'

'That's why I love this job.' said the driver. 'Evening shifts especially. Most students are so glad to return to their bedsitters that they tip like crazy. Two, three times the fare sometimes. All cash, of course, nothing through the books. Soon, it adds up. Last night, for instance, I took over a hundred pounds. All help pay for the airfare. Here we are now, sir. Didn't take long, did it?' He surveyed the properties of the neighborhood. Live around here, do you, sir?'

Solomon passed him a note. 'Friend of mine.'

'Ah. Oh, I see. Fair play to you. See you again soon.' He drove off with a quick toot of the horn. It was too early for curtain-twitching, but Solomon was irritated by the driver anyway.

'Christmas in the Maldives.'

He got into his car, parked nearby, and drove the short trip to his work.

As usual, there were not many people about. He helped himself to a plastic cup of coffee from the vending machine and went to his office. In here, it was freezing, but there was a convector heater. He turned it on, warming himself close to it for a few seconds before sitting behind his desk. There was a pile of papers there...

Time went by. A little after eight, Helen, one of the secretaries, telephoned him.

'Hello?' he said.

'Morning, Solomon.' said Helen. 'Mister Chumwell would like to see you.'

Blast.

'Tell him I'll be up in a few minutes.'

'Okay. Thanks, Solomon.'

Helen Robinson: Everything a secretary should be. Smart, petite. Wide brown eyes and lips set in a permanent smile. Her figure was neat, too, proportional. Immaculately dressed.

And the way she walked - always in high heels. She clip-clopped through the premises, turning heads in every direction. They liked to think she did it on purpose every now and then.

Solomon went into the office. She sat behind her desk, kept apart from Chumwell. His office was behind the half-glazed door in front of them.

'Morning, Miss Robinson.'

'Oh, rather formal this morning. Good morning to you, Mister Swift.'

'Sorry. Can't help wondering what he wants me for.'

'Go in and see. He's waiting for you.'

'Thanks.'

He crossed the beige carpet, knocked at the door, and went in.

'Ah! Solomon. Come on in. Be seated.'

'Thanks.' Solomon pulled a chair over from its place against the wall and sat at the other side of the desk from Chumwell.

'So.' began Chumwell. 'Uh… how was Scotland?'

'Beautiful part of the world, so they say.'

'You don't agree?'

'Hardly saw any of it. Straight up and straight back down.'

'Yes, noticed that. Do you realize that's a trip that takes Pete five days?'

'He tells me he often has time for a little fishing. Salmon, *et cetera*.'

'Oh, quite, quite. Yes. Often brings me some. I am getting a bit sick of it lately, to be honest. Still, that's not the topic for this morning.'

Solomon stopped himself from saying, "What is?".

Chumwell waved a piece of paper. 'Do you realize you were underweight?'

'Yes. Got pulled at Gretna. Chap said it was because I was a new face.'

'Aha, aha. Nonetheless, true for all that. The question is, though, how did you become underweight?'

'No idea at all. Thought about it a lot. The truck was loaded and tagged here on the Friday.'

'Tagged?'

'Yes.' Surely Chumwell knew that the vehicles were tagged? Still, maybe not. 'Yellow plastic tag that goes on after loading and securing the truck.'

'Oh yes, of course. You keep a de-tagger in the glove compartment, don't you?'

'We do. I didn't use mine, but I imagine the Customs people have their own. Re-tag it after inspection, and off we go.'

'Right. Okay.'

'Nobody went near it after I picked it up. Sure, I stopped at the services on the M6, but I didn't get out of the truck. Told them that at Gretna. I had my sandwiches and coffee. And the portable toilet. No need to get out.'

'Aha. Quite. Difficult to say what happened then.'

'Agreed.'

'You realize what this means?'

'Well, I'm not one to drop a fellow worker into the soup, so to speak, but it seems to me that the load must have been lightened before I left on Friday.'

'In other words, the cigars were stolen by somebody here?'

' Not for me to put words in your mouth, but yes. It would seem so.'

'A thief in our midst! Hmm. How well do you know friend Tolman?'

'Pete? Hardly at all. I only know him because I took his place last week. Why not ask the foreman?'

'Yes, I will, Solly. Thanks.'

'Was that all?'

'Hm? Oh, yes. For now, yes. Thank you, Solomon.'

There was clearly nothing more to say. Solomon bade Chumwell a farewell and did the same to Helen in the adjoining office.

'Bye, Solomon.'

He walked down the corridor, busy with his thoughts.

'Morning, Sol.'

'Hm? Oh, good morning, Tom. Sorry, miles away.'

'You wish.'

They carried on in opposite directions.

Solomon got back to his now-heated office and sat at his desk.

So, Pete Tolman was a thief? Alright then, how? He picked up a pencil and twiddled it - a thing people did when thinking. What then? Too much on his mind. Lunch in the pub today, maybe. A pint often cleared his head.

How did you steal approximately two hundred cigars on God's Earth? How long would that take? He tried to visualize it in his mind. He couldn't do it. It must be some kind of trick. People didn't steal just for the hell of it. There must be some kind of, what's the word, "wrinkle". He tapped the pencil on the desk. It reminded him of Fran. Lovely Fran. He hadn't seen her for days! He wondered if he should drop her a text but decided against it. In her mind, whatever had happened, there was nothing wrong. She would come home when she wanted to. For now, she was with her bestie - the delicious Lizzie. Ah, Lizzie... And he was with Jessica. Lovely Jessica... His own personal animal between his legs raised its weary head. 'Down boy.'

As a cover, he pulled his chair close to the desk and tried to continue his work.

Helen's high heels clip-clopped down the corridor. She knocked on his door.

One, two, three, four...

'Come in!'

She did so. Framed herself in the doorway for a second.

'Solomon.'

'Helen. Come in, do.'

'Thanks.' She closed the door.

'Take a seat.' He indicated the other chair, set back against the wall to the side of the office. He would have brought it over for her, but he could not stand.

She gave herself a slight shrug but soon sat opposite him on the other side of the desk.

'What brings you here?' he asked.

'It's like this.' She began. 'Your meeting with Mister Chumwell. I listened to every word.'

As secretaries do, he thought. Moneypenny...

'And?'

She leaned closer. 'Pete and I... Mister Tolman and I are what you might call an item.'

'Really?'

'Yes, really. Often go with him on the trips.'

Not all fishing, then...

'Up to Scotland. Over to Wales for the Irish trips. I don't go to Dublin - I hate the water! There's a Days Inn on the other side of Wrexham, near the railway station. We stay there. Then, he goes to Holyhead, and I get the train back here.'

Solomon wondered why she was telling him all this.

'If Chumwell investigates further, it will all come out, not about the two of us but definitely about the thefts. He's an old hand at it. Been doing it for years. I said he'd get caught one of these days, and now he has.' She'd thought about feigning tears at this point but decided against it now. She looked directly at Solomon with her big brown eyes.

Solomon shrugged. 'What can I do? You heard the conversation. It hardly involves me. I've got no idea how he does it. I'm sorry, Helen. I don't see how I can help.'

She drew a business card from her inside jacket pocket.

'We can't talk here. Why not come to mine this evening, and we'll discuss it further?'

He looked at the card. Tasteful, artistic. "Helen Robinson - Home care." Then, the address and telephone number.

'Home care?' he enquired.

'Just a few days a week. 'she said. 'Started looking after a neighbor, dead now, of course, but he was so impressed with me that he told all his friends at the Civic Centre, and it snowballed from that. I only cook and clean, nothing more.'

'Very good. Well done, you.'

She stood up, smoothing down her bright skirt. 'This evening then. Say six-thirty?'

'Make it seven? I'm all behind here. Okay?'

'Okay. Thanks, Solly.'

She left after replacing the chair against the wall.

Solomon fiddled with his pencil.

They breakfasted at the kitchen table, an organic piece from Oak Loft.

There was tea and toast and, as a special treat, Rose's lime marmalade.

'My secret pleasure.' said Lizzie.

'Amongst others.' said Fran.

'True, true. Guilty as charged. Can't always get it, though. Sells out pretty fast whenever it's in. That's why there's about four jars in the cupboard.'

'Lovely. Reminds me of my grandparents. They liked it too.'

'What are we up to today then? Any thoughts?'

'Yes. Regretfully, I think it's time I went home. If you'd take me over in a few hours?'

'Sure.'

'Solomon will be at work. I'll cook him something wonderful for tonight, and then, when he's fed and watered, I'll tell him what happened.'

'Yes. Makes sense. He's the man you love - and *vice versa*. Well, not *vice versa*. You know what I mean.' She waved a triangle of toast like conducting an invisible orchestra. 'Stands to reason you should tell him. He needs to know.'

'And then what, though?'

'Have to wait and see, won't we? One thing at a time and take it slowly.'

'And what about us? I've loved the times we've spent together.'

Lizzie shrugged. 'Me too. We're best friends, Fran. I'll always be here for you, and hopefully, you're there for me.'

'Always.'

'Always then!'

They touched teacups.

Solomon couldn't help thinking about the black hair.

After work, he got into his car and texted Jessie.

BE LATE TONIGHT. BUSINESS APPOINTMENT

Back came the reply:

BEST GO HOME. MOTHER'S TURNED UP HERE. X

That was that, then. He drove carefully; the roads were already slippy. Again, he thought about the black hair.

It simply didn't add up. He had racked his brains for friends of his, or hers, with black hair, but there were none. It had come to the point where he was almost suspecting everyone - from Helen to Pete Tolman. They both had black hair. Chumwell was out, though; he was bald as a coot.

Of course, it didn't necessarily follow that a stranger had left the hair. It could have come from Jess. Or himself. Or Fran. He decided not to worry too much for now. He could always quiz Fran.

Fran! He hadn't seen her for a long time. Get this meeting out of the way, and he would go home and hopefully find her waiting. No reason why not.

Helen Robinson answered her door, still in her work clothes except for her beautifully tailored jacket, which hung on a hanger over a door frame to the rear of the hallway.

'Solomon!'

'Hello, Helen. Not too early, am I?'

'Not at all. Not at all. Come through.'

She showed him into the lounge. Similar furnishings to his own: large three-seater sofa, large coffee table. A dining table and two chairs are in the corner, with a laptop computer purring quietly to itself. Curtains were drawn at both ends of the room, pulled up tight.

They sat themselves at opposite ends of the sofa. A bottle of white wine and two thin, delicate glasses were on the coffee table.

'Like some wine?' she asked sweetly.

'Yes. Could have just the one, couldn't I?'

'Of course. Why not?' She poured effortlessly. 'Chardonnay.'

'Thanks.' He took a glass.

'Santé.' she said. 'Means, "Your excellent health."'

'Yes, so I believe.' he said. 'Bit of a Francophile myself. Often over there.'

'Really? Where's your favourite spot?'

'Finistère, for me. Easiest to get to. Plymouth to Roscoff on the ferry in three or four hours. Another hour's drive, and you're on the Atlantic coast. Beautiful down there.'

'I'll bet. My favourite is the Dordogne. Takes forever to get there. Takes forever to save up for it, too. Would go again this summer if I had anyone to go with.'

'Wouldn't Pete go?'

She laughed briefly. 'No, no. Little woman at home.'

'Ah. Sorry. Didn't realize.'

She laughed again. 'You men. Never do, do you?'

'Well, I can't speak for any other men, but personally, it's generally best not to assume anything.'

'Oh, quiet.' She put down her Glass and edged closer to him. 'Wanted you here for ages.' she said.

'What?'

'Thought I'd never get you here.' She began to unbutton her blouse. She was bra-less under it. 'How about it, Solly? No, not Solly. Makes you sound like a kids' toy. I'm betting you're so much more than that. Sol. That's what I like to call you when I dream about you. "Oh, Sol!" I'd scream. "Do it to me, do it to me. Harder! Harder!" Oh, those dreams, Sol. You'd love them. Sometimes, I wake up too tired to go to work. Those mornings, I lie in my bed. Thinking about you. This isn't a dream, though. Is it Sol?' Her knickers were scrunched up in her hand. 'Come on, help yourself. You've got me now. I can show you things you've never seen before. Like these... When you heard me sashaying down the corridors, did you ever think that you'd one evening be sat here with me, stark naked? Begging you to fuck me? I have. Dreamed about it forever. Let me finish undressing you, and I'll help you get inside me. That okay, Sol? Sol?'

He didn't need to tell twice. After she'd finished, he laid her back on the sofa and smothered her with kisses.

'I thought you said that you and Pete were an item?'

'Don't see him here, do you?'

Fran opened her own front door and gazed at the Pigletty carpet. Never mind.

She waved goodbye to Lizzie, closed the door, slipped off her coat and shoes, and entered the sitting room.

David stood there. His head was swathed in bandages; he looked like an Egyptian mummy. He was holding a weapon. A Taser. He raised it, leveled it at Fran, and shot her.

She collapsed onto the floor, a terrific pain in her right shoulder. She was bewildered and began to shake uncontrollably. He was soon looming over her.

'Good.' he said. 'CEDs are not too bad. Conducted Energy Device. Ill-effects over in about an hour. Leaves us plenty of time.' He unbuckled her belt and started to undo her jeans. 'Stupid invention, jeans. Difficult to get on, difficult to get off. Never mind. Nearly there.' He leered down at her. 'And then we'll see, won't we? What's the matter? Thought I'd give up on you? Oh, no. Not me.'

Her mind panicked, but she was powerless to move. Pain dominated her, and she thought she might lose consciousness. She lay still, trembling. She could hear her own tears. He didn't care. He had her jeans and pants down over her knees.

Solomon blew his brains out with the Scottish revolver.

In the spare room, Rod was awoken by Lizzie.

'Oh, hello, stranger.' he said. 'What's up?'

'Cold.' She said. Move over.'

In the dark, he smiled but complied. 'Anything to oblige.' She crept in. He held her close. She was right - she was cold. 'No lovers tonight?'

'No. All gone, for now.'

'I hope you're not expecting me to…'

'No, no. Need sleep, that's all. Needed someone to hold me.'

'Always available, wife.'

'Red-raw down there anyway.'

Solomon pulled her trousers up as best he could and pulled her out into the hall. He shut the door behind him, concealing the grisly sight. They would never go in that room again.

He gathered her up in his arms and moved the two of them to the closed kitchen door. The quilt he had used on Sunday was in the cupboard under the stairs. He pulled it out and gently wrapped her up in it. He wasn't entirely sure what to do, so he took her onto his lap, his back against the kitchen door, and hoped she would relax. He wondered if she wanted tea - brandy even? His phone was in his pocket, and he managed to fish it out and look up "Taser attacks" on it. He had seen those stun guns before, on the television. Sometimes, these attacks could be fatal. He held her wrist expertly and reassured himself that the pulse, though fast, was not out of control. The limited entry said that he was doing, more or less, the right thing, and so he held her. Occasionally saying, "Sshhh." It was all he could think of. She shook. Her arms and legs. She clenched and unclenched her right hand - a fist?

Solomon thought about the blood-spattered room. In his immediate memory, there was blood on the sofa, the carpet, the curtains, and the wall. It would take forever to clean. David was dead; there was no doubt about that. Clearly, he had broken in intent on raping Fran, the sick bastard. Jessie had been right about that.

What was the next thing to do, though?

The events leading up to the incident were not extraordinary. He thought back to an hour ago. After leaving Helen warm and sated, he had tucked her up in her own bed and headed home, hardly believing his luck lately. Wednesday evening. He'd had three women this week. Soon to be four, he hoped.

Arriving home, he ignored the Pigletty carpet and went up the stairs, but Fran wasn't in. He heard the smashing of Glass downstairs and froze. Burglars? In his bedside unit was Carter's gun from Scotland. Nobody had taken it from him. He took it out and tiptoed across the bedroom. The door was ajar. He listened, but there were no further sounds.

At that moment, Fran came home. Everything else happened all at once. She entered the sitting room, and seconds later, Solomon heard the shot. He crept quietly downstairs across the Pigletty carpet and opened the door.

Solomon had only ever fired the gun twice and killed two men. Two! He sat with his true love and continued to wonder. Of course, the police would have to be informed. There was too much mess for anyone to clean it up. He turned the situation over in his mind. Alright, a man had broken into his house, shot his partner and attempted to rape her. That much was clear and concise. In an attempt to protect her, Solomon shot the man. That was all he could say. The only difficulty was the police would ask him where he had got the gun.

Well, where had he? The gun was now lying where he had dropped it, in the sitting room, but he had no wish to recover it. He assumed it was a standard police issue. Alright, he had killed the thief in Scotland with it, but there was no record of that as far as he knew. Maybe it would be alright, he thought. The main thing was getting Fran to a safe place to recover. Then he would call the police. He extricated himself from her and smiled. 'Just using the phone.' he explained. He had an idea that she nodded, but he couldn't be sure – she was still trembling from shock and the after-effects of the attack. He crossed the Pigletty carpet, picked up the phone, and pressed LR.

In the detention room, Solomon sat and waited. Detective Schofield had recorded a brief but accurate statement and left the room to get it typed out.

Lizzie had collected Fran and whisked her off to hospital, which was the right thing to do, according to Solomon's phone browser.

122

The police were issued with "removal tools," but the actual removal sounded painful, and these things were best left to medical staff.

Schofield returned, brandishing a folder, which he waved airily at Solomon before placing on the desk. He was more cheerful than Solomon expected him to be. Just as well, he thought. This could be a difficult interview. It was nearly midnight.

'Got in by the bay window.' said Schofield. 'Left-hand side. Glass on the inside, not the outside - that's how we can tell. It's an awful lot of blood, but still. Incredible the amount of blood we carry around with ourselves.' he said matter-of-factly. 'I remember one case once...' He caught Solomon's eye. 'Sorry. Doesn't matter. Anyway, he'd obviously decided that the house was empty and didn't care about Glass everywhere. Clear, he knew what he had come to do.' That look again. 'Sorry.'

He thought Solomon showed a quiet exasperation, which might help his cause.

'What happens next then?' he asked. 'Are you going to charge me?'

'With what?' wondered Schofield. 'Obviously not murder. Nothing pre-planned. Self-defense, in a way. Of course, I'm no lawyer. Few men would do otherwise, though, I'm guessing.' He opened the folder. 'Uh... always keep the gun in the house, I assume?'

'Where else? Is there no point having it if you can't lay your hands on it if you need it?

'I suppose not. Don't get an awful lot of visitors then?'

'Not ones that burst in via the windows, no.'

'Ah. No. Of course not.'

'I suppose I' 'll need a lawyer, won't I?'

'Do you have one?'

Solomon thought. 'There was a solicitor when we bought the house who kept on about "Demised premises." That's not really what he had in mind. This isn't really his kind of thing.'

'That's okay. We have one here, on the premises. I'll send him to you, and you can chat.'

Didn't seem quite the expression to use, but Solomon said, 'Okay.'

'Take it easy.' Schofield left the room.

The lawyer arrived minutes later.

'Mister Swift?'

Solomon nodded. 'Yes.'

'Ah. Good, good. Thought it must be. Mind if I sit?'

'Go ahead.'

The lawyer carried a brown leather briefcase. He paced it on the desk and read the statement in the folder.

After a few minutes. 'Right then. Where shall we start?'

'You have experience of these kinds of cases?'

'Oh yes. Very much so. New one every month, you might say.'

'Right. You tell me then. Where do we start?'

'Open and shut case.' said the lawyer. 'No matters undisclosed. I take it you have a license for the gun?'

'No.'

'No?'

'No.'

'Ah.'

After the slug's removal, the doctor insisted that Fran remain in the hospital overnight. Lizzie sat in the ward at her bedside, wondering what she could say. Her friend looked terrible - as you would, thought Lizzie. She tried to hold her hand, but that wasn't doing anybody any good, so she just sat quietly in case she was needed. Fran stared at the ceiling. She had been given codeine, so she should sleep in a few minutes. Lizzie could only sit and wait.

'Let's see.' said the lawyer. 'Where did you get it from?'

'Shall we say I found it?'

'Hm, could do. A judge will want more, though. Found it where?'

Solomon thought. 'Toilets, up on The Downs. My first thought was, can't leave that there. Never know who might pick it up.'

'A child, for instance?'

'Yes! A child! Well done! Anyway, I was going to hand it into these guys here but thought, well, you never know when you might need a gun, do you?'

'Not these days, no.' agreed the lawyer.

'Good job I did. Dread to think what I'd have done otherwise.'

'No doubt your appearance would have given him pause… Ah, no. Never mind. Yes, alright - you found it. Let's see how that goes down.'

'Will I have to go into a court and repeat all of this?'

The lawyer shook his head. 'Shouldn't think so, no. The courts are too busy to attend to these open and shut cases.' He opened and shut his case. 'Good day.'

Christmas came and went. They stayed with Rodney and Lizzie - at their place. Lizzie chirruped around them happily. Cooking up endless rounds of toast and smearing each slice with delicious lime marmalade. Rodney had given her a coffee machine for the gift-giving season, and they tried a new brand or recipe every day.

One December afternoon, they drove out to the countryside and wandered the Dorset pathways - looking at houses and thinking of moving. He tried walking with his arm around her, but that was never easy. He moved his arm from her waist up to her right shoulder, down her arm, and held her hand.

'Which do you think?' asked Solomon. 'In the village or outside it?'

'Well now.' said Fran. 'Let's think. I imagine that in the village, I'd be making jam and wine all day while the neighbours drop in with homemade cakes for Billy and Betty.'

'Billy and Betty? Are they our children's names?'

'No, silly.' She slapped him playfully. 'They're the sheepdogs.'

'Out of the village though, there's nothing. Look around you.'

'Yes, I know. It's perfect - paradise!'

'Dark at night, though.'

'Isn't everywhere? Besides, you'll protect me. I know you.'

'I'll protect *you*, yes, but what about me?'

'Still got your gun, haven't you? Not only that,' she said, moving swiftly on. 'There will be Billy and Betty, snarling and growling. A friend of mine once had a Labrador cross. Used to growl at anybody who came too near. Our dogs would be like that.'

'How do you make a Labrador cross?'

'Hide his bones.'

'Ha ha. In any event, what with all that snarling and growling and me snoring, we'd be better off out here. In the village, we'd be giving cause for complaints because of the noise.'

'Can't have that. Ruining someone else's paradise.'

'That's settled then.'

'What is?'

'Let's go to the pub and have a ploughman's.'

Jessica stood alone at the funeral. Her mother waited in the car. It had taken forever to finalise what had happened, but to the police, it all seemed straightforward - you might say it was elementary. Whatever the way, he was gone, and nobody was there to pay their respects save for her.

She hadn't seen or heard Solomon since that day and doubted whether he could shed more light on the circumstances than she had already read in the local newspaper report. Little had been made of it - just a few lines. A man had been killed breaking into a house. So what? Happened all the time, it seemed. It is easy to say that the victim, she saw him as that, had the balance of his mind affected. According to his medical notes, the level of drugs in his system was dangerous to anyone outside of a hospital. He had discharged himself, though. The nurses on duty at the time said there was nothing they could do.

The post-mortem had taken an age too. It's hard to see why if it was an easy case. Still, everything took time, one way or the other. Her mother had friends who had waited six to seven weeks for their burials. Jessica decided that she wouldn't have anything to do with that come the time. She'd seen the adverts for pure cremation on the TV; that was the way forward for her and her mother.

Now, she stood in the cold and watched her husband's disappearance into the ground. In her fist was a handful of dirt. Ironic, she thought. That, after all, was all he was - a handful of dirt. She let it fall and wiped her hands clean.

Sam served up the bacon baps. 'Six, was it?'

The foreman nodded. 'It was.' He took off his helmet and wiped his brow.

'How's it going? Be finished soon? Seems an awful tie in the demolishing of a Methodist church. Catholics, are ye?'

'No particular faith myself. Can't speak for the others.'

'Neither should you.' agreed Sam.

'Nevertheless, keep the bacon baps coming, and we'll stay all year.' Sam smiled at this. 'No, another week or two and we'll be gone. Diggers next. Scheduled for mid-January, but we'll see.' He took the paper bag from Sam. 'Thanks. See you tomorrow.'

'On the ice.' said Sam.

Solomon sat in the car and watched.

'Keep coming back here.' she observed.

'It's on our way.'

'Something else though?'

'Hmm.' he agreed. 'Something not quite right.'

'Like what?'

'If I knew that, sweetheart, we needn't keep stopping here.'

The remaining foundations were all that could now be seen. Dug well beneath the ground, they were solid blocks of concrete and, Solomon guessed, would have to be blown out with dynamite. 'What a night that will be,' he reflected. 'like fireworks.'

'They should have known they'd have such trouble.' said Fran.

'Yes, perhaps they did. It's the easiest way all around, though. Still, wouldn't mind a closer look all the same.'

'You should go over there. In your hi-vis coat. Show them your badge.'

'I don't have a badge.'

'You could make one.'

'True. Hmm…'

'Come on. Let's get back to Lizzie's. I can't wait to show her all the properties we've seen today. That second one, the Tudor gabled cottage. Room enough for a family. And guests, too.'

'Guests like Lizzie, d'you mean? Nah, she'd hate the country. See spiders and snakes everywhere. Proper city girl is Lizzie.'

'Heard her called worse. Still, we'd see she was well looked after.'

'No doubt.'

He got the yellow high-visibility coat from the boot of his car and his white helmet, too. Putting them on, he walked into Lizzie's kitchen.

'What do you think?'

'Very smart.' said one.

'Look the part,' said the other.

'You look like one of those Playmobil characters.'

'I'll take that as a compliment if you don't mind.'

'Not at all.'

'Now,' said Lizzie. 'You'll need a badge. Hold still while I take your photo. Put your reading glasses on. Makes you look authoritative.'

'Now there's a word.' said Fran.

'Sshhh, sshhhh. That's a serious face now. Hold on... That's got it. Good. Yes,' She looked at the image. 'Looks just like you. Now, email it to the PC...'

At the desktop, on the kitchen table, Fran was tapping at the keys. The computer went "Ping." 'That's got it. Let's have a look. Oh, yes. Excellent, Lizzie. Now, just export it into the document... Now, we'll need words. Something, what was your word, Lizzie? Authoritative.'

'You'll need to put "Hazardous Substances on it somewhere.' said Solomon. 'Put it in bold. That always makes people sit up and beg. After that, anything will do. Put the marriage service. No one's going to read it all.'

'No, we can't do that. It is bound to be the day someone's on-site and insists on inspecting it. I'll look on the internet, that's full of words. Bound to be something we can use.'

'Remind me,' said Lizzie. 'What are we doing all this for?'

'Simple as this,' said Solomon. 'Back in the day, a few hundred years ago, the church was built for the miners.'

'Gold!'

'Coal, you silly arse. Anyway, there were mines all about. All up and down the Pigsty Hill. Suppose they built the church on top of one?'

'Alright. What if they did?'

'Dynamite could make the rest of the foundations fall into a hole, a disused mine. This could set off a chain reaction that could lead to half the buildings on Gloucester Road being in danger of collapse.'

'Not, Sam, the butcher!'

'Even he. I'm not doing this for sausages, though.'

'Or pasties.'

'No. I'm just going to have a look. See what I can see.'

Later that day, he parked in his usual spot and surveyed the situation. It was a clear day. There is a chance of rain, but nothing to worry about in the early afternoon light. He got out of the car and put on his helmet. He also carried a clipboard. His new badge swung around his neck on a lanyard provided by Lizzie. She'd got it at Glastonbury festival when she had been litter-picking afterward. Fran had soaked the cover in coffee to give it an aged look.

He crossed the road. The church site was twenty yards away. He ambled towards it, looking for all the world, like a man who was sick and tired of his job but had to just keep on

Doing it.

He approached a similarly dressed man.

'Morning.'

'Afternoon.'

Solomon checked his watch. 'You're right, you're right. My God. Where do the days go?'

'What brings you here?' asked the man. A foreman, Solomon guessed.

'Just routine. Updates. You know the kind of thing.' He brandished his badge briefly and then took a pen from his inside jacket pocket, a Parker. He consulted his clipboard. 'You Mason?'

'Me? No. Stewart.'

'Stewart. S T U A R T ? Or S T E W A R T ?'

'The second one.'

'The second one.' repeated Solomon, scrawling rapidly. 'Good. Funny name, Mason, I thought. For demolition, I mean. Can you imagine it, can't you? "I'm a Mason. But I knock things down.' Solomon inspected the hole. 'Have to blast all this. Wouldn't you reckon?'

Stewart shook his head. 'Wouldn't know.'

'Wouldn't tell me if you did, would you?'

'You've got it.'

'Good man.'

'I'll leave you to it. New man on the job. Diggers everywhere. You know how it is.'

'I do indeed. All the best.'

Stewart wandered away, and Solomon wondered what to do next. He could easily step closer to the foundations, but what would be the point? A hole is a hole. There was obviously nobody on site who he could talk to, not at this time.

Maybe he should leave?

He turned back to the street and almost collided with someone he recognised. Those eyes, that hair, that fulsome figure. She stopped.

'Footballer.' she said.

'Nurse.' he replied. 'Thought I recognised you.' he continued.

'In these old things? Prefer me in my uniform, I expect. Most men do. Some women, too.' She was dressed in a grey top and chinos, carrying a paper bag with a baguette poking out. 'Needed bread.' she explained.

'Oh yes.' he joked. 'You always have to knead bread.'

She frowned slightly, unsure if he was joking.

'I'm joking.' he said. 'Should call you "Kneady Edie."'

'Oh! It's a joke. Thought so. Aw… you remembered my name.'

'One of the things I remember, yes.' he said.

'What brings you to these parts?' She looked him up and down. 'Look very official. All badged up. Problems?'

He couldn't remember if he'd told her what he did for a living.

'No, no. Nothing to worry about.'

'Good.' A clock struck eleven somewhere. 'Coffee time.' she said. 'Walk with me. I only live around the corner.'

While they walked, she chatted.

'Father used to be a minister there, so from an early age, I'd always be called upon to help him.'

'At the church? Right.'

'He couldn't get the hang of the typewriter, so there was always something to type up: Table-tennis fixtures, dates for coffee mornings. The dreaded sermon for Sunday. All those kinds of things.'

'Sorry to see it go? I guess.'

'Very. How about you? You don't look like a church-goer.'

'Who does? I was in the Sunday school. Used to play five-a-side football there.'

'In the church?' she smiled. 'How sacrilegious.'

'Oh, I wouldn't have said so. I imagine even Jesus played football when he wasn't out fishing.'

'Last one to be picked too.' She laughed. 'Blasphemy!'

'Sorry.'

They got to the house.

'I'm upstairs.' she said. 'First floor. Or the second floor if you're American. Why do they do that?'

'Do what?' asked Solomon, intrigued.

'Call the ground floor the first floor. It's technically correct, I suppose. It is the first floor you come to in a building. We're wasting time. Come on.'

They climbed the stairs to her door. She had a sensor key that undid the lock.

'Caroline! I'm back!' She walked to the kitchen area of the open-plan lounge and put the bread down.

'Nice place.' he remarked, following her in.

She shrugged. 'It's okay for the two of us. Used to be three, but Suzie's got herself engaged. Suits us though.'

'Great.'

'Tell you what,' she said. 'There's no time for coffee now. Let's go straight to bed.'

'All comfy?'

She smiled in the half-light. 'Always am with you.'

No one else was about, so Lizzie and Fran had decided to take it easy.

'Now, don't go getting all girly with me. Otherwise, I'll have to attack you again.'

'I wouldn't mind.'

'Neither would I. Good.'

They curled up together, cradling each other like spoons. Outside their windows, the world busied itself with what it thought were important matters. Lorries and buses honked and swerved up and down the street while smart cars bumped into each other again. In here, all was relatively quiet.

'Where were we?' Fran wondered.

'Said you'd told him everything. Him too.'

'Oh yes. Forgot.'

'Never mind. Here now. Talk to me.'

'We talked half the night. All out in the open. No holds barred.'

'All sins forgiven?'

'For now. Never know, of course.'

'Funny, we women do that. We say it's all over, but ask again in a month, a year, a lifetime, and these things come back to haunt us.'

'Quite a lot to be forgiven, really. If you think about it.'

'Like you and me?'

'For a start. You and me, him and you.'

'Me, you and Brun.' She guffawed. 'Sorry.'

'Me, you, Hilary, and Rod.'

'Something for everyone!' They both laughed. 'Anyhoo, you can't count Hilary. She hardly touched you.'

'Well, I was being dragged off to the spare room by your husband then.'

'He wasn't husbanding me at the time. Where were we?'

'Just talking.'

'Oh, yes. All sins are forgiven.'

'Hardest part though is the killing.'

'*Killings*. Plural.'

'Yes, I know.'

'How do you feel about that?'

'What? That he killed a man while trying to defend my honor?'

'Yes!'

'Not sure. It's kind of sexy, in a way. Turns me on, thinking about it now. What do you think?'

'For myself, I hope I'm never in a similar situation. He would have raped you, Fran. Done immeasurable harm - mental or physical. So long as he got what he wanted. Bastard.'

'And then, along came Solomon.'

'Yes, it does have a caveman-like feel to it, doesn't it? The call of the wild.'

'Must have done, I suppose.'

'And what about Jessica?'

'What about her?'

'Well, Solomon did offer her... comfort, in a manner of speaking.'

'We'd have done the same. After all, she was in an emotional torment. We often depend on sex to help us get through times like those.' She yawned and stretched, then cuddled closer. 'You know what?'

'What?'

'I kind of wish I'd been there, watching them. You know?'

'Only natural. Two attractive people having sex. Sells all the world over.'

'I bet he was great - her too. Always imagined him with someone else.'

'Why?'

'Just because, when it's me and him, we get locked into each other - there's no one else in the whole wide world. Makes me wonder sometimes.'

'I guess so. They were at it like knives, d'you mean?'

Fran laughed. 'Not really, no. That funny expression. I wonder what it means?'

'From the middle-ages.'

'Really?'

'Yes. The knife-grinder would pass through the streets: "Any knives to grind?" he'd shout. That's where the knives come in. And the grinding, I suppose. One of the metaphors for intercourse that we're always using.'

'Thank you, Miss Knowledgeable.'

'Any time.'

'Anyway, I'd have done the same thing.'

'Francesca, you did. You were there for me, and I was there for you. Simples.'

'Didn't have to let your husband drag me off to bed, did I?'

'Hardly had to drag you, my dear. Anyway, Rod's harmless. I bet you hardly felt it.'

'No. Well, I was exhausted.'

'Not surprised.'

'He liked looking at me while he was doing it.'

'Typical man.'

'Yes, but… after what happened…'

'What *nearly* happened.'

'Or nearly happened; I wasn't sure how I'd feel about it. Being looked at. Like some sort of, I don't know, sex object?'

It was Lizzie's turn to laugh. 'A sex object? Oh, my dear, gorgeous girlfriend. You'll always be that. To me.'

'Yes, but with you and me, it's different.'

'What about you and Solomon?'

'What about us?'

'Well, does he look at you in the same way?'

Fran thought about this. 'Ohh, yes. He certainly does. Like he'd do anything for me. Anything.'

'No, not that. That's just love - getting in the way, as usual. I meant how he looks into your eyes when he's screwing you. That look.'

She thought about this, too. 'Mm, yes. Always dreamed I'd have a man that looked at me like that.'

'Not just a casual fuck?'

'No.'

'Good old Rod, then. Ideal man, given the circumstances.'

'I suppose so.'

'I look at you too, you know. When we're… doing it. Love the look of you when you're in ecstasy.'

'Oh, that's just machinery. With a great big hulking man, it's different.'

'It certainly is.'

'Tell you what,' she said. 'Let's call it two-hundred and fifty. Really, that was twice, but I won't charge you for the second time because I like you - and you remembered my name. We won't charge for Caroline either, poor cow. It's been so long since she's had a shag she's probably pre-decimal.' She laughed at this. Caroline was asleep on her side, her back to them, snoring softly.

Solomon was not sure. 'I'm sorry.' he said. 'Do you expect me to pay you for what we've done?'

'Of course, darling.' she said, sounding like he could be anyone. 'You didn't think I gave it away for free?' She spread her arms out wide. 'All this?' She laughed.

'Well I…'

'Don't you think I was worth it? You liked it when I wrapped my legs around you, didn't you? Gets you in a bit deeper than that. I love it.'

'But you're a minister's daughter!'

'What's that got to do with anything? As you said, even Jesus played football. I don't imagine that was the only thing he got up to. In some of my father's writings, he was married with two kids.'

'Now who's being blasphemous?'

'Well, I mean - look around you - at the world's population. All came from the same place or places.'

'Yes, but do you mean to say that I can come around here, ring your bell - so to speak, give you two hundred pounds, and make love to you?'

'Love? This isn't love. Tell me, is someone waiting for you when you get home?'

Although they had told each other everything, he thought about Fran and felt ashamed.

'There you are then.' Edie had been thinking while rolling up a post-coital cigarette. 'Two hundred? Yes, alright. I didn't put the uniform on, did I? Still, you've seen me in that. I was ready for it and could see that you were too.'

Solomon waved a credit card. 'I don't suppose?'

'Well, of course, darling. You didn't take me for some kind of amateur, did you?' She produced her card reader. 'Thanks for that. Come again. Soon, you'll be able to get frequent flyer points.'

Solomon left the house and wandered down the path. He passed a man on the way; similar to him, they exchanged nods. He walked the short way back to the demolished church. A tiny street connected Edie's with Gloucester Road, sloping and already a little frosty. He observed a young man, jacketed and helmeted at the site, hitting the remaining concrete slabs with a sledgehammer. So, they weren't blasting after all. The young man acknowledged his presence.

'Thirsty work.' said Solomon.

'Not really.' said the young man. 'Trick is to let the tool do the work.' He held the hammer horizontally and then let it fall - with minimal effort. The hammer hit its target, and another block fell.

'Good work.' said Solomon. 'Your boss will be pleased with you.'

The man let the hammer rest and wiped his brow with his sleeve. 'I am the boss.' he said.

He placed the hammer carefully on the newly-disturbed ground.

'So, what brings you here, mister...' He peered at Solomon's badge.

'Noname.' said Solomon. 'Never mind with the jokes. I've heard them all.'

'Sure you have.'

'What's next then?'

'No clue. Eight tonnes of topsoil arriving soon. Of course, you can only get six on a lorry. I said make it two lots of four, but I imagine it'll be a six and a two.'

'I see.' said Solomon, gravely. 'And then what?'

'Ooh, who knows? The plot will be sold off for land green space. They say it's topsoil, but there's ever so many roots and seedlings. Come back here in a month, and you'll need a pair of shears or a gardener.'

'But what if the land is sold for development?' insisted Solomon.

'Why should I care?' enquired the man. Then, 'Alright, suppose it is. They'll dig new foundations, find what's been left there, and act accordingly.'

'What if they do?'

'Well, what if they do? We've had seismic surveys all around here. Yes, there were mines here once, but there's no danger of anything being disturbed underneath.'

'What if they build cellars?'

'Windowless cellars? What for?'

'I don't know. Wine?'

The man was thoughtful for a while. He looked down the hill. 'Wine cellars. Now, there's an idea.'

Solomon left the man pondering. He got into his car and drove to Lizzie's. Unresolved thoughts clouded his mind. Well, suppose they did build cellars? Suppose they blew up half the Pigsty Hill? Like the man said, why should he care? Seismic surveys. What did he know? Nothing. He had a friend who did, but he would be hundreds of miles away, on a dry boat in the middle of the North Sea now. Uncontactable. Still, there was always the internet.

He also wondered about Jess. He hadn't heard from her for a long time and hoped she was getting on with her life. Despite everything, he still had a soft spot for her. One that all the Helens and Edies couldn't compete with. Maybe he should drop in on her one day. Or one night…

He found himself thinking about Helen's breasts. Then Edie's. Then Caroline's! Then Jessica's. His poor heart raced. Why was it, he wondered, that the shape of a woman's body governed and marshaled a man's thoughts. Sure, some sort of cry-back to the nursery, but once a grown man, what did they want with what women kept beneath their blouses and shirts? He drove home in silence.

Sure, women loved their own breasts. Most women, anyway. He supposed it was the same as he was with his penis. All blokes were the same. All had pet names for them, although he had never thought of one for his. "Rocket," probably. Something like that.

That was different, though. A man's appendage was his means of reproduction. A woman's breasts weren't anything like that. Tended to get excited - when they were tended to. He smiled to himself. Especially Fran's… And Lizzie's. And Jessica's. Helen's, Edie's…

He got back and let himself in. He crept quietly up the stairs and peeped through the gap in the nearly-closed bedroom door. Fran and Lizzie were curled up together, fast asleep.

He grinned and headed for the shower.

'Wassa matter? You not tired?'

In the darkness, she shook her head on the pillow. 'Not really, no. Bit worried about our little girl, that's all.'

'Which one?'

'Oh, for heaven's sake, Desmond. Francesca, of course.'

'Oh. Thought you meant the other one.'

'The other one's name is Jennifer, Desmond. As you well know.'

'I know. Heh-heh - could have been Norma.'

'Norma? Why?'

'Norma Desmond. Geddit? Heh-heh.'

'Oh, joking again. Typical you.'

'What's wrong with her anyway?'

'Franny? Not sure. Been through a lot lately. Bound to have an effect on her. I'm waiting for signs.'

'Of what? She'll get over it - people do. No matter what you do to your fellow man, he'll always come up smiling again.'

'Francesca is not a man, dear.'

'Never said she was. Whatever the way, she'll get over it in her own time. You know how resilient she's always been? Remember when that tortoise of hers ran away?'

'It did not run away, Desmond. You sold it to one of your workmates.'

'Well, told her it ran away, and she was fine about it. Got another one the very next day.'

'Which you also sold.'

'Pets. Always die. Prepares you for life, that's what I think. Never mind past experiences. Whatever happens, doesn't mean she's depressed or anything. Fact is, I found her pretty cheerful the last time we spoke.'

'I didn't say she was depressed. Oh, that's the trouble with you. You never listen to what I'm saying.'

'I'm listening now, aren't I?'

'I suppose so. Well, at least she's got Solomon. He thinks the world of her. See it in his eyes, can't you?'

'I should bloody think so! I mean, you don't blow a man's head off for someone you couldn't give two stuff over, do you know? Do you? No. Thought not.'

'I'm just worried that it might affect her. Long-term, you know? Deep down inside. Ooh! Oh, what's the point? You never listen.'

'Hard to hear you sometimes. With that hover-mower or whatever you call it, whirring away under the bedclothes.'

'I make no excuses. It relaxes me.'

'Hope you're thinking of me while you're doing that.'

'Well, I am. In a way.'

'In what way?'

'Well, thinking about you and me in our younger days.'

'That cornfield in summer. Pembrokeshire.'

'Yes. Yes, that was fun. We did have some fun, didn't we?'

'Got two daughters, haven't we?'

'Seems a long time ago now.'

'Well, we're not dead yet. Put it away in the drawer and climb on top of me.'

'Oh, no, Desmond, no. Suppose you had a turn or something?'

'A turn? That's a laugh. I should be glad of a turn every now and again. A turn? Huh. Funny, I don't think. Used to be mad about you, you know?'

'I know.'

'Said I'd do anything for you.'

'I know. You did. I know you did.'

'Come over to my side. Let me take your nipples in my mouth again.'

'No. I know you. You'll bite. I'd be sore for ages afterward.'

'Afterwards. Huh.'

'Sleepy now.'

'Switch it off then. You'll run the batteries down.'

'Okay. There. Back in the drawer. All gone.'

'Who'd you think about this time?'

'Never you mind.'

She closed her eyes.

He put his hand between her legs.

'Oh, no, Desmond. No. Go to sleep. You'll be rubbish in the morning.'

'Not morning yet, is it? Sshhh. This won't hurt a bit.'

'Ohh.'

'Always fancied you rotten, Barbara. Always dreamed I'd have you one day. And now I have.' He ran his hands over her. 'This is mine. And this is mine. And this, and this.' She began to snore softly. 'And now look at us. Only in our fifties. Still life in the old dogs yet.' He tried to get on top of her, but he was unable to; his lithe form was no match for her ample womanly curves. There was so much of her. She wasn't fat but well-proportioned. Always had been. The first girl in the youth club to get boobs. Just appeared with them one evening in her half-cup bra and left all the boys with their tongues hanging out. All had lovers' balls the following day...

All except him. She liked him. He'd had his hands full that evening.

He caressed her full, rounded breasts with his skinny hands. 'Lovely.' He collapsed back onto his own side and stared at the ceiling.

'Fabulous woman. Say what you like.' he murmured.

In her sleep, she smiled.

Later, after showering and shaving, he bedded down in the spare room for the night.

Presently, the door squeaked open quietly, and a voice whispered:

'Solly? You awake?'

The luminescent orange streetlights outside vaguely lit her female form.

'Yeah, of course. What's up?'

'Can I come in with you?'

'You have to ask?'

'Move over then. Here I come. Brrr. Cold. Hate these thin beds.'

'Won't be for long.'

'No, I guess not. Mmm, you're lovely and warm.'

'Soon warm you up too.'

'Smell nice.'

'Showered.'

'Oh. How'd it go then?'

'The shower? So-so.'

She slapped his chest playfully. 'Idiot. I meant at the church.'

Solomon thought back over the day's events. Obviously, some things are better left unsaid…

'Happened to run into the boss-man.'

'Oh yes?'

'Yes.'

'And what did he have to say for himself?'

'Not much. I asked him what would happen if somebody came along and blasted the foundations.'

'Dynamite.'

'Exactly. Remember a friend of mine who was in the seismic game. Mad Angus - remember him? I'm all at sea at the moment, but I can do some research on the net tomorrow. He bored us all silly one night, talking about chain reactions and what-have-you. Something about one explosion causes enough CO_2 that it triggers another explosion nearby. Like a vacuum cleaner in reverse. Of course, all quite pissed at the time.'

'No doubt.'

'Left it like that. Suggested wine cellars to him.'

'Wine cellars? Why wine? Golly, that's not easy to say, is it?'

'Sure. Why not?'

'No, I suppose so. What are you thinking then?'

'That this would make all of the potential new-builds much more expensive. Trouble is, a chain reaction like that could destroy half of the hill.'

'Oh, I see.'

'Wonder why it bugs me? I mean, what is it to me?'

'I don't know. Happens sometimes. You get obsessed with something, and you can't see something else that is under your very nose.'

'True story. Wait a minute.'

'What?'

'You're naked.'

'I know. What's the matter? You never seen a naked woman before?'

'Well, now and then, I suppose.' They both chuckled quietly. 'Not one like you, though.'

'Oh no, Solomon. There's no one like me. Come here… oohhh, is all that for me? Lucky girl, aren't I? Better be on top form tonight.'

'Ohh, come here you.' Her face was softly illuminated by the orange glow from outside. He kissed her and ran his fingers through her hair. 'Crazy about you, you know that, don't you?'

'Had a pretty good idea, yes.'

'First time I saw you naked, I thought, yes, there's somebody I'd like to know better.'

'Felt the same about you too.'

'Crazy. You ready?'

'Think so. Try and see.'

The bed creaked quietly in places.

'Sshhh.' she said. 'You'll wake Fran.'

The following day, Solomon met the boss-man again.

His name was Norman - or, at least, he wore a badge with that name on it. Whether it was his first or last name, Solomon neither knew nor cared. It reminded him of "Psycho II," which was all he could think of.

He offered the man a cigarette, an old trick of his fathers. During that man's employed years, he had been a sales representative for a builders' merchant. If you offered a man a cigarette, he would say you'd bought five minutes of his time. Plenty of time to make a sale. Yes, Solomon used to think, five minutes of his life, that he would never get back again.

Nonetheless, he puffed away happily with Norman and concentrated on more important things.

'No topsoil then?'

'Thanks.' Norman blew smoke. 'No. Out of stock, it seems. How you can be out of stock of soil is a mystery. Fields are full of it.

Still, the driver said he only had five tonnes. I asked him when the other three were being delivered, and he said he didn't know. I told him to come back when he did. Phoned the branch, and they said it could be a week or two. Out of stock. Of topsoil, mark you.'

This monologue seemed to tire the man, so Solomon let him smoke in peace for a while.

'Gives us an opportunity though.'

'Oh? coughed Norman. 'To do what?'

'Have a bit of a look-see. That patch in the corner. Looks like stairs. What is it?'

'No idea at all, as it goes. Stairs leading down to a locked metal door is all I know.'

'Can't you go down and see?'

'No. Confined Spaces Act. 1997. You ought to know that. I do: "No person at work shall enter a confined space to carry out work for any purpose unless it is not reasonably practicable to achieve that purpose without such entry." Had to learn that by heart.'

'I see.' Solomon pondered. 'So, what could be down there, d'you think?'

'Couldn't say. Priest hole?'

'In a Methodist Church? No. Besides, this place was only built a few hundred years ago. They didn't have things like that back then.'

'Could be anything then.' said Norman. 'Who knows?'

Solomon flicked his cigarette butt into the foundations. 'Well, as it happens, I may know someone who does.'

She was surprised to see him.

'Why, hello, footballer.' she said. 'What brings you here? I know, can't get enough of me, hey?'

He smiled and edged past her into the house. 'No, it's not that.'

'Oh. Shame. Always liked you.'

'Something else. It's to do with the church.'

'Want me to convert, is that it?' She smiled. 'Only joking. Just making coffee. Want one? Cold out, I expect.'

'Freezing. Lovely. Thanks.'

'Come through, come through. Park yourself on a stool. Now, mugs, mugs, mugs… Ah! Here we are. Boil, kettle, boil!'

'Shouldn't boil the water for coffee.' he said. 'Just below boiling point, or you'll frazzle the beans.'

'Better tell the kettle that then. Not me. Now then. Something about the church?'

'Oh yes. On the far side, in the corner. Steps go down to a locked door. Any idea what's in there?'

'Yes, of course. Hymn book store.'

'Hymn book store?'

'Yes.' It made her giggle. 'Sounds funny when you say it.'

'But, what for?'

'Well, briefly, too many bugs in the air molder the books. Some of them are of a "considerable age." Apparently, it keeps them more preserved in an underground space. That's what it was built for. A lot of the churches have them. Not just here. All over the country.'

'I see. Yes, makes a kind of sense, I suppose.'

'Suppose away. That's what it's for. Spent many a happy hour down there.'

'Oh yes? Doing what?'

'Not for you to know. Drink your coffee.'

He did so. His blue mug was lettered in white with the slogan, "Save the NHS!" He quite agreed. The coffee revived his senses. She was right - it was cold outside.

'How big is it?' he asked.

'As big as the church is. Or was. The whole length and width. Wasn't always full of books, of course, but there was space for them if we needed it.'

'Why make it so big?'

'Cheapest option. There are no walls down there. Just what's it called? Dexion. Shelving.'

'I see.'

'See a lot, don't you? Tell you what, get that coffee down you, and I'll let you have a free one. That'll warm you through properly.'

'Are you sure?'

'Sure, I'm sure. I've got nothing on this morning.'

'Love you when you've got nothing on.'

'Come on then.'

Barbara laid the white linen tablecloth over her late grandmother's dining table. A family heirloom; the table, not the cloth. Both leaves flat out underneath. She smoothed the material flat with the palm of her hand, her wedding ring catching on the gaps between the leaves. She stood up straight and surveyed her work.

'That's it. Fantastic. It's amazing what a piece of white material will do. Now, a centerpiece.'

In the corner of the room was a sturdy oaken display unit, filled with ornaments in glass that provided... possibilities. Two swans dancing, doing the courtship of love, she thought. The sight arrested her eyes.

'Yes. The very thing.' She carried the piece, almost reverentially, to the center of the table and placed it carefully.

'Thought I might invite them round.'

Desmond sat in his favourite armchair, studying the Sunday papers. The sun shone weakly through the French windows.

'Mm? Who?'

'Don't you ever listen?' She sighed. 'Franny and Solomon, of course.'

'Oh, of course. Yes, why not? Franny.'

'And Solomon.' she reminded him.

'Oh, of course. Solomon too. Mustn't forget him.'

'Good. How about next Sunday? I could do a roast.'

'Ah, yes. Good idea. Love a roast, me. Potatoes in goose fat. Reminds me of Chrimbo.'

'What if he's a vegetarian? People often are?'

'Who?'

'Solomon, of course!'

'Oh, Solomon. Of course. Sorry. Carry on. Love a roast, me.'

'I know you do. That is the only reason I suggested it. Lamb, I think.'

'Lamb yourself.' Desmond coughed as if to cover some embarrassment.

'I'll invite them then. Yes?'

'Yes. Sorry. Invite who?'

She came across the tastefully decorated room, all polished timber furniture, and bright cream walls and carpeting. Various ornaments littered every flat surface. Sporting triumphs that showed Desmond could concentrate if he tried. Used to, anyway.

She perched on the arm of his chair and crossed her legs. Her skirt rode up her thigh. He risked a glance.

'Your daughter, Francesca.' she reminded him again.

'Oh, right. Still, on that, are we? Right.'

'And Solomon. Her intended.'

'Solomon, too. Right. Right.'

'He'll sit opposite me. You'll be at the head of the table.'

'Master of the house. Right.'

'And Francesca will be opposite you.'

'Always was. Bloody tortoise.'

'What shall I wear, d'you think?'

'Ooh, I dunno. What you've got on now. Seems alright.'

'What? These old things? I just wear these for cleaning the house.'

'Good job, too.'

'No. I want something special.'

'Why?'

'Why not?'

'Oh, fair enough. Cards in the wallet there.'

'Thanks.'

'Don't see why we have to make a big fuss anyway. You know how it is with a roast. One slip of the fork, and you've got gravy all down your shirt.'

'You do, yes. I won't. I will be quite the belle of the ball.'

'What for? Not a special occasion, is it?'

'You never know. Who knows what the next year or two will bring. Might be wedding bells in the wind.'

'Not in the wind, no. Bad idea. Continual clonking would drive you nuts.'

She gazed into space. 'I meant a marriage. A beautiful white wedding.'

'White? Alright. You know best. You'll want a new dress for that too, I shouldn't wonder.'

'No, you shouldn't. Well, anyway, I want something nice. Better than these old togs. Something that makes me feel like a woman.'

'Alright. See you upstairs.'

'Don't be coarse! I meant for the meal. I want to look a million dollars.'

'*Pounds* over here. War's over. Remember? Don't see why you want to go to so much trouble for.'

'No, of course not, Desmond.' She stood up. 'That's because you never see anything.'

The barracks still retained the feel of the British army - like it belonged here.

Wendy was prepared for this: She wore slipper socks under her regulation boots.

The Scot in her small troupe took a place opposite her.

'Someone sitting here?'

'Is now.' she said, between mouthfuls. The meals here were generally dreadful; enough to keep body and soul together but only just. Today's specialty was some sort of fish and potato pie. Friday; hence, the fish. For all the cadets who were Roman Catholics, there were many.

'Thanks.'

She studied him haphazardly. Offered him the condiments.

'Salt? Helps. A little.'

'A little salt!' A smile. At last. 'Thanks again.'

'Any time.'

'Right.'

What brings you this far south? Colchester must be about four hundred miles from the Wall.'

'Hadrian's, d'you mean? Yes. Three hundred and twenty-five, according to my hire car.'

'They'd know.'

'Absolutely.'

'You're a good shot. I've watched you. Why the extra training?'

'Standard practice after an incident.'

'An incident? What happened?'

'I got shot.'

'Oh. Sorry.'

'Occupational hazard, as they say. Not a problem. The little shit that did it got killed. Could have been me.'

'Always the case. Still sorry, though.'

'Partner got killed too. I was lucky.'

'Lucky?'

'You know what I mean. Name's Carter, by the way.'

They shook hands across the table.

'I'm Wendy. Sorry, surnames, isn't it? Good police protocol. Bentley. Nice to meet.'

'Vegetarian, me. Sorry, - joke.'

'That's funny!'

'Thought so. Thanks. Again. Seem to be thanking you for everything. Whatever next?' He looked around the half-deserted room. 'Jeez, what a dump. Is there anything to do around here? Saw you wrapped around the pretty blonde cadet the other evening. Partner?'

'Just a friend.'

'Yes. All looked pretty friendly. So, tell me, what is there to do around here? If one doesn't have a pretty blonde in tow?'

'Could always do me.'

'Really?'

'Yes. It's okay. I'm Bi.'

In the afternoons, she took a siesta. Desmond pottered in the garden, grumbling about weeds or birds. It was winter, though, and there was little to do.

No matter. It got him out of the house for a bit. A ticking clock downstairs was the only noise.

Nevertheless, she was restless today. She stretched herself out flat. The central heating was set at twenty degrees. She had got herself undressed, unusually. Usually, she just laid down and drifted off. Not today, though. Someone on her mind…

She inspected herself with her hands. Everything is in the right place - more or less. Breasts and nipples still responded to her touch - or anyone else's, she assumed. She wondered about calling Desmond in, just for a bit of a frolic - like old times. She dismissed this thought from her mind. Old times were old times. Best left in the past. You could never go home again.

She contented herself with the fact that even now, her husband thought her attractive. The trouble was, they were virtually the same age, not like old times at all.

She took the device from her drawer and placed it where the sun never shines.

She relaxed.

'Now then.' she said to herself softly. 'Solomon…'

They lay together afterward. Holding each other for warmth.

'Wow.'

'Thank you. It's a pleasure to serve. You were pretty good, too.'

'Better than a woman?' he teased.

She shook her head. 'It's different, that's all. I've been seeing a lot of women lately. You make a nice change.'

'Thanks. Why both, though? Can't you decide?'

'Clearly not. It's funny.'

'What is?'

'The police force is still so male-dominated. For every WPC that I tell that I'm gay, the look in their eyes. They're like, "Really?" Like it was some kind of brand new thing.'

'Like, "The Untouchables."' he joked. 'You should stick to men. Call me any time. Although the scar's a bit off-putting, I imagine.'

'Seen worse.' she said.

'I suppose you have. Rough town, Bristol. So I've heard.'

'Heard a lot about Scotland, too. Lots of unpunished crime.'

'Same as down here then.'

'Not really, Gangs and muggings. Nothing is out of control. Nothing we can't handle. Tell me more about your incident. If you're okay talking about it?'

'Typical copper. Always on the job. Can't switch it off, can you?'

'I imagine you're the same?'

'Got me. Truce.'

'One or two things on my mind. You know how it is. Thought it might help if we discussed them. Don't have to if you don't want to.'

'No, it's okay. It can't do any harm, will it?'

'Mental scars, maybe?'

'Nah. Scotsman, me. All as hard as nails where I come from.'

'Sometimes that's not enough.' she said, feeling the scar on his shoulder.

'Worse than it looks.' he grimaced. 'They had to cut me to get the bullet out. Glad I slept through that.'

'It'll heal. Get the sun on it. Or a lamp.'

'Good idea.'

'What happened then? You say your partner was killed. Did he shoot the perp?'

'No. Didn't get a chance. He was shot first. As I say, I was lucky. In the squad car with us was the victim. He'd been hi-jacked; the bastard had taken his truck. Jimmy and I set out to apprehend, and I gave the victim our spare gun - just to protect himself, nothing more.'

'Go on?'

'Next thing I knew, Jimmy was shot dead, and I had this tremendous pain in my shoulder. Heard another shot - thought it was the killer, come back for me but, no. The victim had shot the guy.'

'Killed the killer. Interesting.'

'Well, they carted me off to hospital. Never saw him again. Hardly had time to thank him.'

'Who was he?'

'One of your lot - Sassenach. Came from Bristol, actually. Said he did, anyway. Did something with cigars.'

'Cigars?' she said.

'Yeah. Said he picked and packed them or something.'

'Picked and packed. Interesting.'

'Alright, Inspector. Ready for Round Two?'

'Don't tell me you are?'

'Sure. Got you here now, haven't I? All blondes standing aside, for the moment.'

'But you're a man. You should be snoring your head off and dreaming about football by now.'

'Well, I'm not. Feel.'

'Armed and dangerous.' she said. 'Nice.'

Edie sat at the kitchen bar top, brooding.

'Morning!' It was Caroline. She breezed through the flat like a sea breeze. 'Paper come yet?'

'Not heard it.'

Caroline looked at her watch. And then at the clock. 'Should be here by now. Shouldn't it?'

Edie shrugged. 'Who knows? Maybe there isn't any news today. Maybe nothing of any great importance has happened in the last twenty-four hours, so nothing's been printed. Yes. I expect it's that.'

'Oh dear.' said Caroline. 'Whose bed did you get out the wrong side of this morning?'

'Nobody's.'

'Well, that's even worse. Hate waking up alone.'

'Thought you'd be used to it by now.'

'Spiteful, Edie. Spiteful. Come on. Tell your auntie Caroline what's wrong. As if I didn't know. You've got that face on again.'

158

'What face? What are you talking about, crazy nurse?'

'Go on. Say it.'

Again, Edie shrugged. 'I've fallen in love.'

'Oh dear. Not again.'

'Yes, again. Happy now?'

'No, of course not. Hate to see you unhappy. You're such a bright and cheerful person. Cheer all souls up. You're just no good if you're miserable.'

'It's not my fault. It's men that make me miserable. Blame them.'

'Who is it this time? Anyone I know?'

'You may have a memory of him. Still, you weren't really awake at the time.'

'Oh. Him.'

'What do you mean, "Him"?'

'Didn't catch his name. I'm too busy catching my breath instead. God, he was huge! That the one?'

'Yes.' said Edie wretchedly. 'The footballer.'

'What are you going to do?'

'Same as ever - what can I do? Men don't want prostitutes who fall in love with them. It's too complicated.'

'For the last time, Edie, you are not a prostitute.'

'I know, I know. I just offer my "services" to men for money. It's quite different.'

'Keeps you out of trouble, doesn't it? Don't I? Saves creeping around bars at night, covering your drink with your hand and trying to get lucky. You get to pick and choose.'

'Yes, and every time I pick and choose, I end up miserable. I have got a good mind to give it all up. Just stick to the nursing. None of the men who come here mean anything to me, not on an emotional level.'

'Apart from the footballer?'

'Apart from him, yes.'

'Go on then. Tell me he's the most wonderful man you've ever met. How you're going to get married and raise a family. Somewhere in the country, possibly. A cottage with roses around the door and a horseshoe overhead.'

'Oh, shut up.'

The following morning:

'Breakfast in bed? Luxury.'

'Bet you don't get this in bonny Scotland.'

'Salty porridge is all. What's this? Bacon? Told you I was a vegetarian.'

'You did. Made me laugh.'

He crunched and then munched. 'Well, this is lovely. You've been lovely. Thanks a lot.'

'Any time.'

'If you'd told me I'd spend the night with you, I'd never have believed it.'

'Oh, I can be unbelievable sometimes.'

'You sure can. It's funny. In your cadet uniform, you're all sort of staid and prissy. Underneath it all, though…'

'I know. I'm fantastic!'

'That too. And you can pull blondes faster than I can. With your black hair and blue eyes. Every inch of your perfect skin. Love the socks, by the way.'

'I shall always wear them.'

'Good. Settled then. Tea in the pot?'

'Of course. I know Scotsmen. Traditional Scottish breakfast, isn't it? Cup of tea and three fags.'

'Three? You're spoiling me.'

'Can't smoke in here. Detectors.'

'Freezing outside, by the look of it.'

'Stay here then. You're quite safe. I won't bite you. Unless you want me to?'

'No, no. Just tea, thank you.'

'Thank *you*. I've been thinking.'

'Thought you might be. Go on?'

'Can I ask you something?'

'Just did. Sorry. Go ahead.'

'About the date.'

'A date? Is this a date? Well, heaven preserves us.'

'No, silly. Your incident. What was the date it happened?'

'Mind telling me why?'

'Just got an idea about it. A hunch, you might say.'

'I might. What's it about, this hunch?'

'It's what you said about cigars. A friend of mine has a partner who was away in Scotland last year. Delivering cigars.'

'Aha. And?'

'She used the very same words to describe what he did for a living.'

'Words? What words?'

'You said - and she said, "He picks and packs cigars."'

Carter shook his head. 'Not so strange. I mean, if you picked and then packed cigars for a living, how would you describe it?'

'I suppose so.'

'Anyway, the population of Bristol is about three-quarters of a million people, including the Greater Urban Sprawl. What makes you think he's your guy?'

'Thing is, a few weeks later, he shot and killed an intruder in his house. With a Colt forty-five. Scottish issue, correct?'

'Correct. So?'

'Of course, it never made the news; these kinds of crimes are more or less commonplace. Justice appeared to have been done in this case. There is nothing further to report. But we get to hear about things sometimes. The intruder tried to rape the female in the house. That's why our guy killed him. Just one shot.'

'Still got four left then, ain't he?' said Carter devilishly.

'Seriously though. Made me think.'

'Aha. She's a friend of yours, is she? The wife?'

'They're not married. Not yet. Well?'

'Well, what?'

'I'm guessing.' she began. 'That your incident was on or about the second weekend of November.'

'Saturday.' He whistled, impressed. 'How the hell did you work that out?'

'I'm a police officer.' she said. 'So are you.'

'Well, what about it? Don't you think the killer got what was coming to him?'

'Emotionally, yes. But there's still such a thing as justice, Carter.'

'Please - call me Jim. We're well acquainted now, ain't we?'

'Wait a minute. I thought your partner's name was Jim?'

'It was. That's why they call me Carter.'

'I see. Where were we?'

'The punishment should fit the crime. I think that's what you were driving at.'

'Oh yes. That's right. Don't you think so? I mean, I'm all for vigilante action. God knows we hardly have the man-hours or officers for the current crime levels.'

'Your Bristol intruder - shot with the same gun as our gangster was. What were the charges?'

'There weren't any. Sometimes, we just do what we do for a quiet life. Peace and quiet.'

'So, what about justice?'

'What about it?'

'Exactly.'

'Well? What were the charges in your case?'

'None at all.' he said. 'You know these gang members - same down here, too, I expect. They're all no more than kids just out of school or borstal. Prison even. Nothing to live for. Do anything for cash or heroin. Strange the effect that stuff has on them.'

'Cash?'

'Heroin, funny girl. They all think we can't smell it. Stinks the cars out some nights. I keep one of those Christmas tree air fresheners on the rear-view mirror… Where was I?'

'Gangs and their members.' she said helpfully.

'Thanks. Anyway, there might be a missing persons' report, but generally, no more than that. It's like swatting flies. Glad to see the back of them. Never amount to anything, will they?'

'That's sad.'

'So it is, Wendy, so it is. But then, life is sad. Being a police officer soon teaches you that.'

'Wait a minute.'

'Now what?'

'You're saying your name is Jimmy Carter? Like the U.S. President?'

'He was okay.'

'Still is, I think. Must be about a hundred by now.'

'He's... wait now. What am I? Yes, he's ninety-eight. Still going strong.'

'Parents were Democrats?'

'His or mine?'

'Yours, you fool!' She laughed. He made her laugh. She liked that. He had always made her laugh. Ever since she had... befriended him.

Befriended. Now there was a word...

'Nah.' he said in reply to her question. 'Parents barely had an education between them. Originally, the father's family were carters. That's all I know.'

'Oh. Okay.'

'Story of my life there. Didn't take long, did it?'

'Not over yet, is it?'

'I suppose not. Not yet a while. What are we doing today? Is there a module?'

'Ten-thirty.'

'Right. Knew you'd know. I don't know why we have to have one every single day. Gets tiring; boring even.'

'Poor you. Gets it all out of the way at once, doesn't it? Otherwise, we'd sit around all day, bored to tears. Playing games on our stupid p[phone apps and shagging each 0other.'

'thank you.'

'I'd sooner get it all done and go back home.'

'Home?'

'Where the heart is.'

'So I believe.' Carter looked around. 'You've got this little place turned out nice.'

'Thank you. Suits me. Didn't do a thing, actually. It's the same as the last person left it. Bit basic, but what can you do?'

'Just put up and shut up, I guess.'

'Quite right, may as well. It will all be over before we know it. What's your like?'

'Oh, pretty much the same as this. I'm on a higher floor, and we have to share a shower. Not all at the same time, you understand.'

'I understand.'

'Still, a bed, a sink, table and chair.'

'Sounds charming. You must have me round some time.'

'"Have you"?'

'You know what I mean. Saucy.'

'Like a prison, really. I imagine.'

'Good job, I'm around then. Don't get this kind of action in Holloway.'

'Holloway is a women's prison.'

'I know.'

'You would.'

'Think I might go and see her.' she said.

'The partner? What for?' he said, keeping up.

'Because, sometimes, Jim, justice has to be seen to be done. A man has killed two others. Don't you think there should be more investigation than what's passed? Otherwise, what the hell is the point of a law-enforcement department?'

'Better just keep our noses to the grindstone; learn what we can. Why rock the boat?'

'Because it isn't a boat, James. This is real life, yours and mine. Don't you think we owe it to ourselves to investigate further?'

'Wait a minute, wait a minute... I begin to see how your mind is working. You just want to contact your friend and offer her comfort and solace. Don't you know? Is that it?'

She lay back and smiled. 'Maybe, maybe. A little comfort and solace can go a long way.'

'"Won't be long." they said. Hah!' She collapsed next to him on the sofa. 'If I know those two, they'll be gone for an hour. Two probably. Ah well. Time to relax for a while. Takes it out of you; all this entertaining.'

'You'll have to come to ours another time.'

'Another time? Thank you, Solomon. I'd enjoy that.' She smoothed her skirt down with her nail-polished fingers and folded her arms.

'It was a lovely meal, Barbara. Genuine Dorset lamb. Delicious. Thank you.'

'Any time at all, Solomon. Any time. Just ask. It's lovely to see you. Both. I say, "Any time," but you'd have to give me advance warning. I always forget how much work has to go into these occasions. Tablecloths to iron, potatoes to peel, carrots and swede to grate; everything planned to the very last inch. Then there's the laying of the table. You should have seen me this morning, spreadeagled across the table with my arms stretched out as far as they could go. What a sight I must have looked.'

'I can imagine.'

'You should do.' She smiled, sat back, and unfolded her arms. She placed them on either side of her. Her fingers clenched the Velour material. Then she said:

'Would you like to kiss me?'

Solomon was astonished. 'Me?'

'Yes. You. No one else here is there? They won't be back for ages. Desmond is very fussy about wine; so's Fran, as you know. The grape, the grain, the origin. The *appellation contrôlée*. Drives me mad. That's why I always make him go alone.'

'He's left you alone with a strange man in the house. Anything could happen.'

She laughed. 'You're not so strange. Not to me. Anyplace, he knows he can trust me. What about you, Solomon? Do you think you can trust me?'

'I'm not sure.'

'It's alright. I won't tell anyone. And the chain's on the door so no one will disturb us. Well? What about it? I know you've thought about it. I can see it in your eyes sometimes when you look at me. "Hello," I thought. "May have to watch this one."'

'And have you?'

'Have I what?'

'Watched me?'

'Oh, yes. Very, very closely, I've watched you, Solomon. Well? Don't be coy. Now's your chance. Kiss me. Go on. Who's to know?'

He leaned closer and put his lips to hers, awkwardly at first. She accepted him easily. Their mouths were soon a torrent of tastes and scents. Their senses whirled.

After a while, they broke to catch their breath.

'Mm, delicious.' she said. 'You taste of mint sauce.'

'So do you. Sorry.'

'Don't be. I liked it. All my own work. Thanks. You're a good kisser. Licked the back of my teeth with your tongue. Well, sexy. Hold on, let me unbutton myself. Then you can have a good feel. You'd like that, wouldn't you? All men like the feel of a woman's breasts. Women love it too.'

'Unhook your bra.'

'No. We can't. We'd get caught. Not that I haven't dreamt of it. Do you like my tits, Solomon? Nice, aren't they? All the men I've been with say so. "Lovely tits, Barbara." They'd go. Then they're all over me. Just like you could be if you play your cards right.'

'I'm no good at card games.'

'Lucky in love, maybe?'

'This isn't love, Barbara. What you're thinking of is sex.'

'Am I?'

'See it in your eyes.'

'Be quick then. Take what you want. It's alright; no one will ever know. There. Now, put your hand in there. It's better without a bra, but you can't have everything. Not unless you come back another time? Wednesdays are good. He always goes to the city to play snooker with his stock-market friends, so I'm here alone all day. Nobody for company save for myself.'

'Wednesdays?'

'Wednesday.' she said, decidedly. 'I'll get myself all dressed up for you. Can you imagine me in black silk, satin, and lace? I look phenomenal. Every man's dream but all yours for just one day. You won't be able to resist me. And I'll let you. I'll let you look all you want. And then you can fuck me. In my own great, big, double bed. You could fuck my brains out! Can you imagine? And then you'd go back home to Franny.'

'Your daughter.'

'Don't. Don't confuse the situation. Sorry, I shouldn't have mentioned her. It's only a sexual fling. Nothing serious. Like a set of tennis or badminton.'

'Okay. Wednesday then. What time?'

'As soon as you like. I take a lot of satisfaction. Desmond generally leaves about nine a.m., so come after that. And you will come, Solomon. I'll make you. I'll make you so hot and hard you could go off inside me like a rocket. Kiss me some more. Put your hand up my skirt and stroke my pussy. I've got no panties on. Go on, pussy wants you. Oh, poor, poor pussy.' His hand slid up her thigh. 'That's it! That's it! Oh, I love the feel of a man's hands on me. Stroke me, baby, stroke. That's it... Oh damn! You're making me come already.' She shuddered with the ecstasy of the moment. Then: 'Better stop now.'

He pulled her skirt back down smoothly, transferred his hand back to her breast, hidden beneath her cotton blouse, and put his tongue in her mouth. She moaned like no one had ever touched her before. It made her climax.

'Oh! Oh, God, no. I'll have to go and get cleaned up now before they get back. Take the chain off the door, or they'll get suspicious, and we can't have that.'

She gathered herself up and headed for the door, her high heels pock-marking the carpet as she walked.

After taking the chain off, he followed her up the stairs, mesmerized by the swing of her hips. In the shower room, shoes off, she turned on the hose and waited for the water to warm. He approached her from behind.

'Oh, a strange man in my bathroom. What on Earth could he want, I wonder?' she joked. He took both her breasts in his hands and kissed her neck, his nether regions hard against her buttocks. She enjoyed it for a few moments. Then, he broke away.

'Stop it.' she whispered. 'Go away. You can't do me in here. We'll both get soaked. You'll have to wait.'

'What am I supposed to do with this?' he asked.

'It'll die back. They always do. Till Wednesday.'

'Wednesday.'

'Wednesday. I'll be waiting.' She pushed him away and closed the door.

On Wednesday, he was early. He watched Desmond leave for the city in his casual attire. Desmond always went to these occasions by train - there would be drinking involved, and so his beloved Sierra Sapphire remained garaged at home, safe and sound.

She was holding the door open for him as Desmond disappeared around the hedge-lined corner.

'You're early.' she said, a housecoat covering whatever she was wearing underneath. She looked like a suburban housewife. Just as well...

'Shall I come back later?'

She giggled a little; the morning Martini doing its job.

'No, no. Of course not. Give me a few more minutes, and then I'll be ready for you. There's coffee in the cafetière. Have that, and then come upstairs.'

'Thanks.'

'Oh, and better put the chain on. Just in case he's forgotten his keys or portfolio. Don't think he has, but better not take any chances.'

'Don't you think your neighbors might be wondering? Net-curtains twitching? All that?'

'Why? A friend of my daughters comes by to do a few odd jobs for me; what could be more natural? Don't worry, they're not the sort to pry; none of them.'

She went up the stairs. Solomon wandered into the kitchen and thought about coffee…

Nah. Better not. He was minty fresh for her. No point in spoiling that. He decided to give her five minutes and then go up.

Looking out of the window, he noticed that the lawn had been mowed recently. Desmond's weekend chore, he imagined, quite rightly. He wondered why it was that people devoted so much time and effort to small patches of ground and patterned them with greens and browns, reds and blues. He'd never seen the attraction himself, especially since what he had come here for was waiting for him in her bedroom. He'd thought about her a lot since Sunday. Yes, he'd always fancied her, in that way that men do, about their girlfriends' mothers. Never dreamed she felt the same way. Well, he was free today to give her the time of her life. His too…

He softly paced the hall and climbed the stairs.

The bedroom was ajar. Inside, an apricot light suffused the room as the sun filtered through the curtains.

She lay reclined on her side, on her bed. Her hourglass figure swathed in the sexiest garments he had ever seen. She was delectable in Victoria's Secret black underwear. Her hair swept away from her face and ears. Her eyes blazed with passion. She smiled her sweetest smile.

'Well?' she asked.

'Barbara, you look wonderful. Good enough to eat.'

'Might be time for that too, hopefully. Come here.'

'Hang on, hang on. Let me look at you.'

171

He walked across the deep-pile carpet, shedding his clothes as he did so.

'Wow!' she said. 'Is that all for me?'

'Stand up.' She did so. 'Turn around.'

'What are you going to do?'

Skilfully, he removed her brassiere and took her breasts in his hands - as though weighing them.

'Oh!' she said. 'Good job, you've got warm hands.'

'Wanted to do this for ages. How does it feel?'

'Lovely. Feel free.'

'Always wanted to do this.' he said huskily. 'To take these ripe pears in my hands and feel the full weight of them. Gorgeous. Your previous partners were right, Barbie. You do have lovely tits.'

He kissed her neck and helped her out of her black basque. 'Stockings and shoes staying on, for now.' he said. 'Then I can screw you like a whore.'

'I am a whore.' she whimpered. 'Oh, I am such a whore.'

He turned her around to face him and kissed her deeply. She lay back on the bed, her legs parted.

'Come on then, I'm ready. Oh, Solly, I am so wet for you. Give it to me!'

On the bedside table, her mobile phone rang.

She answered it, as people do.

'Hello?..... Speaking..... Yes?' She gathered the covers around her. He rolled away. 'A crash? But trains don't crash. Not these days, anyway. Sorry, I am talking rubbish. Shock talking. Where is he?..... Uh-huh, I know it. Okay. Be there in half an hour.'

She disengaged.

'I've got to go. Where are my clothes?' Solomon hadn't watched her undress, so couldn't say. She opened drawers and wardrobe doors and clothed herself. Despite everything, it turned him on even more.

He stood up.

'I'll go make some coffee.'

'No, no. There's no time.'

'I'll make some anyway. Could do with one.'

'Right.'

She was down the stairs and out the front door before the cafetière had finished filtering. The kitchen wall shook as she opened the automatic garage door. The Sierra made the walls reverberate too. Then she was gone. It occurred to Solomon that he needed a shower. He still wasn't entirely sure what had happened.

Later with Fran:

'You're late.'

'Ain't I always?'

'Not generally. What's wrong?'

'Might ask you the same. Who's on the phone?'

She realized she was holding it, cradling it against her neck.

'Oh. No-one. Trying to get hold of Mum, but there's no reply.'

'Okay. Gone out maybe?'

'Not on a Wednesday. Never on a Wednesday. Never goes out.'

'Never?'

'Hardly ever. Worried about Dad. Heard about the train crash on the News. Paddington - that's his line. Always.'

'Want to pop round?'

'Not really. If there's News, then someone will call.'

He took the phone from her and sat her down on the sofa.

'You're right. I suppose so.'

He sat down, too.

'Maybe he's out in the back garden, collecting lawn trimmings?'

'What? No. Why would you say that? Wednesday is his London day. Always has been. A chance to blow off steam with his old pals.'

'Of course. Sorry. I wasn't thinking. Although…'

'What?'

'Maybe your mum is out there, doing the same.'

'No, no. She wouldn't. It's Dad's garden; it always has been. He's cut every blade, pruned every shrub, dead-headed every Rose.'

Sounds like an obsession.' Solomon remarked.

'No, not really.' she replied. 'You know people and their gardens.'

'Not really, no. We always lived in flats. A window box here and there, but that was all.'

She'd been thinking.

'What makes you think he's cut the grass?'

'Usual weekend chore, isn't it? Wash the car, mow the lawn.'

'Depends on the season. But, yes. And then collect trimmings. For composting.'

'Sure. Why not? Same as ours. Can't just leave them on the lawn. They discolor it as they rot.'

'Makes me wonder why you said it, that's all. We were around there on Sunday. He hadn't done it then.'

'Maybe didn't have time. You know, with us coming.'

'Still… Why would you be thinking that he's out collecting lawn trimmings when, in all probability, he's lying somewhere critically injured.'

'Just jumping to conclusions, sweetie. Get back on the phone. See if there's any reply.'

'Alright.' She grabbed the phone again.

'What are you doing?'

'Calling Mum again. It's not like her. She loves her Wednesdays. Nothing to do and all day to do it. A chance to catch up on all the things she's been meaning to do.' There was no reply. 'No. Still not answering.'

'Try her mobile.'

She shook her head.' No. She never answers it. Either out of charge or credit. Bought it for her one Mother's Day, but I might just as well have saved the money.'

'Try it. You never know.'

'It's ringing! Hello Mum?….. Where are you?….. I know! I heard it on the News….. Is he okay?….. Hang on. Let me write that down.' She found a pen on the coffee table and scribbled furiously to wake it up. 'Damn pen! Okay, it's working. Go on…..' She wrote on an ornamental notepad - a gift from her mother. 'Right….. Got it. Okay. I'll see you there.'

She put the phone down.

'What's happening?' he asked.

'He's at St. Mary's Hospital - they all are. Something called ICU?'

'Intensive Care Unit.'

'Thanks. Coming with me?'

'If you'd like.'

She thought. 'No. Better if you stay here. Then I can get hold of you. Or Mum can.'

'Why would she want me?'

'She likes you. Don't you realize? Sometimes, we need people we're fond of in times of trouble. A reassuring voice on the other end of the phone.'

'Okay. Let me know if there's anything you need.'

'Lizzie'll be home soon. Cook some pasta.'

'Fair enough.'

'Right.'

She disappeared out of the front door in a bluster of keys, purses, and front door issues.

'Cancel the milk!'

'No, that's okay. You'll be back in no time.'

Lizzie arrived at the garden gate of the old house. A gang of demolishers stood around, smoking and peering at plans.'

'Seems fairly straightforward.' said one.

'What's happening, orange chaps?' said Lizzie.

The head man shrugged.

'Pulling the place down. No one wants to live here since the murder.'

'Not surprised. Do me a favor?'

The man eyed her up and down. 'Anything. What is it?'

'That carpet in the hallway. Roll it up and put it in my car?'

'The Pigletty one?'

'I've always liked it.'

They sat in the cold, white waiting room, waiting for News of their ailing husband and father. In the echoey corridor, a clock ticked ominously.

Outside, muffled by the triple-glazed windows, steamy, the world continued about its business. Traffic sounds filled the air: many, many honks and horns.

'Been some time.' Fran observed.

'Takes as long as it takes.' said Barbara.

'Mm.'

'Where did you park?'

'Next to you. Saw the Sierra there and thought, "That's Mum."'

'Oh. Good. Fifty pence an hour, mind?'

'That's London. Anyway, I saw. I've got it on an App.'

'Apps for everything these days. What a time to be alive!'

'Slightly sardonic, but, okay, yes, it is.'

'Still.'

'Yes, I know. Everything costs. I wanted to be here. That's all.'

'Why wouldn't you? You only get one father.'

'So I believe.' said Fran.

They were teasing each other, anything to mitigate the tension.

Barbara looked around at the other long, red nylon-covered benches. At the staff notice board, the vending machine with extruded foam cups, the doors that led left, right, and who-knows-where.

'I hate these places.' she said.

Fran nodded. 'Don't we all? Still, what's the alternative? A hundred years ago, all those passengers would've been left for dead.'

177

'Not really, no. There were hospitals - and First-Aid, back in the days of steam railways.'

'And Florence Nightingale.'

'And, as you say, Florence Nightingale. When was she born?'

'Nineteenth Century. Ooh, I don't know - about two hundred years ago?'

'Wonder what she'd make of this place.'

'She'd be trolling about with her lamp.'

'I suppose so. Who was Saint Mary anyway?'

'I can throw some light on that. There's a plaque on the wall back in reception. Built in 1866. Fleming discovered penicillin here. Roger Bannister - the four-minute mileist was born here, as well as countless members of the Royal family.'

'Yes, but who was Saint Mary?'

'Probably named after the Spanish port, *Santa Maria.* Named after the virgin Mary, of course.'

'Thanks for that. Love a bit of history. Must be a million memories here.'

'I imagine so."

'Not much more, though.'

'No.'

'Amazing what they can do nowadays, though.'

'Let's hope so.'

Fran sighed. The clock ticked. It was as though time was standing still. Waiting, waiting…

'I hate these places.'

'Me too. It's frightening to think that this is where we all end up. Cold and alone in a draughty corridor. Just waiting for the life to ebb out of you.'

'Hey, don't think that way. We don't know anything yet. Just think; life is for the living. Talk about something else. Take your mind off it.'

'No! I'd hate that! Suppose we were just chatting away, and a nurse comes along with News?'

'Wouldn't be a nurse. Nurses just come along and say that everything is fine and you can see him in a few minutes. Any news would have to come from a doctor.'

'News? What d'you mean? Bad News?'

'Could be.' said Fran, sagely. 'Taken long enough.'

'Thank you. Cheerful Annie, aren't you?'

'Cheerful Annie? Who's that?'

'One of those dolls you used to collect. The whole set of them, weren't there?'

'I don't remember.'

'No. That's the trouble with kids - hardly remember anything.'

'All too busy growing up, I guess.'

A door opened, and a doctor emerged from a room, seemingly cluttered with surgical implements. He approached them.

'Mrs. Faircox?'

'That's me.' said Barbara.

'Ah! Good, good. Not to worry.' the doctor said. 'We think he's going to be okay.'

Fran asked, 'What exactly were his injuries?'

'Difficult to say, exactly. The main issue is his spine. There is a slight risk of paralysis, I'm afraid. Still, I am lucky to be alive at all.

Dreadful crash. Signal failure, the police are saying. Of course, that's just their opinion. There will have to be a full-scale inquiry. Your husband is suffering from temporary whiplash at present. We'll keep him here for a few days and see how he improves. Normally, we'd move him to somewhere less busy, but it's a risk to move him too much. He's fine, here with us. Hopefully, he'll pull - to use a train analogy.'

The women were not amused.

'Feel free to visit when you like.'

Fran sprang up.

'Thank you, doctor. Come on, Mum. Let's get you home. You need a good night's sleep before you do anything else.'

Grumbling, Barbara got to her feet.

'I can't sleep. I won't. I'll be up all night worrying. Besides, there's too much to do. I've hardly done a thing all day.'

'Leave it all for now. You need to rest. Once we're back, safe and sound, I'll send Solomon around. See what he can do for you.'

'Barbara smiled a slow smile.

'Would you?'

It was late when he knocked at her front door.

She was seductively dressed adorably in comfortable nightwear. Black, like she was expecting somebody. Her eyes shone. She smiled, her lips red.

'Lovely to see you.'

'You too.'

'Come in.' She opened the door wide.

Somewhere, a clock counted the seconds, but that was the only sound. They were alone.

'How is he?'

'He'll live. Not forever, but then, who does?'

'No idea.'

'No. Nor me.'

The two of them padded along the carpet of her hallway. The house was empty but warmly lit.

'Well?' she asked.

'Pretty good, actually. I've been thinking about you.'

'Really?' She brushed her hair back behind an earring with her nail-polished fingers. It glowed in the half-light. 'That's nice. Been thinking about you too.'

Suddenly, he gripped her sumptuous body and held her close to him. She gave a slight gasp. 'It's alright. I'm not going to hurt you.' He grabbed and held everything that he could get his hands on. She stood still, six or seven inches below him, and let him have whatever he wanted. She smelled of Muscadet and sunshine. His breath was hot on the nape of her neck. She hardly resisted.

'God! I want you.' he whispered.

'Want you too.' Her breathing was unsteady.

'What about everybody else?'

'Not here, are they? To hell with the consequences. Got me where you wanted me.'

'Not quite.'

He began to unlace her. Strips and straps of lingerie. Victoria's secrets. Insubstantial things. Black, revealing her beautiful, tanned-white skin. Not a mark on her; these things aren't worn tightly, no need. He tore away at the clothing, and the remnants fell to the carpeted floor. He gazed at her, drinking in the sights. His erection was already a rampant beast. She felt for him.

She was perfect. She stared at him with wide-eyed innocence. He kissed her softly, his tongue in her mouth and hers in his. Her hands reached for his shoulders. At first, he thought, to stop him, but it seemed otherwise. She guided his hands. He caressed her. He loved the feel of her breasts, the soft weight of them. He took one in each hand gently. God gives a man two hands and a woman two breasts. It all makes sense.

She gazed back at him as though no one had ever done this to her before. Nobody. Not in the hallway, whatever next?

'So beautiful without your clothes on.'

'That's nice. Say nice things to me, and I'll let you do anything you want.'

'Anything?'

'Everything. Take me to my bed.'

'Sure?'

'I want you - stupid. Want to feel the weight of you on me. You want me to; said so. That's why you're here. Can't wait to wiggle up inside my tunnel, hey? Thought so. Oh! You're all hands! Take me upstairs. I can't wait to feel this great big cock up inside me. I'm going to enjoy this.'

He kissed her again. 'Me too.'

'Okay. This way.' She smiled sweetly, took his hand, and led him up the stairs.

'Solomon, not about?'

Fran shook her head at Lizzie.

'No. I've sent him round to my Mum's. She's got a few things that he can be doing for her.'

'Sent him? Never trust a man, Francesca.'

'Oh, he'll be alright. I know Solomon. He'll do whatever he wants to do, and Mum's crazy about him. They'll fool around, I guess. Tease each other, that kind of thing.'

All the same - your own mother?'

'What's the difference? Besides, I wanted to spend some time with you. Not being alone with you for ages. What you have been doing?'

'A demolition gang.'

'What? All of them?'

'Pretty much. Got me a Pigletty carpet.'

'Have a good time?'

'Not really. Too hard. Too fast. Too quick. You know men sometimes. Want me some kind and tender loving now.'

'Want to go to bed.'

'Very much so.'

Afterwards:

'How was that?'

'Perfect.' She exhaled softly. 'Beautiful.'

'All things bright.' He lay back on his pillow, exhausted. 'You're tremendous.'

She smiled. 'Practice makes perfect.'

'Seems so.'

She brushed the hair from her eyes with her fingers and lay back. Her hands inspect her body for any signs of damage. There didn't seem to be any. Solomon was a careful lover.

'Man o man! I can see what she sees in you.'

'Your daughter, d'you mean?'

'Sshh, don't. Don't trivialise it. Tonight, it's just you and me, me and you. Doesn't matter where we came from or where we're going. Let's just enjoy these moments.'

'Okay.'

'Thank you, Solomon. This was wonderful. I've never been taken like that before.'

'Taken?'

'What then? Given?'

'Well, you did kinda throw yourself at me.'

'I did, didn't I? Saw what I wanted and thought, "Why not?" Threw me at you, and you caught me, my great big handsome lover. Look at you - all over my best sheets.'

'Black satin. Suits you. You look absolutely gorgeous against them.'

'Question is, how will I ever live without you now?'

'Don't have to. I know where you live.'

She laughed raucously. Her laughter blazed away across the high ceiling of her bedroom. 'Like The Godfather?' She slapped him playfully. 'No, I don't mean that.'

'What then? Do you want me to come around here unannounced and screw you whenever I want to?'

She giggled. 'Unannounced? Yes, of course, that's what I'd want. Don't you know anything? Women love that. Love being taken by surprise, off-guard. Love being wanted and lusted after. Fawned over, leered at. Didn't they teach you anything at school?'

'Not much. Not about girls, no. Well, yes, about girls. But not about women. Not about women like you, Babs. You're fantastic. Beyond my wildest dreams.'

'Don't.'

'Don't what?'

'Don't call me Babs. I don't care for it.'

'Beautiful Babs.'

'Stop it! Reminds me of another Babs, the famous one.'

'No longer with us, as it goes; what then? What do you like to be called?'

'Oh, I don't know. You think of something.'

He ran his smooth hands over her. 'Mmm, Thunder Cat.'

'Too sexy.'

'Alright. You tell me.'

'Um… Priscilla.' she decided.

'Like The Queen of the Desert? Alright. That's what I'll call you from now on. That way, if you phone and somebody else answers, you can leave a message: "Tell him Priscilla called."'

'Why would I phone you?'

'When you get horny.'

'They'd recognize my voice. I could text you.'

'Better idea. I always delete messages once I've read them.'

'Good computer buff could easily find them. Isn't there a "recently deleted" file?'

'Could be. Anyway, I hardly ever let anybody else touch my phone. Why would they?'

'If they didn't trust you?'

'Maybe. But your daughter knows me only too well.'

'What about me?'

'You'll be alright. I'll protect you from the Hooded Claw.'

'Who?'

'You'll be my closely-guarded secret. Anyway, let's not talk about these things, -Priscilla. Where was I?'

He maneuvered himself on top of her. She parted her legs.

'About there. And there. Ooh, yes! And there.'

The following morning:

She fingered the hair on his chest. It woke him.

'Okay?' she asked.

'Wonderful. Worn out, but wonderful. How about you?'

'About the same. Let's lay here for a few hours and watch the sunrise.'

'Sounds good.'

The sun was slowly rising through the closed curtains. They watched as its light filled the room. A warm, suffusing light. They lay in each other's arms.

'Are you going to the hospital today?'

'Should do. The doctor said he'd need time to rest and recuperate. But I should show my face.'

'Taking Fran?'

'No, I don't think so. Won't she want to know where you've been all night?'

'Gathering lawn trimmings.'

'Lawn trimmings? But the lawn hasn't been cut.'

'I'll do that too.'

'In the dark?'

'In the moonlight.'

'Okay. That's up to you.' She moved her hand further down. 'Are the two of you happy together?'

'Not sure. The murders didn't help.'

'Not murders. Self-defense. Manslaughter, at best.'

'Whatever. And she's very much in love with Lizzie. On a purely physical level, I mean.'

She laughed. 'Just like you and me.'

'Me and you.'

'Me and you.'

'We were talking about the new house, and she's already got a room marked out for her. "This will be Lizzie's room!" she announced, grandly.'

'When do you think you'll move?'

'Up to the solicitors. About eighty days, they reckon. Searches to do, contracts to exchange. There's a bit of a chain, but we're in no rush. I'll bet you ten-to-one they'll both be curled up together now.'

'I like Lizzie.'

'So do I.'

'Ever had her?

'Once, and once only. She was there for me when I needed somebody.'

'Will you tell her?'

'About us? No. Victoria isn't the only one who keeps secrets. Fancy an early morning one?'

'Trim my lawn?' She stretched herself out. 'Why not?'

Lizzie was relaxed and enjoying herself, too, in her nice and warm double bed.

'Mm, oh, it's you,' Fran pandered to her. 'Oh, that's nice. Fingers. Warm hands. Where have you been?'

'Nowhere. Downstairs. Pottering about.'

'Pottering. Mm, keep pottering. Throw me like a pot. I'm clay in your hands. Oh, God! I'm coming already! What in the world was I dreaming about?'

'Who knows. Awake now. Just me.'

'Mm, keep doing that. Keep on doing what you're doing…'

'Always be here for you, sweet one.'

'Mm, hope so. What about Solomon, though?'

'I think we're nearly at an end, him and me. Done a lot and seen a lot. Enjoyed every moment. Well, apart from three or four. But, when love affairs come to an end, there's nothing you can do but run.'

'Run?'

'Well, walk away. Find somebody new. Your body, for instance.'

'I see. Is that why you sent him around to your mother's?'

'Nah. He wouldn't dare. Besides, she's not really his type.'

'Oh, Francesca. Silly, silly girl. All women are Solomon's type. Would you mind though?'

'Mind?'

'Yes. Mind. Could you be with him again, knowing that he'd screwed your very own mother?'

Fran thought about this.

'Not "screwed". Solomon wouldn't just screw. He'd… make love to her… Softly, gently, carefully. Oh! Getting jealous now.'

Lizzie laughed. 'Concentrate.' she said.

'Alright. Sorry. On reflection… No. I don't think I could. Not that I'd been betrayed or anything.'

'No. What then?'

188

'It's just… not decent.'

Lizzie laughed some more. 'Decent? Oh, Francesca. You're priceless, you know that?'

Fran giggled. 'Yes, I suppose I am. But that's how we are with sexual relationships these days. They change us. Make us different people. Sometimes that's unforgivable.'

'Seems to me that if you think of sex as something so important that you have to be forgiven for taking a wrong step, it must be something that you hold extremely dear.'

'Well, it is, isn't it? I mean, look at us. We're not the same good friends that we were a while ago.'

'No. we're lovers now. It's different.'

'That's what I'm saying. It's changed us. Hopefully into better people…'

'Closer friends.'

'That too, of course. I think we're ready to take our relationship to the next stage.'

'And what is that?'

'We will see.'

On the other side of town, the two lovers relaxed.

'You okay?'

'Why wouldn't I be? A little out of breath, but that's just my age.'

'Nonsense. You're in the prime of your life. Why do you think I'm here? Never had a woman like you before.'

'Not even my daughter?'

'No. She's a child compared to you. You're softer, more giving. Know all the tricks. I can tell you've lived and loved before. You're lovely and soft. Safe and warm. I feel that I could do anything with you.'

'She's crazy about you.'

' Was once, I agree. All things come to a close, though. Seems we're heading that way, her and me.'

'Tell me, how do you feel about us?'

'About us?'

'You and me.'

'Me and you.'

'Me and you.'

'Okay. It's secret, exciting. Wish it could always be, but it won't. Your old man will recover; Fran and I will move to our house in the country.'

'And Lizzie.'

'And Lizzie. You'll go back to normal: coffee mornings, jumble sales, knitting patterns, council meetings. You'll be fine.'

'Sounds awful.' What's Plan B?'

'Plan B is where I take you somewhere you've always wanted to go - and be. We'll kiss goodbye to this crummy town and start a new life.'

'Marvellous! Could you afford that?'

'Between us, we could. Depends where it is, of course.'

She sat up in bed. The covers fell from her voluptuous body; he drank in the sight. 'The south of France!' she announced boldly. 'I've always wanted to be there. Went to Marseilles once, with the girls, shopping. Cheap flight. I loved it there. The architecture, the eateries and orangeries. The beautiful blue Mediterranean means 'Middle of the Earth,' you know.'

'I know.'

'Let's do it, Solly! Let's go there! I love it there! Imagine, after a morning sunbathing and sipping Pina Coladas, I come home, shower first, - hose myself down and then let you make mad, passionate love to me in the golden afternoon sunshine. God, it gets hot down there; thirty degrees most of the time. White curtains flutter at the windows. Bed linen rustling. Not another sound to be heard, save for the fishermen, returning from their day's labors and the songs of the hungry birds that follow them in on the tide.'

'The Med's tideless.'

'Well, you know what I mean. What could be better? Paradise on Earth!'

'Sounds incredible.'

'My aunt Nelly was the same.'

'Nelly?'

'Short for Eleanor, but everyone called her "Nelly."'

'Okay.'

'She'd go with any man for about three gin and limes. Got involved with a Boulanger in Montmartre once - Paris, you know? Well, that was the beginning of the end. Always fresh bread on the table, but she ballooned in size. Heart went in the end.'

'We should go!' exclaimed Fran. 'It'd be brilliant. I love Paris!'

'Me too! Tell you what, as well.'

'What?'

'We should get married, you and I.'

'Married? But you're already married. To Rod.'

'Oh, he won't mind. I don't know if it's Christmas or Easter at the best of times. And this is the best of times. Isn't it?'

'Yes! You're right. I suppose it is. I, for one, have never been happier.'

'Me neither. I love you,' Cesca. Pretty sure you feel the same. You can get divorced online these days. I'll fill in the form and be free in no time! Oh, we'll marry in Paris.'

'At Notre Dame?'

'If we can. Lots of rebuilding going on since the fire.'

'Only trouble is… Solomon.'

Well, he'd have to know. It's only polite. You'd have to tell him.'

Fran lay back. 'Alright. I can do that.' She sighed. 'Poor Solomon.'

'Poor Solomon, my arse. He'll get over it… Always does, doesn't he? Whatever life throws at him, he comes up smiling.'

'Lovely smile, too.'

'There you go. He'll be fine. Probably tucked up inside some lucky female even as we speak.'

It was noon in Paris, the hottest time of the day. It's the best time to see it, some say. It was hot. She held on to his arm as they bundled through the platforms at the Gare Saint-Lazare. Trains rustled by. Each one is intent on their future destinations. Discarded newspapers flew, as they do everywhere.

Barbara was dressed favourably: A cream-colored cheesecloth blouse and a medium-length linen skirt that she had thought too thin when she was purchasing it. Glad about it now. It was patterned with images of fruit, which seemed to add a cooling effect, too. Although this was only Paris, she was baking hot already, and the glow of her occasionally trickled down her bare legs and into her open-toed sandals. Solomon appeared not to notice.

'Where next?' asked Barbara.

'The *Chemin de fer* takes us to Perpignan.' said Solomon. 'After that, we'll see. Gotta love that Channel Tunnel. Never been through it before. Forty-five minutes. Didn't feel a thing.'

'Perpignan? That's the south of France?' she asked innocently.

'As close to Spain as you can get - without actually going there. Previously, I drove through the Pyrenees to Andorra and then down into Spain. Didn't think much of Spain, as it goes. Saw Dali's house and went back home. We were staying at Castelnaudary; friends there. Nice little town, you'd love it.'

'Is it near where we're setting up home?'

'Close enough. You'll see. Tell me, have you ever had sex on a train?'

She grinned. 'Not yet.'

The sale of their property was in the final stages. There were papers to be signed before they could move in, so Solomon had booked them into a nearby *Pensione* for a couple of weeks. To Barbara, it sounded adorable: Views across the Mediterranean, hot and cold running water, room service. Sounded like the lap of luxury.

Yes, there was a lot of work to do on the house once they'd moved in, but not just yet. For now, it was a romantic holiday. She loved it.

Once seated in their compartment, they let the train rumble and grumble through the French countryside. The furniture was shabby, and the smell of tobacco invaded their senses. There was only one other occupant. A foreign-looking man in his forties or fifties, asleep in the corner, back to the engine. Everything was as they had expected. The vinyl coverings had peeled over the years at every corner, and the windows were stained with nicotine, an oily orange. Attempts had been made to clean them but ineffectually.

Their traveling suitcases, one each, were stored over their heads, safe and sound. A kind of hammock arrangement. Their journey was about nine hundred miles; it would take a day and a half. Could have flown down for thirty Euros, return!

He stared across at her.

'I want you.' he said.

She glanced at the other occupant and then back at him. 'I know.' She read her magazine. Cross your legs. It's a long trip.'

'Can't help that.'

She looked at him again. 'But we're really doing it, aren't we? Getting away from it all. Starting over, as John Lennon would say.'

'We sure are. Unbelievable.'

'What is?'

'You are. Go on - loosen your blouse. No one's looking - except me.'

'No. It keeps me cool. Besides, I can't imagine where you think you're going to do me on a moving train.'

'I'll find us somewhere.'

'I'll bet you would. Control yourself. Imagine you see a red flag.'

'Meaning "Stop"? Okay. What are you reading?'

'Don't know, really. It's all in French. I'm just looking at the pictures. It's all fashion, I think. *Modes de jour,* whatever that may mean.'

'"Fashions of the day," broadly.'

'Okay. Thanks.'

He undid his collar. 'Hot down here already. Don't get this in England.'

'England?' she smiled. 'Where's that?'

He read from his phone. 'Twenty-eight degrees. That's hot!'

'What's that in Fahrenheit?'

'Eighty-two.'

'Makes me wonder what we're going to do with ourselves all the day.' She sounded wistful.

'It's not that hot first thing in the mornings. Afternoons are for siestas. And lovemaking.'

'We'll have to see about that.'

'Yes. Of course. Promise you - you won't be able to resist me - stripped to the waist every day.'

'Or me.'

'Yes. I can imagine that. I'd love to see you with a nice, deep bronze tan.'

She smiles at him again. 'Said you liked my "perfect white skin."'

'I do. I love it. Crazy about you. Trying to prove it.'

'Cross your legs.'

'Easy for a woman to say that.'

'I know. That's why I said it.'

'Love you with your knickers off.'

'I thought it was my tits you liked?'

'I do! It's true. The first time I set eyes on you, I thought, "Wow! There's a pair."'

'I know you did. I could tell.'

'You're very proud of them, aren't you?'

'Always have been. When I first noticed them growing, I thought, "Hello. I'll bet we'll have some fun with you two."'

'And did you?'

'Once or twice.'

'Once or twice?'

'Well, three or four times. Seven or eight, now, I come to think. Just as I thought, all the boys wanted to see me naked.'

'Naked?'

'Well, topless mainly. To start with. After that, who knew what might happen?'

'Let's have a look at them. What have you got on underneath? The red one? Or the black one? Love you in both, by the way.'

'"Love"? Hah! You're not talking about love. This is just sex.'

'Just?'

'You know what I mean. Anyway, you'll have to wait. You might disturb our other passenger. You never know; he might understand what we're saying. Might be listening to every word.'

'I doubt it.'

The man in the corner suddenly shook himself awake.

'Please, you may not speak French, but I have perfect English.' He raised a battered trilby in greeting and extended a hand. To the male, of course. Not the female.

He introduced himself.

'Name's Bond.'

'James?'

'No, no. Too obvious. I call myself Colin.'

'Interesting.' said Solomon. 'Originally, Colle. From the old French for Nicholas.'

'I couldn't say, wouldn't know.'

'Do now. Back in Henry the fifth's day.'

'May have been, may have been. Possibly. Most popular names have to do with stones, pebbles, rocks, *et cetera*.'

'Pierre?'

'There you go.'

'Where are you heading, Colin Bond?'

'Further south. Looking for a place to stay. Just somewhere to lay the head. A change of clothes in the wardrobe. Peace. Quiet. Stranger in these parts. As are the two of you. I gather.'

'Gather away.'

'Your wife is very quiet. All is well?'

'She's reading. And a little shy.'

'She seems to have, how you say, dropped off.'

'Been a long day. Plus, it's hot. We're from England. Never this hot over there.'

'No. I imagine not... She has a fine body. Very full in the chest. What's her name.'

'They don't all have names. You're living in the Stone Age.'

'What do you call her then? When you want her.'

'I generally say, "You ready yet?"'

'Ready for what?'

'You know.'

'Oh. That… She does have a lovely figure. Lovely breasts.'

'You should feel them in your hands.'

'Could I?'

'I'd kill you if you touched her.'

The man laughed. She didn't wake. Either feigning sleep or wishing that they'd both go away.

'Go on. She's asleep. Let me feel her up. She'll think it's you.'

'She knows my hands, not yours.'

'Said you'd kill me.'

'I would.'

'Would it surprise you to know that I have a gun in my pocket?'

'How funny. So do I. Always carry a piece when I'm overseas. Force of habit, you might say.'

'You Englishmen, crazy bastards. Do anything for a woman, wouldn't you?'

'This particular woman, yes. Anyhow, we are not crazy bastards. Check your history books. We always win through.'

'It is said that history books are written by winners.'

'True enough. After all, if you've lost, you've lost. Nothing much more to say. Whereas winners tell tales of battles and skirmishes, retreats, and surrenders by the other side. The spoils of war, enemies vanquished, and women surrendered. Victory in the end!'

'Most of the time.'

'Correct.'

The man stood, preparing to leave.

'Tell your wife I loved the look of her as she slept.'

'No. Take your gun and fuck off.'

The sliding door creaked open.

'I have a feeling we will meet again.'

'Can't wait. And, for the record, she's not my wife.'

'Should be some man's wife. Beautiful creature.'

'As I said, touch her, and I'll kill you.'

'Ever killed a man before?'

'Twice.'

'With a gun?'

'Twice.'

He left the compartment. The sliding door sound woke her.

'Has he gone?'

'Yes.'

'Good. Creepy, creepy guy.'

'Aren't we all?'

'No. You're not.'

'Despite what I always want from you?'

'That's okay. I want it too- from you. Love being with you in that way.'

'Keep talking.'

'No, you're okay. What d'you think he wanted?'

'You, I think.'

'Me? Why me?'

'Why do you think? "Beautiful pair of tits," he said.'

'In his broken English. Yuk! Horrid man.'

'Said so. Much as I could do to keep his hands off you.'

'Why?'

'I don't know. Turned me on a bit. The thought of him rubbing his hands all over you, all over your tits. Had an appeal.'

'Well, I'm glad you stopped yourself. I'd never have forgiven you.'

'All women say that. And yet, they let men get away with pretty much anything they want to do. Strange really. That's a thing, isn't it? Female fantasy?'

'Being raped, you mean? No. Not at all. Yes, we love being made love to or with. But, for me, it has to be warm and tender too.'

'I'll bear it in mind.'

'You always do. It seems to anyway. How soon till we get there?'

He looked at his watch and adjusted to French time. 'Long time yet. Try to sleep. I'll wake you when we're close.'

'Alright. But, no touching.'

'Can't promise anything.'

'Okay. I'll just have to trust you, won't I?'

'Good luck with that.'

'What do we do once we're there?'

'I'll hire a car. They do that down there. About a fifteen-minute drive, and we're home free.'

She smiled. 'Home. Free. Can't wait.'

The scenery rustled by.

'All looks the same.' she observed.

'Guess so. Farmland. Arable crops, mainly. See where they line the roads with trees? That's to keep the horses cool. Same as on the canals. The big thing in France is canals. We'll see a few down our way.'

'Our way... I love canals.'

'Me too.' He looked out of the window again. 'Hardly ever see another soul about. You get that with train journeys. Everything looks the same. They may as well put up cartoons of the Eiffel Tower on all of the windows.'

'Once they're clean.'

'Well, quite. So, you've never been this far south before?'

'No. Never.'

'Wait till you see the views. You're looking out over the Mediterranean Sea, the sun basking warmly in the near-distance, the fisher-folk going about their business, hooks and rods, fishes and eyes. That smell. Beautiful. As the catches are hauled in. Always have a glass of cold white wine at your nearest elbow. Chardonnay, perhaps. Magnifique!'

By the time Lizzie and Fran got to Paris, it was midnight. Shivery cold. Neither were dressed for this kind of weather, so they headed for the nearest coffee bar for a reviving cup.

'Hate that tunnel.' complained Lizzie bitterly. 'Now we're out of Europe, I think they should flood it. Then we could call ourselves an island again.'

'Never mind. We're here now. It's far better than slopping about on the Narrow Sea for four or five hours.'

'I suppose.' She sipped her cappuccino.

'Where's our first port of call?'

'Hotel first. In the morning, we have to find a register office and post the banns.'

'You need a ban to marry me?' she kidded.

'Stop it, you're funny. Come on. Let's be off. It's only a few streets from here. Paris is concentric, so every street is linked to another. I've got the map App.'

They were booked in at *Le Metropol*, a swanky Paris hotel. 'What the hell.' said Lizzie, who had no intention of paying the bill. They made their way up to the room and inspected it. Fran was first to the French windows. She threw them open wide and looked out at the sprawling metropolis.

'Wow!' she said. 'It is truly beautiful!'

'Just what the Germans thought.' said Lizzie, in a voice dripping with irony. 'Still, that was a long time ago. Forgive and forget. Try to anyway.'

'Where do you suppose the nearest Register Office is?'

Lizzie fanned herself with a small, pocket-size guidebook. 'Don't have to suppose.' she said, reclining on the big double bed. 'All in here. I imagine there's an App you can download, but I saw this at the railway station and thought, yes, that'll do.'

The Chunnel had deposited them at Calais, so they'd had to get a second train to Paris.

'Clever you. Alright. Fancy a bite to eat?'

'Why not? We'll use the restaurant tonight. Don't fancy room service. Stink the place out if you're not careful.'

'There's menus here.' said Fran.

'Good thinking. By the hotel, I mean.'

'Yes.'

'Always give the customers what they want. Or what you think they want. Works for me. What looks good?'

'Ahh… Everything!' she said simply.

'Show me.'

Fran came and sat by her side. Lizzie read the menu.

'Yes. All very nice and good. I'm going to try the *moules marinière*, followed by the steak *au poivre*. I've heard they do it well here.'

'What's *Lof*?'

'Monkfish. You don't want that.'

'Don't I?'

'No. horrible gristly stuff. Probably wouldn't agree with you. Can never tell when it was caught, either. We're inland here, so no doubt it was fished out early this morning in Normandy or Brittany. Trust me, stick with the steaks. This place is famous for it.'

'Alrighty, I'll have a steak too.'

'And mussels?'

'Not sure. What's the *soup de jour?*'

'Soup of the day.' joked Lizzie.

'Oh, you!'

They laughed.

'And a lovely baked potato - a Maris Piper. Or *Maris Piper*, as they say in France.'

'French, are they?'

'No, no. Just a joke. Come on. Let's go down. I'm going to enjoy this.'

'Me too!'

'Come on then.'

They left the train at the station. It was unseasonably warm, lovely. The hot Sun began working on their tans. They could smell the scents of the sea - though it was just out of sight here. The city of Perpignan was not busy; nothing much of interest to see, but the fact that they were here at all cheered their spirits. There was a Hire Point for cars for English people.

'Who was he anyway?'

'Oh, just some guy.' Solomon said. 'Why? Who cares?'

'Not me.' She smoothed herself down, her blouse, her skirt. God, it was even hotter down here. Hotter than the sticky, smoky train. She imagined herself bare-naked, diving into their very own swimming pool. The crystalline waters below her. All bought and paid for.

'Wait here.' he said confidently. 'I'll go and get us a car.'

'Okay.'

He strode purposefully to the car hire place. She watched and waited.

There was a low stone wall that encircled a green space. She perched on it and watched the people scurrying about; some with dogs, some flying kites, and some sat eating ice. There was a stall. She fancied a raspberry ripple. Maybe when Solomon came back.

Everybody seemed wrapped up in their own little lives. Different to Britain, she thought: In Britain, everybody wants to know what you're doing, what you're up to. Here, though, people disregarded each other and let each other get on with whatever they wanted to do. It was reassuring, in a way. She watched two women, scantily clad, flirting with a group of young men playing football. One was blonde, the other a redhead, both with hourglass figures. The redhead is the larger of the two. Size wasn't at all important, of course, she thought. Still... All seemed well with the world at large.

The stranger from the train appeared at her side and followed her line of sight. He observed the two girls.

'Beautiful, aren't they?' he said. 'Young and sexy. Perfect.'

'Depends what you're looking for, I guess.' she replied.

'What about you?'

She sneered at him, avoiding direct eye contact. 'I am not available.' she said.

'I think your husband was about to offer me lodgings.' said Mister Bond.

'Not without asking me first, he wouldn't.'

'Maybe not. And he's not my husband.' She thought. 'Not yet, anyway.'

'And you are not his wife. Bon. There is still a chance of the rest of us rampant males.'

'Rampant males? That's a laugh. Five-minute wonders; that's all you ever are. All think you're Casanovas or Don Juans. Ridiculous.'

'And what about you women?' he asked loudly. 'What are you? With all your primping and preening, dressed up, painted, and pampered. Bits and pieces of clothing clinging to you or hanging off. You'll never be men, none of you.'

'Don't shout at me!'

'I wasn't shouting. Merely raised my voice.'

'Well, don't. I don't like it.'

'Pardon.'

'I said, I don't like it.'

'No, no. By *pardon*, I mean sorry. *Excusez-moi.* Excuse me.'

'Oh. Alright then.'

'Tell me, what are you doing here?'

'None of your beeswax.'

'Waiting for your man friend with a car, I'm guessing.'

'Good for you. Leave me alone. Go and try your luck with one of those two over there. I'm sure you could charm at least one of them.'

No. They are mere girls. I am interested in a woman. You, in fact.'

'Hard luck. Like I say, I'm unavailable.'

'Oh, come on. I know life. Everyone is available. You just have to find the time.'

'Forget it. I am not interested.'

'It could be fate.' he continued. 'Here is me, looking for a vibrant, sexy woman, and here you are, everything I dream about. Your looks, your form, your figure. The way your body curves in the most interesting of places, I think I am in love with you.'

' Love again. Ha! You men and your ideals of love. You don't know what you're talking about. You just want a quick shag, that's all.'

'Well, I wouldn't say no.'

'I would. Go away.'

Well? What do you like? What are you expecting to find here in France?'

'Not you. Nothing like you. You said some nasty things about me on the train.'

'I thought you were sleeping.'

'I was listening. It's dangerous for a woman to sleep in a compartment full of strangers.'

'I suppose so.'

'Anyway, I'm wide awake now. I can see you for what you are.'

'What did I say that upset you?'

'Never you mind.'

'Was it because I was admiring your breasts?'

'Yes. That was rude. No matter whether you thought I was asleep or not. Very rude.'

'I apologize.'

'Now I'm awake, and we can indulge in polite conversation. Is that what you want? Is that good enough for you? Or would you rather have me flat on my back with my knickers bunched up in my hand? Naked, powerless, comatose. Yours do to whatever and whichever you wanted to. Is that what you'd prefer? No. It's never going to happen. You disgust me.'

'We did.'

'I've known men like you before.'

'And you could again. Of course, you could. I could come to your new cottage home while your so-called husband isn't looking - away on business or whatever. I could come up into your bedroom, into your bed, and smuggle myself up inside of you.'

'Remarkable grasp of the English language, you have. Not a traceable accent. Tell me, where are you from?'

'I'll tell you after sex.'

'Don't hold your breath.'

'My dear,' he said. 'I never do.'

Fran & Lizzie

The car was a Nissan Micra. No power to it, but it would do for now. They drove up into the hills to where their new property was.

'What did he want anyway?'

'Not sure. Wanted to see my tits, of course. But that was out of the question.'

'Of course.'

'Said you'd offered him lodgings.'

'Me?' said Solomon. 'Perish the thought. 'The last thing we want is anybody else on the premises, At least until we get settled.'

'Mm, could let a room or two. Help with the mortgage.'

'No, no. We'll be alright. We have money. Nothing but trouble, tenants. Never know where you are with them. Better off on our own.'

'So you can do what you like with me.'

He risked a glance at her and smiled. 'I like.'

She lowered the sun visor to inspect her appearance. God, she looked rough. It had been a long trip. What she really wanted was to get to the hotel and take a nice, long, hot shower. And after that, a lovely afternoon. Lying on crisp, clean sheets with the love of her life. She wondered, for a moment, what he saw in her? What did any man see in her? She lowered the mirror some more. Well, there were these two, of course: her bosoms, peaches, and cream. She was proud of them both. Why shouldn't she be? What would she be without them? She thought of the two women in the park. Probably hard at it by now - both of them. She felt Solomon's thigh lovingly with her right hand.

'Don't!' he said, but she knew he was joking. 'Not while I'm driving.'

'Oh, go on. You're a good driver.' Her left hand tugged at his zipper, that familiar sound. 'Want me to suck you off?'

'You wouldn't dare.'

'Oh, wouldn't I?'

'Anyway, I'm all sweaty.'

'So am I.'

He drove steerlessly as she moved into position.

'Now then…'

She was all lips and tongue. He tried hard to keep his eyes on the road, but, well, you can't under those circumstances. Tried his best, but she was doing her best, too.

He caressed her hair with his free hand. Her mouth was full. She bit, she tried to swallow, but it was too soon. He felt for her, her private parts - her lady parts beneath her skirt. She gave a muffled squeal, but it was no good. He couldn't reach her like this, not properly.

For her, it was all she had ever wanted. At any moment, she imagined a patrol car passing them and wondering what the driver was doing. Why he didn't have his hands on the wheel. Solomon had spotted a layby on their right-hand side and slowed the car, then pulled in and stopped. He couldn't reach the handbrake, so he kept his foot on the brake. They were on fairly level ground.

He ripped the blouse off her, tearing it. Buttons flew. Beneath it, she was naked, her two perfect breasts in his hands and elsewhere. She concentrated on what she was doing, oblivious to the rest of the world. He felt the climax rising inside him, and, in a moment, he was all over her: in her mouth, in her hair. Boy, she would need that shower now.

She sat up and found tissues in her purse, of course, and after a few minutes, they set off again. She felt strangely peaceful and didn't feel the need to talk. His left hand felt for her on the straight road. She was contented. She loved him.

'What else did he say, though?' he asked.

'He was a bit scary. We were watching two young women flirting with the footballers. He made some unkind remarks about them, too. Then said he'd prefer me. He gave me the creeps.'

'Why? Because he fancied you? I would have thought you'd be used to that by now.'

'Not really, no. Made me feel uncomfortable.'

'That's settled then. If he makes you feel uncomfortable, next time I see him, I'll tell him to clear off.'

'Sweet.'

There was a gap in the hedgerow - where a gate had been removed. This was their cottage. A stone-built farmer's dwelling. No more than six rooms; three up, three down. They parked right outside. There was no one about, although the immobilièr had said that he might be in the vicinity.

'Just as well he isn't,' she said. 'Look at the state of us! Everyone would know that we'd been at it.' She burrowed in her handbag. 'I've got a scarf in here somewhere.' She found it. 'Here we are.' She tied it around her disheveled hair. 'That's better. Now we're presentable. Now we can meet people.'

He chuckled. 'Come on then, I've got the key. Let's see what we've bought.'

They had bought it blind. Online, there were a dozen photographs, but none of them really did the place justice. She ran her hands up the banisters as they made their way up the stairs. It was perfect, she thought. Rudimentary was the word used to describe it, but already, she could see herself doing the decorating. Touching up, making good, all of those kinds of things. Everything needed doing. The Sunlit every room, but it wouldn't always.

As promised, the scene from the upstairs windows gave views of the sea.

'I wonder,' he said. 'if we could make the living rooms upstairs and the bedrooms down? Seems a shame to waste these views.'

'What about the chimneys?' she asked. 'It would be wonderful to have a wood fire in the colder months; plenty of timber in the trees surrounding us, and the farmer said he would be grateful for any pollarding that we could do. Let's face it, it won't be this warm all year round.'

'No, I suppose not. Okay. I'll get an axe and pollard the hell out of them. Should keep us going for a few years.'

'What are they anyway?'

'Lime and Plane.' he said.

There was nothing much to see in the upstairs room - all the furniture had been stripped out. They went downstairs.

'First thing is a new kitchen.' she declared. He agreed.

'You're right. There's a place in the city that can supply all of that. Called, *"Oficina Inglesa."* Deliver too. I can fit it.'

'My hero!'

Mister Bond appeared at the doorway and surprised them both.

'Welcome!' he exclaimed. 'Welcome to your new home! Mine too, maybe.'

Solomon was ruffled. 'What the hell are you doing here?'

'You followed us?' asked Barbara, indignantly.

'Of course. Not a crime in this country. Wanted to see where you were heading, where your new home was. Yes, I followed you. Ahem, even when you stopped for a while. A strange driving style you English have - the brake lights stayed on the whole time.'

Solomon was forceful. 'Alright, you've seen where we live. There's no place for you here. Suppose you clear off and never darken our doorway again?'

'Harsh.' said Bond. 'I so hoped that we could be friends.'

'Don't count on it.'

'Besides,' interjected Barbara. 'We won't be moving in for a month or two. I'm sorry. You'll have to make alternative arrangements.'

'Very well. There is a hotel in Perpignan. I am to stay there for a short while.'

'Us too!' said Barbara, regretfully.

'Perhaps we will have tea together in the coming weeks? Good day, for now.' With a tilt of his hat, he walked to his car and sped off.

'Dear me, that's torn it. He knows where we live now.' she said

'Don't worry. I guess he was just looking for lodgings, as he said. He'll find somewhere. There's no reason for him to drive all the way up here.'

'I hope not.'

'So do I. Come on. Let's get you back to the hotel and into a nice hot shower.'

'I could do with one.'

'I'm sure you could.'

'Brake lights. Hah!'

'What do we do now though?'

He shifted his weight from herds and sprawled back on their bed, comfortably numb.

'Whatever we want!' he exclaimed. 'Or, to put it more correctly, whatever it is that we first intended to do. While we were back on the dismal, grey, untidy - unhealthy streets of England.'

'England, my England.' she said, dreamily. 'How I'll miss it - one of these days.'

'All changed now, isn't it?' he continued. 'No places that I remember. No familiar sights. Even the Tower of London is emblazoned with dayglo "street art." I'm using that term in inverted commas, of course.'

'Of course.' she agreed. 'Emblazoned, - cute word. Want a smoke?'

'Go on then.'

She lit two cigarettes from the scented candle at the bedside, sandalwood. She passed one across to him. He took it on his lips, inhaled, and blew grey smoke at the badly-artexed ceiling of their bedroom.

'Incredibly difficult job, artexing.' he commented.

'Go on.' She snuggled her head to his chest.

'No matter what you do, you can never get it exactly right. That patch is just there, for instance, and example.'

'Sure, you're right.' she said, sleepy after sex.

'Different mixes, different drying times. Call any tradesman for repair, and they'll all generally say you have to board it over and start again.'

'Lowering the ceiling height. Uh-huh.'

'Then, of course, same or similar problems.' He blew more smoke. 'Never liked it as a finish, personally.'

'Nor me. Used to be all the rage. Everybody had it.'

'True. That or polystyrene tiles. Huge fire risk.'

'Mm. Stank as well. Of course, everybody smoked back then. But like we're doing now.'

'Well,' he mused.' You have to smoke after coitus. There are rules, you know.'

She chuckled. 'Always reminds me of my first time. Or times.'

He kissed her forehead. 'Were you any good back then?'

'Never had any complaints.' she smiled. 'Anyway, I wasn't as good then as I am now.'

'Happy to hear. You're a bit of a fire risk yourself.'

The world buzzed by outside. Everybody was in their own world out there doing their own things before the Earth turned again and the Sun shed its light on other parts of the globe. Giving the people here a few night-time, pitch-black hours. Dark, satiny nights. Dreamy. He puffed and sighed contentedly.

'Was I good for you? This time?' she asked.

He ran his free hand over the curve of her hips.

'Fabulous. Always were, always are. Like a favourite feast from the fridge.'

'Best served cold.'

'You're always good. Best I've ever had. Quite a woman.'

'And you've had my daughter.'

'Sshh. Don't mention it. There's no need. That was then, and this is now.'

'I'm never sure.' she stammered nervously. 'A little too hot down here as well.'

'Love you when you're hot. Feel the sheets. We're both soaked to the skin. Beautiful. Listen.'

She listened. 'To what?'

'Nothing. Afternoon silence, afternoon delight. Love it here. Love you too.'

'Oh, you.'

'You too.'

He kissed her as they extinguished their cigarettes in the square glass ashtray on the bedside table. An anomaly in laminated chipboard; once white. It would have to go.

'Mean it, though.'

He caught up, remembering at once. 'As I say, whatever we want to do. I've wandered all over the place, all around the house, making mental lists of what we could be doing or what needs doing. It'll all take time, lovely time. No need to prioritise. There's nothing that needs doing straight away. It mustn't make it feel like a job of work or something that we HAVE to do. Let's just enjoy it and think ourselves lucky. After all, it could all be a whole lot worse.'

She stretched herself out, gloriously naked beneath the white cotton sheets.

'Want me again?'

'Again and again. Every time.'

After showering, she dressed herself comfortably. Sensible pants or *panties,* if you prefer. And blue dungarees. No brassiere. She didn't seem to need one these days. That was Solomon, of course. He seemed to have... invigorated her in certain areas, certain places. She remembered his hands all over her the previous evening. She fingered her own nipples. These proud beauties, one and two. Loro and Sublanne. Yes, they both had names. 'Where would I be without the two of you?' she wondered out loud. 'I know I'm a woman, but you turn me on, both of you. Especially you, Loro. Big sister. Ooh! You're bigger, aren't you? Always were. Lovely Loro. Men love the sight and the feel of you, don't they? But don't worry. Nothing's going to come between us. You belong to me, the two of you. Don't you worry about a thing?'

She fingered herself briefly - down there. She wondered if... but, no. There was no time. The breakfast tables were laid.

She giggled to herself. 'And so was I!'

Downstairs, he was making coffee and toast.

'No croissants. Not this morning. Wouldn't fit in the toaster.' he explained or complained.

'Ain't it always the way.' she said.

'No matter. Once the roaster is up and running, we'll have a proper feast.'

'Roaster?' she asked. 'What's that?'

'At the moment, it's an old farming barrel that had been left lying

around. I've power-hosed it clean, and once it's dry, we can load it with pruned ivy branches and cook whatever we want.'

'Like a barbecue.'

'Yes.' he supposed. 'Exactly.'

'Good. I'm famished.'

'Not surprised.' he observed. 'We both burned some calories last night.'

She blushed a little, as she was supposed to. He grinned.

'Here. Drink a cup.'

The coffee was hot and strong, just the way she liked it. Did

he already know that much about her? Probably, she admitted to herself. After all...

'For animal feed once, I suppose. No use for that anymore. Just need to hinge a lid on it, and we'll be firing on all cylinders, as they say.'

'Oh no. Not today. There's a thing on in town that I thought we might go to.'

'Thing?'

'Some sort of carnival. Annual event.'

'Oh. Okay. If that's what you'd like to do.'

'There was one thing…'

'Go on.'

'What did people say? Your friends, I mean.'

'I don't have any friends. I'm a very unpopular man…'

'Work colleagues then?'

He crumpled a frown. 'What are you getting at?'

'Oh, you know. How the conversation went. "Lovely mum, you've got there, Franny. What is she? Forty-two? Forty-four?"'

'Know now, don't I? Double D. Diamonds are forever.'

'Oh, stop it. You'll set me off again. I've just showered.'

'I know.'

'Watching, were you?'

'Yes. Of course. Wouldn't you?'

He turned towards her. The hot Sun gazed down on them.

'Do you want a firework?'

She laughed out loud. The sound echoed through their hills.

'A firework! Never heard it called that before.'

He smiled and raised the smoking-hot griddle stick from the fire.

'This. I meant.'

'Of course, you did. Sorry. Thought you meant something else.'

'Maybe I did. You are my very own Catherine Wheel.'

'You must give me a spin sometime.'

He shook his head.

'Not in this heat, no. Wouldn't put you through it. What's this about a carnival?'

'Mm, later. I'll rustle up some lunch first.'

'Carry on, matron.'

She arrived half an hour later, laden with trays full of nourishments. She reminded him of an English milkmaid, which one he couldn't say.

'What'cha doing?'

'Ah! The woman of the house. Beautiful in blue jeans - and a few other places as well. Beautiful Babs.'

'Please, don't call me that. I don't like it. It undermines me. There's more to me than these two.'

'I know.'

'Lucky you.'

'Sorry. Fair enough. One of Ronnie Barker's, if memory serves.'

'Well, bring him here, and I'll tell him off.'

'Okay. What have you got there? Tea or beer?'

'Both. Never know with you.'

'Yes, but, handsome female, if I have beer, I can't drive.'

'We're not driving. We'll stroll down. Besides, this is France. Everybody drives drunk down here.'

'And back?' asked Solomon, aghast.

'Sure. Why not? Knowing us, we'll be three sheets to the wind by early evening anyway. Be a nice walk home.'

He thought about this.

'Yes, yes. Of course, it would. Romantic.'

'Steady!'

'Sorry.'

'Here.' She proffered a cup. 'I've brought tea. Mint and Coriander.'

'Parsley.'

'Broadly. Agreed. Can't tell them apart sometimes.'

'Touch of Cinnamon?'

'Of course. I know you so well.'

'Already. Hmm, could be right.'

'Hot out here.'

'Take your jeans off.'

'I thought you said I looked good in them.'

'You do. Gorgeous. Better out of them, though. Tan your legs. You'd look better with some color on you.'

'How very multi-racial of you today so! Anyhoo, - too many English winters. I doubt I'll ever tan again.'

'Try. Don't panic. I'll just watch.'

'I bet you will! Come on, finish off. We need to get moving.'

'I'm moving already.'

'Button your fly.'

'It is buttoned.'

'It thinks otherwise. What you have been doing anyway?'

'Unearthing stones.'

'Strange word, "Unearthing."'

'"Depriving the stone of soil, turning the rock. Smooth, basaltic. Some volcanic remnants, worn clean by time and tides. Once tilted, reveals scuttling small creatures - too numerous to document." OED. Life all goes on.'

'I see. What are you building?'

'Nothing much. Just thinking. Can't just rush into these things - like they do on the TV Shows. Plastering over every single thing. Putting up insubstantial plywood shelving and flopping magnolia-colored paint onto every wall. I hate it! Hate it all. Things will be different here. Everything will be "Just-So" as Kipling would have said.'

'Lions and tigers everywhere. Under the bed, under the chair.'

'Was that him?'

'No. It was me.' She simpered. 'I've never kippled, - but I understand it's ruddy -hard.'

'An old joke.' he nodded. 'But well received.'

'Good. Tea's nice.'

'So I believe. Three o'clock.' he agreed. 'Everything stops.'

She blew on her cup with her ruby-red lips. Well, the wrong lips to his mind, but that was the effect she had on him. He was always considering her form and figure, the parts she painted, the parts left unfettered. No matter what it was they were doing. And in bed, she was dynamite.

'What about tonight then?' she asked innocently.

'No.' he said huskily. 'Want you now. Over there, under the lime trees. Naked in the golden sunlight, stripped bare-naked for all the gods in the world to see. Can you imagine? What do you think they put you here for?'

'I don't know. Ooh, you've made me all wet again now.'

'Now you know. Besides, that's how I like you.'

'I'll have to shower myself - again. And then we'll be off. Eat your meats.'

'That a euphemism? Alright, I will. Imagine you with your hair wet and scattered about you. Have your shower, and then, let's do it.'

'Songwriter now, are you?' she smirked. 'Seriously, what do you want to do. And don't say "Me". That's not going to happen. Maybe later.'

'How much later?'

'Wait and see.'

'Too small for a carnival.' he said. 'Not what we'd call one anyway.'

'Oh, shush. Everyone's enjoying their selves.'

'Never was a fan, myself. Of carnivals, I mean. Not people.'

'Good.'

'Always too noisy, too smoky. Gypsies calling themselves "Travellers" - whatever the hell that means.'

'Gypsies is what British people referred to Egyptian migrants as - a few wars ago. Somehow, the term stood.'

'British people are not at their best at public occasions. Listen to cricket crowds. English carnivals are shitty and gritty.'

'Look nice on a banner?'

'And, in most cases, "littery."'

'That a word?'

'Is now. And filled with brightly-colored majorettes you've never seen or heard of before. The whole town stinks of diesel and fried onions. There is always someone in a kilt on a bagpipe, too. God knows why.'

'My uncle Jim.' she reminisced.

'Sure he does.'

She looked around. 'Here, though, it seems more peaceful.' She rubbed his arm. 'Home. More peaceful.'

'Tranquil.'

'If you like.'

'I like. Are these toffee apples?'

'Look like them. Could be. Ask him. You know French.'

'Not that much. I'd message, *"Est-ce-que Pommes de toffee?"* Something like that.'

'Who knows?'

'Well, another time then. When we're more familiar.'

'"More familiar"? That'd be hard.'

'You'd have to hope so. So would I. You make me feel so…'

She patted his hand affectionately. 'I know. Always do.'

They walked hand-in-hand along the less-than-busy village street. These events were held fortnightly in the summer months and were color-coded. This time, the emphasis was on yellow: Everything was daffodil or primrose. Sometimes fat and French butter. There were flies everywhere; annoying, irritating. People swatted their hands aimlessly. Flies moved in a different time zone, however, and saw the hands coming from seconds away. Tattered bunting fluttered between the unlit street lamps. Rudimentary stalls had been erected at appropriate intervals - in front of the patrons' very homes. Laundered-white cloths covered what were actually wallpaper tables in their days, and the fares they supported were kindly labeled for an explanation, all in French, of course. There were pâtés and cheeses - Comte! Pickles and chutneys. Jams, *bien sûr.* Made from last year's summer berries. There were cakes aplenty - everybody made cakes. Here and there, a neighbour took a chance with works of art or craft. Images and representations of sunrises and sunsets smudged in chalks. Reasonably priced, though. Somewhere, there was music of a kind. A recorded sound - not a live band, but its tones lulled the visitors into a gentle ambiance, whereby they'd purchase, more or less, anything. *Souvenirs* of time well spent.

Barbara purchased a snow globe of the Eiffel Tower.

'Well, saves actually going to Paris.' she said. 'All the roads look the same to me, I've heard. All go round in circles.'

'Well, if you're going to go around, circles should be your first choice.'

She linked arms with him.

'Correcting me. I said, "round". You amended it to "around."'

'Just my way. I don't mean anything by it. Why make mistakes when you don't have to? Bet you were a right cracker at school.'

'At school? Never paid it much heed. Just wanted a man, - someone like you.'

'I'd have been about twelve.'

'Not far off it now - inches, I mean! You're funny. Where are you taking me?'

'Why? Where d'you want to go? The weather is not too good anyway, according to all phone reports. May as well go home to bed.'

'Okay.' she said. 'I'd be up for that.'

'I know. You are incredibly sexy. You know that?'

'I seem to be with you. Let's enjoy it while we can.'

'They do say, "Make a woman laugh, and you're half of the way home." Whose home is not made clear.'

'Oh...'

'What?'

'I've wet my knickers - again.'

'So have I.'

'That's what I meant.'

'We'll have to think of something.'

'Thinking about it already. It's the heat, I think. Puts ideas into my head.'

'Keep them

there - for now. See that guy over there?

'What guy?'

'That one. Look!'

'Oh, the guy without a shirt?'

'That's him. Mayor of this town. You can tell by the gold chain, his chain of office.'

'You men are so weird. Still… goes well against the white hair on his chest.'

'Knew you'd like him.'

'Why is he not even wearing a shirt?'

'I don't know. Too hot, I guess. Why don't you ask him?'

'I don't speak French - why don't you? Idiot!'

'You or me?'

'You! Of course. You're right, it's too hot. Who could live here? But, the white does go with the gold, in a way.'

'Now you're thinking.'

'Very regal, in a way.'

'That's how revolutions start!'

'Ooh, don't. Not all that again. Poor Marie! Who needs it? Haven't we grown up after all of that?'

'Let's hope so.'

Bond appeared behind their shoulders.

'Thought I might find the two of you here.'

She stiffened. Solomon continued to peruse the various stalls. Nobody spoke. Bond offered a gift.

'Pomme d'amour? Or, "toffee-apple" as you say in England-land.'

'Thank you, no. I'd get it everywhere.'

'All over your clothes, you mean?' He smiled. 'I can only imagine such a thing.'

'Imagine away.'

Solomon reappeared with ice cream.

'Quick! It'll soon dissolve.'

Hers was a raspberry ripple. She loved that.

'Got you one too.' Solomon said to Bond. 'Vanilla. Mind you, don't get it on your shoes… Suede, aren't they?'

'Easily suede.' said Bond.

She laughed. They pretended not to notice.

'I believe so. They were bought for me, so I cannot be sure.'

'You have people who buy your shoes for you?' He was intrigued.

She shrugged. 'Don't we all?'

A tinny voice echoed over proceedings briefly. The multi-colored bunting fluttered in the sea breeze. A number was called.

Bond tugged Solomon by the shoulder.

'It is you!' he exclaimed. 'Your ticket has won. See? *Trente-et-deux.* Thirty-two. Is that your number, my friend? I am sure it is. Nobody else seems to be coming forward.'

'Oh, Solomon. You clever thing.' Barbara interjected. 'Go up and see what you've won.'

'Well, I don't know…'

'Of course, it's you! I was behind you, and I'm thirty-four!'

'Much more than that, surely.' said Bond, eyeing her up and down. 'I am sure.'

'Cheeky.' she said. 'Go on, Solly. Before they draw someone else.'

'Alright.'

He waded off through the crowd.

'Hopefully, it will be Champagne. Then we can really celebrate.'

'Celebrate?'

'Our new-found friendship. You know the French; any excuse to celebrate.'

'What makes you think that we are friends?'

'I know how to read women.'

'Oh, you do, do you? We will see.'

Bond took his chance as he saw it…

'I can't help thinking about you now, like toffee in my hands. Me, nibbling at your softer parts. And your harder parts, glistening in the Sun.'

'Dream on.'

'I do. Don't fight it, honey-pie. You were meant for me, and I want you.'

'Guess again. I am not your "honey-pie". Never will be.'

'We will see. Nature has a way. Imagine this: wherever you are and whatever you are doing, I will be watching and waiting. Imagine that.'

'No, thank you. We seem to have got off at the wrong door; excuse my French. I am not interested in you. Not at all. And if I find you on my property, I will take my shotgun down from the wall and, afterward, summon a gendarme.

'But I am interested in you, lovely, sexy woman. Fate has crossed our paths.'

'Paths? It was a railway line!'

'And yet, here I still am.'

'Alright. Be still.'

'I have dreamed of a woman like you since I was…' he indicated with the flat of his hand. 'That high. I am a man that never gives in and always gets what he wants.'

'In England, we have a name for people like that. Begins with a double-yew.'

'But, we are not in England. This is France. I have a home advantage. Familiar soil.'

'Try Vanish! Or Domestos. Exterminates all known germs. Good luck with everything else in your infantile mind.'

'It will not be a matter of luck, Madame. More of a twist of fate. Look out, here comes your lord protector. Back from the hunt. We will meet again.'

Bond, at once, seemed to disappear.

'Look at what we won!' said Solomon, seemingly astounded. 'More scented candles! Can't make out the scents; I need a translator. What's this one? Châtaigne. That's to do with cats, isn't it?'

She laughed. 'No, that's chestnut. Everyone knows that.'

'Oh. What is it with these things? They're everywhere! Am I missing something?'

'Maybe it's to make France smell different to what it really smells like.'

'Yes, maybe. Same as all perfumes, I guess. Coming down here on the train, I kept getting the whiff of French onion soup.'

'Well, of course you did. That's pretty much all that was on the menu. That, or cassoulet, of course.'

'Inherited racism, I guess. There was always a Frenchman on a bicycle in England when I was a boy. A string of onions hanging around his neck. Black and white Breton jersey.'

I love those! You should get one.'

'Not down here. Too far south. You're thinking of Brittany.'

'So long as there's cassoulet.'

'Of course. Specialty of our region.'

'Good.'

'Somebody said once that the olfactory sense is stronger than language.'

'Quite true.' She agreed. 'I love the smell of cassoulet. And the taste. Toulouse sausage. Am I right?'

'Quite correct, my dear.'

'*Mon ami.*'

'Mine too. You'll do for me. Where's your friend?'

'Standing opposite me.' She smiled engagingly.

'Not me.' He semi-scolded. 'That bloke from the train. What did he want?'

'What do you think?'

'Hmm. Hope you told him where to go.'

'I told him where he'd never go.' She blushed, only inwardly. 'He's not my friend, either way. Never will be. He's creepy.'

'Thinks the world of you. Can see it in his eyes. Wants you anyway.'

'Hard cheese. Who wants the rest of the world when I have you? You're my Sun, my moon and stars.' She leaned closer and stroked his cheek.

'Good answer.'

'What are they cooking? Smells delicious.'

'Tastes delicious too. Food often does. Hogget, they say. A young lamb. Aged between one and two years. Never see a third spring. Or summer.'

'Men are such barbarians.'

'Smells good enough to eat. Roasted tomatoes and celeriac. Plenty of coriander - or parsley. Virtually the same stuff. Two of your five-a-day.'

'Five-a-day? Does the rest of the world think that we do nothing but sit around all day eating?'

'Well, you're allowed to stand, I believe. Particularly for the cheeses.'

'You're funny. Mint sauce though - or jelly?'

'My dear companion. Mint jelly is an English invention. Here, it's a little mint, a little vinegar. Normally mixed with plain yogurt.'

'Kaita!'

'Bless you. Originally Japanese, but they love it here.'

'So do I. Cools every meal or snack.'

'Originally brought here by Marco Polo. Born in Albania, some believe.'

'Solomon?'

'Yes?'

'Shut up and eat.'

'Okay.'

After eating, they walked back to their car.

'What's up?' he asked. 'Gone rather quiet.'

She shook her head; her auburn curls caught the afternoon sunlight.

'I don't like that man,' she said.

'So? Don't worry about him. He won't do anything while I'm around.'

'What if you're not?'

'I'll always be here. Get used to it. He will, too.'

'What does he want anyway?'

'Well, if you like, the same thing I wanted the first time I saw you.'

'Not the first time.'

'Yes, the very first time.'

'Even though you were seeing my daughter?'

'Hey, we said we'd never speak of it. Come on, let's get you home.'

'Our home.' She smiled sweetly.

'Exactly.'

'What's the speed limit here?'

'Who cares?'

But...

It was only a matter of time before Bond made his way onto her property, her own private dwelling.

She was cooking in the farmhouse-style kitchen; onions, zucchini, and peppers slowly fried, ready for the red kidney beans to be added. She was using Mexican chipotle flakes, and the air smelled of chili and stung her eyes a little. Solomon had gone to the village, hopefully, to collect their new garden mower. The grass was too long, and they couldn't see what it contained if anything. There were bears in this part of France. Foxes, too, of course. It put her chicken run on the back burner. She'd always wanted chickens, just a few hens, eggs daily. Fence for the foxes - or bears.

She turned back to the stove - *la four*. It hissed and spitted with olive oil. There were plum tomatoes, mushrooms, and real olives at hand, too. Olives, ready-pitted, green and black. She loved Kalamata olives, but this was France, and they hadn't seen any. Besides, what if the mayor dropped by? Said he might. Anyway, Kalamata olives were Greek and didn't belong in her current recipe.

And knives — Sabatiers. She didn't like the look of him.

'What are you doing in my home!'

'Your husband.' He explained. 'Saw him leave. That's it for the two of you, is it? Makes you available.'

'No, it doesn't. He's just in the village doing some business. Back any minute. Better flee before I take one of your ears off with my favorite knife!'

'Flee?'

Means, go. Desist. Stop calling around here. Go away.'

'I see.' he said, amused. 'Yes, yes. It's much easier to just say flee.'

'Don't move!' she shouted. 'I may not be a dead shot with these knives, but I could easily give you something to think about. Once the bleeding stops.'

He laughed. 'You're funny.'

She was serious. 'Try me.'

'I'd love to.' he said, candidly. 'That's why I'm here.'

'Well, you can just push off. You'll get nothing from me.'

'What are you doing here? What do you want?'

'You, of course. You're my obsession. I saw your husband leave and thought, Why not?'

'I'll tell you why not, you loathsome individual. I can't stand you - the look or the smell. Go and bother somebody else. I don't want you here. My other half will be back before you know it.'

'Hmm. Left on the Paris train. The earliest he'd be home is eight o'clock tonight. We could do a lot before then.'

'Spying on us now, are you?'

'Of course. One has to be sure of one's ground.'

'Okay, sure. You like the look of me. That's all. Speaking personally, I can't stand the sight of you. So, go on. Get out of my house, or I'll make you sorry you ever called on me.'

'Fiery stuff. Typical redhead. Spits fire. Enchanting.'

'Go on, fuck off.' She was half-dressed in a chef's white blouson, buttoned right to left, he noticed. The swell and curve of her bosoms filled the uniform perfectly. God, he wanted her. Couldn't she tell?

She went on;

'How would you like it? No, don't answer that. Just get out of my house. What do you think you're doing here? Okay, my partner is not on the premises, but rest assured, if he found you here, he'd kill you.'

'He's killed before. Told me that on the train.'

'I know. For me.' She thought about this. 'Well, the second time anyway.'

He skulked around her kitchen table, putting his fingers where they didn't belong.

'Mm. Mint, Marjoram, Basil, Rosemary, Turmeric. Good for the skin.' He appeared to concentrate. '"Doing in your home"? Well, now, what do you think? It was only a matter of moments before he left you alone for a while. Thought he could trust me, did he?' Bond laughed a short, evil laugh. 'And now, here we are. He'll be gone for several hours more. We can do anything we want to do.'

'Like what?'

'You know what.'

'Forget it. It's never going to happen. Go on, push off!'

'Plenty enough time.'

'For what?'

'For me to visit your bedchamber, strip you of these meagre clothes and make mad and passionate love to you. Imagine that.'

Behind the stove, stirring gently, Barbara coloured slightly. 'You wouldn't dare.'

'Daring me? I was at a public school. We never resist a dare.'

'He'd kill you.'

'But he is not here. And you'd have no reason to tell. I'm sure you'd be worth it.'

'Worth more than life itself?'

'I am sure. We all hang by a thread, madame. The breathing in and out could stop at any time. Who's to say? Why not enjoy life as we can every step of the way? Go on. He need never know. Even if you fake it. I'm sure you've had to fake it before.'

She bristled. 'There's nothing fake about me!'

'I am sure. Come on, take that top off and let's have a look at you.'

'Want to wank over me, do you? Thought as much. I can see you for what you are.'

'Au contraire madame. I want you pinned to the bed, flat out. Want to penetrate you in the fullest fashion, as they say en France. Want those gorgeous breasts I keep dreaming of. Want my hands on you. I want to watch the colour of your face-cheeks change as I transport you to the gates of ecstasy. Don't tell me you're not considering it. We're all only human.'

'Rubbish. You appal me with your creepy, horrid ways. Give me one chance, and I'll slice off your member with my largest knife. Although, the smallest one would probably do.'

'Size is not important.'

'Hah! Shows what you know.'

'Fighting talk, typically English or British. Best to keep this table between ourselves until your mind is resolved.'

'Resolved to do what?'

'To sleep with me, of course. What else?'

'Never going to happen. Go on - get out. Before he gets back.'

'Show me your breasts first. I've come a long way to see them. Longed for them. The pair. I've imagined how they caress each other.'

'Case of having to.' she said, half-jokingly. 'Not any room for a third.'

'Want me to masturbate over them? Some women like that. I'd like that.'

'Really? Done that, have you? You disgust me.'

'You wouldn't have to be directly involved. You stay on that side, and I'll stay on my side.'

'You don't have a side. This is my house! You wanker.'

'Go on. Just strip off. I can imagine you unbuttoning that blouson. Exposing yourself. Thrilling. And then, give me about thirty seconds, and I'll leave you alone. Unless something further occurs to you... Come on. What harm could it do?'

'What about my pride?'

'What about it? There's nobody here but us. There are a few curious mice behind the wainscotting, but that's all. No other body.'

'No. Not in a million years.' She appeared thoughtful. 'Unless...'

'Yes?'

'If I do what you say, will you go away and never come here again. All puns intended, of course.'

'What about your mate?'

'What about him? He's not here, is he?'

'You'd tell him?'

'Why would I?'

'I'll tell though. I'll tell everyone I meet. "You know that new English woman that lives up on the hill. With her husband? Badger her enough, and she'll do anything you want. Show you everything. Those fantastic tits - you should see them! Magnificent. Makes you believe there's a God."'

She embedded a knife into the butcher block.

'Forget it then. Had your chance, and you blew it. Never going to happen now. Go on, fuck off.'

'You mean you would have done?'

'Never know now, will you. Arsehole.'

'Ah, how the scales are tilted. On the one hand, you think it's a small price to pay. On the other, it's your reputation that you long to keep unsullied.'

'And in the other?'

'Sorry, forgetting myself. You excite me. Only natural.'

'Tissues over there in the corner.'

'You think this is a joke?'

'I think you are a joke. Alright, you took a fancy to me on our train journey, but that should have been that. This isn't a "Brief Encounter."'

'Hmm?'

'It's a movie. A romantic one. No sex in it at all.'

'Never seen it. Still, these things happen.'

'Not to me. I hardly use the train. I mean, it happens to lots of people. Strangers meet. Fleeting glances. "What ifs". Then, we move on. Doesn't mean anything at all. Look at you and me. You don't know anything about me. Don't even know my name.'

'Names are not important. It's seeing that's believing.'

'Well, they are to me. I wouldn't go with any man who hadn't tried to find out everything he could about me. We are not animals. We are sophisticated people. Well, I am.'

'You say, "You wouldn't". You mean to say you were considering my offer?'

'No. I'm not considering any such thing. Just want you out of here, that's all. There'll be hell to pay when my man gets back and finds you here. I wouldn't want to be in your shoes. God knows what he will do.'

'There is much room between God and hell. Let's wait and see. My presence here might lead your man to the conclusion that whatever went on here today, he missed it.'

'I believe he trusts me.'

'Wrongly, my dear. Quite wrongly. People mistrust everyone. From years of hard lessons learnt.'

'Be that as it may.'

This was an expression that was new to Mister Bond. He sifted the words carefully with no result. He didn't know what she meant.

'Please take off your clothes, madame, at the very least. You may never get a chance like this again. Not at your age.'

'Age? What has age got to do with it? Men! You're all the same. Either we're too young -jailbait, inexperienced. Or we're too old and incapable. Well, I'm neither. I'm in the prime of my life. You must think so too, or you wouldn't be here.'

He shrugged. 'I only know you at this age, as you are now. If you had been a sweet sixteen-year-old when we first met, maybe I would have fallen for that girl. Instead of the fulsome womanly creature who meets my gaze now. I could imagine pleasuring myself with you in your sexy promenade dress, but right now, I want you to remove your blouson.'

'Either way, your luck is hard. You'll get nothing from me. The back door is where you left it. Now use it.' She pointed with the sharpest of her knives.

'Very well. We shall meet again, madame. You can be sure of it.' He bade her farewell, and she turned and watched him as he stole through the landscape of cherry and apple trees, fingering the Hebe bushes as he strolled. Green leaves, white-flowered. They captivated him, airs of mystery. Each bud is a tale as yet untold.

Satisfied that he was gone, she went up to her room and thought about herself.

In here, there was quiet; coolness, calmness, - serenity, if the need arose. The colours are carefully chosen and calculated to ease the mind or spirit. She loved it here - so different to England.

Eyes down, curtains half-closed, the radiant sun in abeyance. She slipped off her loose-fitting clothing.

She smoothed her naked body down and checked her breasts for lumps or bumps - nothing of the sort, thank God. To her, they were perfect. As for her thighs, her good waist, her eyes and hips, all good. What was it that men saw in her? Can't just be these, surely? Lovely, sumptuous mounds, though they were. Lovely, rounded flesh. Her nail-polished fingers prodded and proved. Evidence that we live and thrive. Feel good, too. Mmm…

Still, all people have breasts. All women anyway - most women. Without them, we'd be powerless. What was it that men saw? Reminders of infanthood, she'd heard, but men, with their rough hands, just wanted to feel them. And then penetrate her naturally.

God, I'm horny now. Who's about? No one in particular. Oh well…

She lay down on her very own bed. Her fingers moved. Thank God we have fingers. She looked out of the window. A tree had died. Weak, lacked the sufficient nutrition that it had needed. Sunlight and soil. Care and attention. Same as all the rest of us, as we all do.

Not that Bond cretin. Not Solly either, at this moment. Obviously not Desmond, the person who she had claimed as her husband back in the day.

"Husband?" she wondered. "To share a house and resources. Frugally." Hah! No, never the twain. Like all efforts at the English language, the writer meant one thing and the reader another. But how do we communicate otherwise? Her fingers moved again…. Man. Here and now… Oh well, anyone would do. Let's see now…

Solomon couldn't concentrate. He sat at the sunlit, tabled bar in the early afternoon and tried to piece things together. He was pretty sure he didn't know anybody called Wendy - or why she should be trying to blackmail him. Nevertheless, he had come this far. May as well see how it all panned out.

The Sancerre was cold on his tongue. Elsewhere, the world revolved around him - as it always did. He felt desolate, alone. Longed to be with Barbara again... Of course, he worried about Bond. Who wouldn't? But she wouldn't entertain him. Perish the thought! He knew that. They both did. All three of them, really.

He pulled himself together - self-pity never worked. Never mind that. What next? How long could he stay in Paris? He wasn't made of money.

A woman approached, a burly woman. She looked him up and down and seated herself at his table.

'Yeah, see what she meant.'

'What she meant?'

'What she means.' She held out a hand. 'I'm Wendy.'

'Good for you.' He refused the shake. 'What do you want?'

'Just to talk.'

'So talk.'

'About a trip to Scotland.'

'What about it?'

'You killed a man.'

'Obviously, I would dispute that. Who says so?'

'Your friend Carter. Saved his life, he reckons.'

'So? He saved mine, too.'

She nodded. 'Yes, I guess that's true. Where's your friend?'

'Where's yours? Got a warrant, have you?'

'Don't need one. Out of my jurisdiction, as it goes.'

'Good. Go away, then. I've got nothing for you.'

'But you did kill a man.'

'Prove it. Anyway, not in this country. Nor the next one to it. Wasting your time here, I'm afraid. How did you find me anyway?'

'I'm a police officer. It's what we do.'

'You mean Interpol. That kind of thing?'

'Kind of.'

'I must admit to being slightly amazed when the telegram arrived. Who knew that France still had a telegraph system?'

'I did. You have to think - France is roughly four times the size of England. They can't holler to each other over the garden walls.'

'I suppose not.'

She stood.

'Rest assured, I will not let the matter rest.'

'Carter told me that nobody would do anything. That the police would rather all of those gangs were wiped out rather than brought to justice.'

'The law is the law, Mister Swift. No point in having laws if people don't obey them.'

'It was self-defence, though. Ask Carter.'

'The second one wasn't. More a crime passionel. Give my regards to Francesca.'

So, maybe this was the long dark hair on his pillowcase? Who knew?

'No. Tell her yourself - if you can find her.'

'Au revoir.'

'Goodbye.'

The waitress was pretty in her black and white uniform; collars and cuffs all matched. Low-cut cleavage and boobs dressed up to the nines. Long, nylon-clad legs to die for - and what a way to go! She carried trays of drinks in her upturned hand like a juggler. Nothing was too much trouble. She was super-attentive to Solomon - he knew what that might mean. Her smile could light any sky. She lit up his bare table with an infuriating scented candle.

'Anything else?' she enquired, possibly for the thousandth time - this was just a job.

'Up to you.' Said Solomon, in his best getting-to-know-you voice. 'What time do you get off?'

She fluttered her black eyelashes. 'Who? Me? Oh, I never get off.'

Depends how hard the other person tries, I guess.'

'Maybe.' She

turned and left, but Solomon knew what a "Maybe" meant. He could picture her over a freezer or up against a Frigidaire (all puns included). But no, no. No need for romantic illusions. He had a hotel room. How hard could it be?

In the kitchens, Océane continued her duties. Her colleagues rattled pots and pans and called, "Service!" but she was seemingly oblivious.

'What's matter, Océane?' said one of the staff, Marie. 'Cat got your tongue?'

'No, no. Océane replied. 'Nothing.'

'Fine-looking gentleman you're serving.' Goaded Marie. 'Think there might be something else being served in the future? And I'm not talking about racquet sports!'

The rest of the kitchen staff responded with laughter. Océane's cheeks coloured.

'No, no.' she repeated. 'Nothing like that. Looks nice, that's all.'

'Don't they all? Until they get what they want.'

'See to it then!' commanded the chef. 'Service!'

She went about her duties.

Bond kept on coming back, whatever she did, and she thought maybe there was one way to get rid of him. She imagined it. It might be good for her too…

'Could be your lucky day.' she said brightly.

'Oh? Why's that?'

'I've been thinking. And you're right, in a way. It really doesn't matter to anybody but the two of us.'

'You mean?'

'Uh-huh. Come here.'

He moved closer, around the kitchen diner. 'Well?'

'Why not?'

'No reason why not. Got you're here now. Got everything I've wanted.'

'You haven't got me - never will have. I'm doing this to get rid of you - if you're as good as your word. What is it you wanted?'

'Just you - naked. Your beautiful, rounded breasts, your lovely, rounded arse. The colour of your gorgeous blue eyes. What else have you got? Let me see.'

He helped her out of her simple clothing. Cheesecloth shirt; bra-less today - well, she didn't need one. Particularly in this weather. Shorts and sandals. Nothing much...

'Nothing below my waistline.' she warned.

'We will see. Loved you in that white blouson. Kept me awake all night dreaming about you. Could imagine unbuttoning you.'

'I know. I saw. Anyway, clothing's overrated. It's what's beneath that matters'.

He gently exposed her ripe and willing breasts and buried his nose between them.

'Mmm. Fabulous.' came his muffled voice. 'Knew they would be.'

'Don't...'

''You mean, "Do". It's okay. I want you. Want all of you. No one will ever know. Just enjoy yourself. That's what we're all here for. We're all a long time dead.'

'I, I suppose so. What if...'

'There are no "What ifs". Your mate is away in Paris - on business, he told the ticket master. I overheard. Don't worry; we'll have no interruptions. Live for the moment. It's just me and you.'

She stroked his back. 'Always wanted me, didn't you? From the first moment, you set eyes on me. I could tell. What was it that you wanted?'

All of this. The look of you, the curves and shallows of you. The whole of you. These two beauties. Wanted it all.'

'Want me to put my blouson on? It's all washed and pressed.'

'Not now I've got you here like this.' He stroked her with both hands, his thumbs raising the inquisitive nipples, hard as frozen peas.

'Mm, that's nice.'

'Didn't I tell you?'

'Why me, though? Strangers on a train.'

'Looked at yourself in a full-length mirror lately? You're everything I've ever wanted in a woman. Life's a bowl of sweet fruits and berries. Nothing more. Take what you want and eat it whole.'

'And what am I? Fruits and berries?'

'Very much so. Hang on.' He removed her shorts, pants and sandals. 'Mm, nice bush. Neatly trimmed. All your own work?'

'Of course. I said, nothing below the waist!'

'Said no but meant yes. You want me. I can smell it on you.'

He pushed her gently back against the worktop. She hoped it would bear their weight. No matter, it was solid.

Solomon fished with his steak. Océane pondered unnecessarily.

'Enjoyable?'

'Very much so. Need a pick, though.'

'A pick?'

'Mm. For my teeth. I'm actually training a team of small birds to fly in whilst I'm sleeping and pick them clean, but, God, it's hard work. Who sleeps anymore? So much to do, so little time. Whatever the way, sometimes I don't think they understand a word I'm saying. Birds, eh?'

'You're joking.'

'I know. What are you doing later?'

'Later? Legs up with a book and a drink, I'd expect. Squeeze,'

He resisted the temptation.

'Could it be something more lively'?

'My evening? Or the steak? Like what? Want to take me dancing?'

'Some call it dancing. Definitely want to take you. For a start.'

'Hah! Got you. Sshhh, I'm working. Call me later.'

'I don't have your number.'

She smiled. A slow, seductive smile. Her hair caressed her face as she wiped the table clean.

'Yes.' she said, breathing heavily. 'You do.' She dared herself. 'Do you want me?'

'Rare, or well done?'

'Either or both. We will see.'

She skipped away in her sensible shoes.

'Thought so', said Solomon.

Pans and plates were scattered onto the floor, knives and forks too. The noise didn't bother them; it didn't oscillate. She was perfect and smooth against the granite top; she felt it herself. Cold and hard. Naked as the day she was born. She fondled his erection. Firm. Smooth. Long... God, he was hot!

'And now I've got you, I'm going to fuck you across your kitchen table. You'll remember this every time you're cooking.'

'I'm cooking now...'

Her legs were all over the place. She couldn't really tell left from right. She spread them as wide as she could. Dug her heels into the butcher block for purchase, lay back and got herself comfortable.

He was all over her in seconds. She felt her senses heightening. Just like she'd been in her school days. Now, she just wanted a good seeing, too.

He penetrated her easily; she was soaking wet.

'Ooh! Oh! Yes! Oh my...'

Twenty minutes later, he was gone. Just a memory. She wiped herself dry and redressed. Men - all the same. Promised the Earth, moon and stars, but where were they when you really needed one? Hmm, it's nice to have nine inches up inside her, though. Felt good. More memories of schooldays...

There was a beautiful, bountiful tree outside her kitchen window. Promising the Earth. All new foliage. Like all of us, she supposed. The tree foraged its way back to Heaven and didn't much care what it had left behind. Its hands spiralled skywards, but there was only one way home, and they all knew it.

'You awake?'

He grunted back into life, loving the sound of her voice already. She wrapped herself around him like a reptile might do.

'What are you thinking?'

'Same as you.' He hugged her. 'Just about you.' he said.

'And how fabulous I was?'

'Of course. You inspire me. If that's important to you. Pleased me, anyhow. Can't get enough of you.'

'Good answer.' She stroked his hairy chest with her nail-varnished fingers - and more below... 'What else, though? Something troubling you?'

He nodded briefly. 'Kind of. Hard to explain.'

'Take your time. What's in the past is best left there - Nietzsche. Take it from me...'

'I just did.'

'You're in the best place in the world. Naked, in the arms of your recently vanquished lover. Sweet dreams at your command.'

'Vanquished?'

'Well, I pretend to be hard to get, but I'm not. See what I want and have to have it. Spoilt girl. You know that now.'

'I sure do'.

'Now I know.' She fingered him gently. 'Come on. Do me again.'

'Anytime.'

'Good a time as any.'

He clambered over her.

'First time I saw you, I thought, beautiful eyes, lips. The way you wear your hair.'

'Hair. Why do men think that's sexy? We spend half our lives shaving it all off.'

'Leaving your perfect pale skin unencumbered. Beautiful for all to see.'

'Not all, no.'

'Your breasts, your hips, your thighs. Your ankles in flat shoes. Thought to myself, oh yes. I want her. Every inch of her.'

Océane stroked him some more.

'Every inch. And now you've got me. Want me some more?'

'There's more?'

'You betcha. All kinds of different things I can do. You've hardly scratched the surface.'

'Mm. It is such a beautiful surface, too. All gleaned from previous encounters?'

'Gleaned? Naturally. I suppose so. I'm no virgin. Not anymore.'

'Neither am I.'

'What started you off, tell me? The honeyed tones of some glamour girl with her top off. Next, - oh my! Down below the waistline? You tell me. What else could it have been?'

He shrugged a shoulder. 'Not sure. I was a boy once. Woke up one day and realized I had grown into a man. Wanted a woman.'

'Any woman?'

'Some. Not as hard as it looks.'

'There's me you could have fooled.'

'Girl in my class; I can picture her now. Bright and blue school uniform: smart blazer, short skirt. Ankle socks and platform shoes - all the rage back then. I wouldn't have said, "No".

So I didn't.'

'Carried her books from school? All that?'

'Of course. Least you can do.'

'What about me?'

'You're not a schoolgirl anymore.'

'No. I'm "legal" now. Would you, though?'

'Maybe. You're different.'

'That's what I like about me. Never know what I'm thinking.'

'Said she - flat on her back, naked with her legs in the air. Got a pretty good idea.'

'Good. It's what we do here, and now that counts.' She got up and dressed herself in a simple robe. He loved the way she sheathed her breasts from sight, such a thin material: silk. She put on her black and white uniform again and came across and kissed him on the nose.

'Wait here. I'll be five minutes.'

'Five minutes?'

'About that. Got to tell the boss I need a couple of hours off.'

'And then you'll be back?'

'Oh, yes, lover, I'll be back. Not done with me yet.'

She blew him another kiss and left the room.

By the weekend, he was back. This time, he had her in her bed. She smelled of roses and cologne. Almost as though she had been waiting for him, which she had. The back door was left unlocked and everything. He knew the way. Come on in and help yourself...

Dave Jeanes

The blinds were nearly closed, despite the heat of the day, but she knew he would be back; she couldn't keep away. She just knew.

Yes...

He wore a painter's robe, but not for long. He knew what she wanted and what he wanted, too. He was all over her in seconds. His hands, his arms, his brilliant strength.

'I'd hate to be raped by you. God couldn't fight you off.'

He kissed her. 'Don't worry. I'm not going to rape you. Why would I? God, you're beautiful naked.' He explored her. 'So much of you.'

'Not one of those skinny types.'

'No. Handfuls.'

'All yours!' she gasped. 'Take whatever you want.'

He did.

Afterwards, they slept. Morning came, as mornings do.

'Coffee?'

'No. Come back here and do me some more.'

'What for? I'll make you redraw.'

'Stupid question. We're here, and it's now. Why wouldn't you?'

'You get to a point when sex doesn't mean much anymore.'

'Could've fooled me.'

'There's nothing you haven't seen before, and all women do is lie there and take it. Well, that's the female side. The male wants to dominate, seduce, procreate.'

'Don't you dare!' she cried. 'You're not procreating anything in me. I'll be straight down the pharmacy before you could say knife.'

'Fair enough so. Any woman who puts a man's cock in her mouth is dreaming about her father, alive or dead - ask Freud! They paint their eyes black and their lips red, truss their selves up in all kinds of extravagances, high-heeled shoes so their breasts stand out and their arses are all behind them, and still they get irritated when we don't take them seriously. Ridiculous.'

'And yet, you still keep coming back for more.'

'What else is there?'

'Our tits, our arses. Come and feel. I've also got a juicy wet cunt that wants you inside me. Again! Don't say no! Don't!'

'I won't. You're a gorgeous piece of white flesh that my hands can't get enough of. But my God, I'm going to try...'

'Mmm, love your rough hands on my tits. Oh! And down there, too. On my pussy.' She spread her legs for him. 'Don't do this for every man I see.'

'Why me then?'

'Because you wanted me.'

'Mm. Fabulous.' He ran his hot hands over the curves and creases of her body.

Dave Jeanes

'Stop it! You'll get me at it again.'

'Let's have you then.'

'Ohh... take me, take me again, my lover... Take me back to the stars!'

He did. Loved the look and the feel of her. Loved those magnificent breasts under his hands, loved her below the waist. That small, perfect, triangular piece of paradise, waiting patiently, warm and moist. Calm and vibrant. Knowing that he would be back eventually. He loved being inside her. In short, he was in love with her, love and lust, and he didn't know nor care who knew about it.

She entranced him. He gorged himself on her. She lay back and took it like only a woman could. Threw back her arms, occasionally marking his back with her sharp fingernails - men loved those scars.

She liked him, liked the way he moved through her. All her nooks and crannies. Why wouldn't he be standoffish? What was there not to like? She still had it all, plus years of experience. Both Desmond and Solomon had agreed to that. Indirectly, of course.

He seemed to be interested in every inch of her, touching her in places that she couldn't remember being touched before.

'Ooch! Ouch! Oh! That's nice. Do that some more. Just there.'

Felt good.

Thirty minutes later, she lay back again, exhausted and fulfilled.

'Wow!' she said.

He fancied a cigarette. Passed one to her.

'Smoke?'

'I thought I just did.'

He laughed and kissed her on the nose. 'You did. Post-coital.'

She wasn't entirely sure of the meaning.

'No, thanks. Kill you, those things.'

'All gotta go sometime.'

'No need to rush things. Not this morning, hey? Thanks.'

He smiled and stroked her free thigh. 'Thanks are not required.'

'No, I didn't mean that.'

'Who does?' he teased.

'Let's talk.'

Inwardly, he sighed. Still...

'About us.'

'Who?'

'You and me.'

'Here now, aren't we?' He caressed one of her buttocks. 'What do we need to discuss?'

'Just this and that.'

'Oh.' He was relieved. 'What's on your mind?'

'Just, where do we go from here?'

Bond already knew, but he wasn't letting on.

'Who was your first love?'

'Mine? Love or lust?' he joked.

'Whichever. Both.'

He thought. 'My English teacher. I mean, by that, she taught us English, not that she was actually English. Which she was.'

'Okay. Got that straight. Go on.'

'The first time I saw her, I wanted her. Didn't know exactly what it was I wanted, I was only fourteen, but I wanted to see her naked, run my hands over her, kiss her, snog her, smooch her - fuck her! Oh my! She seemed so clean and pure. I could never concentrate on English after that. Read the whole of "For Whom The Bell Tolls" without absorbing a word of it. Shame really. It's a great book, in retrospect. I know that now. She gave me, unconsciously, a great rush of blood to the head. "Don't you like Hemingway?" she'd ask. I couldn't tell her the truth. I knew what she'd say. Still, every time she stepped into the classroom in her high-heeled, navy blue shoes, click-clacking across the wooden floors, I'd be thinking, "What if? What if?" She'd look at me like she knew. As if to say, "Never mind Hemingway. I've got you in my sights. Kapow! I know what you're thinking, but you've got no chance. Never in a month of Sundays. Like the swell of my bosoms, don't you? I know. I've seen the way you look at me. I get this all the time. Every fourteen-year-old boy who comes into my class every term looks at me the same way. Some girls, too. Think you can ever have me? Have to try harder than that. Show me something I've never seen before.'

'And did you?'

'No, of course not. These things are just a part of growing up. Something for the memory banks, that's all - deposits and withdrawals. They don't interfere with everyday life. I did suggest that her husband need never know. Know what she said? "He'd know."'

'Seems so. Bet you wish you had now. Bet she does, too.'

'Nah. These things don't matter.'

'But they do!' she insisted. 'Of course they do. Romance and love tell you that there's more to life than at first meets the eye. Take me, for instance...'

'Spread your legs then.'

'Why, Mister Darcy.' She adopted an Austenesque accent. 'Oh, you. Go on, then. Be quick! Oh! My word!'

He leered over her. 'And what is your word?'

'You'll find out in a minute.'

'A minute.'

'It only takes a minute.'

'Lizzie was less than impressed.

'Have to marry me now.'

'Pardon?'

'Oh, nothing. Just a joke.'

She got up and scouted around for her clothing: bra and pants - check. Knickers, knickers. Ah! The carpet stank of his feet. She redressed herself and made for the door.

'Any time!' her voice rang out. 'Maybe see you again someday.'

She closed the door behind her.

He closed his eyes and began snoring.

'Yeah, in your dreams.' she said to herself. Men! It's all the bloody same. Only want one thing. Still... women only want one thing too, long and lovely though it is, sometimes.

She was aware that she needed to shower. Imagined the smell of him on her. She made it to the hotel.

'Bin men have been?'

'Just gone. Didn't you hear them? Bin and gone.'

'Noisy shower. Couldn't hear a thing.'

'They certainly are.'

'Did they take all that glass?'

The cullet? Yes. All goes to landfill, you know that much.'

'So you say.'

'Seen it. Packed into trains and heading for Scotland. It must be early full by now - the landfill site. Don't be surprised if one day, Scotland breaks off and floats away before sinking without a trace.'

'Oh. Okay. What really happens though?'

'They barrel it up into container ships and send it off to China. Being going on for years.'

'And what do they do with it?'

'Who?'

'The Chinese!'

'Oh, them. Well, there are recycling possibilities. Broken glass can be added to cement or tarmac; it has an everlasting quality. Well, I say, "everlasting." Takes about four thousand years to decompose.'

'Why don't we use glass instead of plastic?'

'Number of reasons. Weight, fragility. Talking of which, are you coming back to bed?'

Indignant, she replied: 'There's nothing wrong with my weight!'

'Absolutely.' he concurred. 'Love you when you're on top. Come on. Get over here.'

'I've just showered.'

'Then you'll be squeaky clean for me.'

'I don't know if I'll squeak.'

'Let's see...'

Fran took her pills. Sixteen this time; she'd heard that was quite enough. Sweet sixteen...

Ah well. Life had begun to suck lately, and she wasn't having any more of it. Not a religious woman, but surely there was more than this? Sure, Lizzie could go from partner to partner and enjoy herself, but it bored Fran in every sense of the word. She sat on the edge of the bed and looked out at the Parisian landscape. Or portrait.

Towers loomed, skyscrapers did what you thought they might. Diggers drove, and drivers in hi-vis vests delivered. Life went on indefinitely.

'Ah well,' she thought again. 'We'll always have Paris.'

"Life wasn't anything," she'd heard it say. 'until you've seen Paris." Or was that Naples?

1.   Didn't matter anymore. Goodbye Elizabeth. Goodbye, Solomon.

She lay back on the bed and fingered herself.

She thought about Solomon, her very last thoughts. 'So, this is suicide? The end of a life. Unsuccessful. Unfulfilled. Just a bag of old and tired bones, longing to be away to the next dimension - whatever that was. Never know; it could be even worse. Never mind. She closed her eyes. All been a waste of fucking time. She'd never achieved anything - nothing at all. Not even childbirth. Never won anything. Sure, kidded a few people into loving her - uncomfortable though it may have been, but only on a temporary basis. Her thoughts drifted to Lizzie. She loved being in Lizzie's arms, but no! Solomon had been her lover. The only man for her.

Basically, though, she just didn't care anymore. I'm sick and tired of just breathing in and out all day and night.

What did it amount to? "As much as a hill of beans." Clark Gable had once said. And he'd know.

She felt cold and hot one second and not the next. Pills, she supposed. The immune system closes down.

So what? No big deal. All gotta go one day. And if you're shot, you'll never drown, as they say in Dublin's fair city. Life comes and it goes, as it does to all things.

She considered Solomon some more, warm and moist. He'd love it if he was here now. But he wasn't. God knows where he was - or with whom? She had a faint idea but didn't want to spend her last few minutes thinking about that possibility.

He had always turned her on, but that was then, and this was now. Times had changed, and he was gone.

She thought some more.

They had been great together. If things were different, they could have conquered any obstacle. Any place, anything. Whichever. Remember those road trips? Just the hard and fast grey road ahead of them. In the old Austin Maxi, his father's, she knew. Circa nineteen seventy-one, if she remembered correctly, And she usually did. Nothing, nothing in their way. Heavenly! She loved the time that they had had together. The leaves, the lanes. Sex in the hedgerows... The open road ahead of them. They had promised each other the world. And look at the two of them now. He'd deserted her for the first woman with nice boobs that had looked at him twice. Even worse, it was her own mother.

She opened herself up and lost the fingers of her left hand inside herself. Always the left - felt like someone else. Her small hand was almost entirely lost to her now; her thumb, too, thinking about Solomon. Oh well.

Why not? Her parting thoughts, her parted thighs. Goodbye, world.

Of course, on the other hand, Lizzie might be upset - might blame herself?

Probably not, though. Lizzie could always find some other body. Always seemed to, anyway.

It's not as if they made each other happy. Not long-term, anyway. It was just sex. Nice sex, but just that. Solomon had fought for her, killed for her. Saved her life. He'd loved her. There was a time when she wanted nothing else but to be with him, close to him. Now, though, those memories repulsed her.

She thought about it again. No, nothing much else to dwell on. Anybody else would do for him. Lizzie too. She realized that she was wet through, her mind spinning in circles. What would the coroner say? Ah well. Doesn't matter anymore.

She closed her eyes again and drifted away.

'What are you wondering?'

She was lounging at her dressing table, quite the lady. Ornaments and jars as far as the eye could see. Reminded her of names and places, and faces, April, Paris, Cologne. She powdered her face, pouted and plucked. She ached in places she'd forgotten existed, but she'd had a great time. Liked to think he had, too.

She watched him from the vanity mirror as she re-blacked her eyes. God, he was hot. She'd never been...

'What'cha doing?'

She started on her red lips.

'Me? Nothing. Just repairing.'

'Ready for next time.'

She smirked. 'Maybe. How about you?'

Also nothing. Just watching. You know Barbara, you are a beautiful creature.'

She laughed this off with a shrug.

'I know. People have said.'

'What shall we do today? I know! Come back to bed.'

'Oh no. We can't spend all day in bed again. Apart from anything else, Solomon could be back soon.'

'Will he?'

'No way of knowing. No signals. He could open the back door at any time.'

'Come here then. Let him find us screwing.'

'No! I wouldn't do that to him. Such a thing as respect, you know.'

'I suppose. Anyhow, he won't be back.'

She looked surprised, even in the mirror. 'Oh?' She turned and stood, revealing her beautiful naked body. Her breasts longed to be kissed and f0ndled again. Her nether regions, black as fur; inviting, enticing.'

'And why's that?'

'Because he met with an unfortunate accident.'

'Who did?'

'Solomon. Lucky for me. I met him when we were out walking. Bade him look over a high promontory. Pushed him and watched him fall; five hundred feet! He never moved again.'

'You killed him!' she shrieked.'

'Shush, yes. So I did. He had something I wanted.'

'What?'

'You.'

He lay back and smoked half a cigarette.

She was agog. 'What?' She clutched the rear metal bedhead and tried to think straight. 'You killed him? Why? How? When?'

'Couple of days ago now.' he said, ignoring the previously already-answered questions. Only natural, she'd be shocked. 'Came straight here, that first time. Wanted you out of your snow-white blouson.'

Thoughts raced through her head. What on Earth was happening? She had to try and fool him, but what did she have?...

'Why, though?' she tried. 'What for? What did he ever do to you?'

'It was simply because I wanted you. You and your gorgeous body... Still do. You're a perfect, wonderful woman. Yes, full of wonder. Never seen anybody like you. Everything I've ever dreamed of. I wanted you to myself, for myself. Every last inch of you. Every inch of me. He was in the way - you know that now. He's in a ditch a few miles from here. It's the best place for him. He'd killed two men himself and thought nothing of it. Chances are, he would have killed me, too, given half the chance. Why take the risk? I thought. And that was that. People like that don't deserve to live.'

'But... he was my lover.'

'And now, I am. So it goes.'

'You act as though he thought nothing of it!' she shouted. 'He did! Of course, he did! At the time, he didn't have any choice!'

'Sshh, come here, quiet down.'

'No! They were troubling times and difficult circumstances. You weren't there. You don't know.'

'I'm here now.'

'You'd probably have done the same.'

'I did... I have. That's human nature. Anything that gets in the way of what we want kill it before it kills you.'

'No! We can't live like that. What about love? Companionship, friendship?' She was aware he was ogling her breasts. 'Stop doing that! Murderer! Rapist!'

He shook his head. 'No. I never raped you.'

'What am I to you then? I'm calling the police.'

He shook his head some more. 'I doubt you will make yourself understood. The gendarmerie gets calls each and every day. There's nothing that they will do.'

'What am I then? Just cheap, free and easy sex?'

'I wouldn't say easy, no. You seemed to be available. I can always tell. Cheap and free - yes. Why? What did you think you were?'

'Available?' She shuddered. 'How? Why?'

264

'Fancied you, that was all. Same as he did once.'

She needed time to think. She came across the room to him and lay on the bed. She was without clothes.

'There's my girl.'

'Men! You're all alike!'

'Why worry then? Some women, too.' he murmured.

He held her like an animal, pinning her down. Luckily, she still had her nail scissors in her hand. She stabbed him repeatedly in the back, again and again, until her strength eluded her. He bled red and white all over her and the bedclothes.

She threw him away from herself. He rumbled to the floor. He lay on the brown domestic carpet and died. More quietly than she'd imagined. Still, there he was - gone.

Outside, the sky was parchment-white. She took it all in. The sun and the sky - beautiful. In the distance, people were organising their wares and fares. Falling over one another for prominent positions. She turned and stepped over his remains. In a rush of rage, disgust and adrenaline, she pulled him out through the French windows and over the balcony to the largely overgrown flowerbed below.

She turned back and went and sat at the dressing table. Her lips needed painting again; she smudged. And her eyes also needed attention.

What next, though? she thought as she painted. What could she do now? All the people that she had loved had taken what they wanted and left her alone.

Bastards!

What else was there?

'Why, though?' Lizzie was appalled.

'Who knows?' replied the coroner.

The body bag was zipped, and two burly fellows carried its contents away. That was that.

'She never said she was contemplating anything like this!'

'Often the way.' said the coroner candidly. 'Sometimes it's the only thing that makes sense. Had a friend one time that had just purchased twelve feet of rope. Never seen him looking so contented. He hung himself the very next evening. Well, goodbye.'

Lizzie and Fran had discussed circumstances like this before briefly. What they wanted, what the other one should do, and so on. Not at any great length, lives were complicated enough, but sometimes the subject would arise. They'd imagined it would be years before any plans were put into practice.

The coroner stuck around outside, smoking, but Lizzie didn't feel like talking. She'd looked for a note, a card, a text message - for God's sake! But no, nothing. She'd come, and she'd gone. That was that. Rubbish.

Maybe for the best, on reflection. After all, Lizzie thought. We can't often explain our lives - let alone our own and unexperienced deaths.

She opened the windows and looked out.

Paris went about its business. Vehicle horns tooted in angry or friendly greetings; it was impossible to tell. Bicyclists rang their little bells. Here and there, a dog barked, and the sounds of birds filled the plane trees that skirted the concentric boulevards. A newspaper vendor waved at a prospective customer. There was little news today, though. Not even of Fran. Maybe tomorrow: "English woman ends own life.".

Something along those lines. In French, obviously: Femme Anglais est mort. Pas de problem."

A train hurtled towards its next stop, the noise or vibrations scaring a murmuration of starlings into the bleached-white sky. Lizzie watched them swoop and fly. It began to rain. City rain. Big, heavy drops, as grey as pebbles. Suited her mood.

This was Paris. Same old, same old, Lizzie pondered. Each sunrise and sunset is equally quantifiable…

And what about her? What could she do next with her life? Take it home? Well, where was home anymore?

First things first: She felt she should make contact with Solomon. They had been lovers once. Well, sexual partners… But, he had been Franny's lover. He deserved to know. She lit another cigarette and stared through the window.

How though? She wondered. She had no idea where he might be. Or, for that matter, why he would be at all interested in news of the death of his former lover - no matter how much he was involved.

She thought…

And he was involved, bottom line. Franny had loved him. But it had never worked out the way they would have liked. What with killings, rape, well, attempted rape, etcetera. Who could hold it all together after traumas like those?

She flicked ash from the window sill. God, hotels didn't even have ashtrays anymore.

All stolen, she supposed. She remembered a student bedsitting room of hers, which was festooned with ashtrays stolen from public houses in England. State Express 555 was her favourite, a thing of comparative beauty in royal blue and gold.

Posters of Guevara on the wall and David Essex. Job for her to tell them apart. Milk bottles on the doorstep downstairs; empty or full.

'Festooned!' she exclaimed, not too loudly. Making herself smile. Happy days.

She sighed. Flicked out her fag, lay back on the bed and thought for a minute.

Where did she see Solomon last?... No, not that. Not now. Nice while it lasted.

Concentrate!

Paris' cold wind began to blow through the streets, but she liked that. Made her feel safe. Where on Earth could he be? And, come to that, why would he want to know?

She rolled over. She loved this hotel's sheets. They seemed to hold her in their snug embraces, perhaps forever...

Solomon...

Yes, yes, they had been lovers once. Purely spontaneous. Not like it was with her and Franny, she remembered fondly. Solomon and Francesca had promised the world to each other, but it had all gone wrong. Such is life: 5h1t happens.

Solomon sat quietly in the barely-furnished room. His head thumped with an anxiety headache. He wondered what the hell was going on. He had been out walking when two uniformed gendarmes had literally picked him up and swept him into the back of their squad car. As far as he was aware, he had done nothing wrong, apart from sleeping with a waitress. Which wasn't a crime, surely?

Suddenly a man was at the door.

'Ah. You're awake. Ready to come with me?'

Solomon guessed so. He stumbled to his feet. The chair was hard and had cut off the circulation to his lower legs a little, so he stumbled a little. Still, maybe the next event would shed some light on his predicament - whatever it was.

His escort was lightly dressed, necessarily so. It was now hot after the rain. And still. As though the entire city was holding its breath. They walked down a dimly lit corridor to another closed door.

'Hold on.' said the man pointlessly. 'I'll knock.'

He did so. A commanding voice bade them enter.

Inside, the room was bright. Venetian blinds cast parallelogram shadows on every surface. Solomon could not see the occupant seated behind the desk, who commanded him to sit at a convenient chair in front of the desk.

'Now then.' it began.

'Well, make up your mind.' said Solomon, using humour as his weapon of choice. It was a woman's voice, but that told him nothing more.

If the person had had an angle-poise lamp, she would have shone it in his face around about now. She didn't, of course.

'Hold on. Chivers, would you close the blinds, please?'

His escort complied. 'Thank you.'

Now that Solomon could see her more clearly, she turned out to be a strikingly beautiful female with long, fair hair. She had probably never been called a dumb blonde in her whole life. She'd coiffured her hair up behind her ears. She thought it made her look professional. He drank in the sight. It is strange how the colour of a person's hair endears us to one another.

She arranged herself, smoothed everything down behind her desk and smiled.

'You look surprised.'

'Why wouldn't I be?'

'Well, now.' She examined an open file. Let's see where we are.'

Solomon was unsure; he didn't know what time it was. Her image entranced him. He wondered about all the parts of her that he had yet to see. Those full breasts from her semi-revealing cleavage. Possibly a pair of child-bearing hips, long legs, high-heeled shoes…

'Stop it.' she said roughly.

'What?' asked an innocent Solomon.

'You're imagining undressing. I don't like that.'

He shrugged. 'Dress down a little then.' he suggested.

'Don't tell me what to do!'

'Fine.' He wondered what it was that she wanted, what she usually did for a living. Yes, she was brisk, business-like. But to what end? No insignia on her sleeves or uniform to indicate rank and status. She hadn't introduced herself. Solomon didn't know and couldn't guess.

'Are you listening to me?' Barked. Cross.

'Sorry. What?'

She snapped the file shut.

'You do realise why you're here?'

1.   'No.' he responded with.

She sighed. He imagined her sighing in different circumstances. Lovely... - he would. What was it she was looking at?

'Stop doing that!'

'What?'

'You!'

He shrugged. He could do no more. 'Can't be anyone else.'

'Does the name Bond mean anything to you?'

'Yes, of course. Does to anyone my age and fighting weight.'

'Colin Bond?'

'Oh. That fella. Yes. Met him on the train going down.'

'And since?'

She wasn't English, and her accent was irritating.

'What?'

'Have you seen him since?'

Not that I recall. Although, wait, yes. He was at the street carnival we attended a couple of days ago.'

'What did you talk about?'

'Oh, Christ, I don't know. This and that. Nothing special. Why? What's this all about?'

She re-opened the file and perused it silently. Then...

'Where you were found, a man's tracks led there.'

'Found?'

'Seems you'd fallen. Or were you pushed? You tell me.'

'I remember I had fallen. Staggered home. Had a telegram waiting. Just said, "Come to Paris". From an... acquaintance of mine. Police officer, as it goes.'

'It goes.'

'Sorry. Can't help you any further. No idea what you're talking about. Or me.'

'The tracks were made by one Colin Bond.'

'One?'

'Now deceased. Found in your flowerbed.'

'Impossible! How would he have got there?'

'Judging from his injuries, pushed from the balcony.'

'Well, not by me. You'd need the strength of ten men to heave him over the handrail.'

'You'd be surprised what a person can do with adrenaline coursing through their veins.'

'Well, hardly goes without saying that it couldn't have been me, not in my current state. It must have been somebody else. An intruder, maybe?'

'Who else was in the house?'

'I have no idea. I wasn't there.'

'Lady friend? Lover?'

'No idea.'

'Is there anyone who could vouch for you?'

'Vouch? Why? What am I supposed to have done?'

'You tell me.'

'No. I've already told you everything I know. If you're not going to charge me, I take it I am free to leave?'

'What are you doing in Paris?'

'None of your beeswax.'

'Beeswax?'

'It's a colloquialism. Means business.'

'Why not say business then?'

'It's an English way.'

'Ah.'

'Well, good luck.' He stood. 'I'm afraid I can't help you any further.'

'Afraid? Another English colloquialism?'

He smiled a thin smile. 'In other circumstances, I'd ask if I could see more of you. There seems to be so much more of you to see...'

'Close the door behind you. Thank you, Chivers.'

Solomon made his way, via lifts and stairs, out of the building.

Outside, it was blindingly white. Must be mid-morning, he hazarded a guess.

He hadn't a clue where he was and didn't know which way to turn. All the signposts were un-French. The streets all looked the same. He wandered aimlessly. Every place he looked, he saw stall-holders and sales-people plying their wares. An inordinate amount of foodstuffs and playstuffs were gaily waved before his very eyes!

But he had no money to buy a thing. He wondered where his home was. Well, he knew where his home was, but he was eight hundred and fifty kilometres from it. Something had clearly gone on there that he didn't have a clue about. He needed to sleep and rest his mind. Where was his hotel? What time was it? Perhaps he could ask somebody? His

French was none too good, but if he tapped his wrist and said something like, "Temps? Temps?" Maybe that would do.

He approached a woman: young, fair, slim. Reminded him of his recent acquaintance a little. Nicer tits, though - little left to the imagination.

He tapped his wrist. She looked at her watch.

'D'accord.' she said, at length. 'Mais, il fait chaud. Une demi-heure, cent Euros.'

Solomon nodded his acceptance of these terms.

'Yeah, you'll do.'

She walked into the nearest gendarmerie she could find, as bold as brass. The operative stood to attention; he knew class when he saw it.

She didn't beat around any bushes.

'I have killed a man.' She said.

'Oh yes.' said he, his mouth agape.

She was irritated. These words surely meant the same in any language? She drummed her fingers on the countertop.

'Well?' she enquired.

The man shuffled some forms. He was relatively new to the post and wasn't quite sure how to proceed. He looked into her eyes.

'When was this?'

'Just now.'

'Aha. And what was your... motive.'

'We were having sex. He told me he had killed my lover. I stabbed him in the back with my nail scissors and threw him off the balcony. Easier if I show you. You know the back road up into the hills?'

'I do indeed.' he replied. 'Often go hunting up there with my friends. Deer, partridge. The occasional pheasant. Just for sport, you must understand.'

'Not really, no. Why men kill is a mystery to me.'

'To eat. To survive?'

She shook her head. 'There are always legumes - good for crop rotation. Allons y - Let's go have a look-see. We'll take your car.'

The man put on a peaked cap for the show.

'Bien sûr.'

They set off

Lizzie thought...

So, what could they say? What would he say? What would she say?

All seemed a little too complicated.

Would they just fall into the nearest bed for a... remembrance coupling?

1.   Sounded nice...

No.

Lizzie wasn't sure that that would help in any way. She got up and moved to the window again, watching the world passing her by. Everybody is wrapped up in their own personal stories. Likewise...

What then? How could they possibly meet? Where could he possibly be? She had tried her Bristol landline; he still had the keys and could be there. Predictably, there was no reply. She'd left a message:

"Hi. It's me. Where are you? Bad news, I'm afraid. Maybe you've heard? I'm on the mobile."

Through her blink of cigarette smoke, she happened to spot WPC Wendy, who seemingly would know her anywhere. What the hell was she doing over here? - no jurisdiction.

The Wendy seemed to be heading for the train station, - Le Gare du Nord. Lizzie gave chase...

Luckily, she was right.

She didn't know why Wendy was in Paris. Again, just assumed. Sometimes, these things are meant.

She caught up with her and grabbed her upper arm.

'WPC!' she said proudly.

Wendy recognised her straight away. Puzzled though.

'How did you know it was me?' she asked.

Lizzie shrugged. 'You have a memorable figure.' she replied, without hesitation.

'So do you.' Wendy grinned.

'Time for coffee?'

They made for the nearest café bar, Wendy continually checking her watch.

'Train to catch.' she explained. 'Eurostar.'

'So are you!'

Which made them both laugh.

'How did you know Solomon was in Paris?'

Wendy sipped and blew her cappuccino.

'I didn't. Found out from Passport Control that he had come to France. After that, he trawled the hotels, pensiones and immobiliers and discovered that he'd bought a place in the south. Sent him a telegram saying, "Meet me in Paris. Let's talk." That was that.'

'Cute. Okay.'

'Didn't think he'd show, but there he was.'

'What does he have to do?'

Wendy shrugged. 'Who knows? You know what happened?'

'Kind of.'

'Me too. Chances are, it was self-defence, but I guess I'll report back saying I know where he is and see what happens. In a way, he's quite right; who cares what happened? Life goes on.'

'Amen. So be it.'

At the cottage, there was blood everywhere.

'Nice job.' said the officer, whose name was Pascal. She'd discovered this on the trip up. Also, his fine muscular figure and frame. He fitted into his summer uniform, shorts, of course, quite well...

'Any questions?' she asked in what she hoped was a coquettish manner. He'd been casting furtive glances at her since their first meeting. Felt his eyes on every inch of her. Every inch... She knew what that might lead to. She knew men. Should do by now...

Where though? There seemed to be blood everywhere. He outthought her.

'I grateful for your attention.' he said in his broken English. 'However, I have a close friend.'

'Don't we all?' she enquired coyly. 'Can't see anyone but you though. How about you? What can you see?'

'No. This is impossible. You are a murder suspect at a crime scene. Natural causes will have to wait.'

'Why?' she complained. 'I'm horny now! Want you. It's the scent of blood. Puts me in mind of the times when a man saw what he wanted and just took it.'

'Ooh, yes. Take me. Do that to me. I can feel your eyes on me. I know what it is that you want. Brrr.'

'Is there a cleaner room?'

There was, of course, a spare room on the property. It was sparsely furnished. Merely an inflated inflatable bed which Solomon had left where it lay, in the centre of the timber-floored space. She had tried to reconcile the fact that Solomon was gone, but it somehow didn't seem real. Maybe one day she would see him again. Who knew?

The pair collapsed onto the bed, only one thing on both of their minds. She fumbled with his starched uniform trousers. He, with his hands full of her. She was dressed appropriately for the season: a thin cotton dress, plain and white - just like her own sweet self. Knickers and brassiere; easily removed. Gratified by his gasps of astonishment, she became naked. She still had it all, and she had no resistance. He bunched her knickers up into her free hand; she loved that. His penetration thrilled her. The remaining faint scent of blood filled her nostrils and inflamed her senses. She acted brilliantly, taking herself to ecstasy and climax more times than she could keep count of. O my!

She gazed down at her. There was so much to be admired. Her beautiful face and spaces. Her eyes, her hair, her gorgeous breasts, her long and lovely legs, now curled around his back.

Solomon wandered the boulevards. The Paris streets echoed about him. Traders bade him purchase their various items, hewn over long and crowded hours at their living quarters. Here, a stall full of embroidery, their colours glinting in the sun - cushions, covers, curtains. He nodded and smiled at the trader but wasn't inclined to buy. Where would he put it? Barbara would have to advise him. He waved the traders away, confidently English or British. What was the difference? They had all fought on the same side; they said they did anyway...

And won!

She caught up with him unexpectedly and linked their arms.

'So this is Paris!' she shrieked, causing heads to turn. 'I knew I'd find you here!'

He stopped, astounded. 'Lizzie?'

'I know! And you're Solomon.' She laughed, excited to see him again.

'What are you doing here?' he wondered. 'And how did you find me? All of Paris looks the

same.'

'Depends what you're looking for.'

'Not like London.' he continued. 'London is a shithole. Filthy. They say you're never more than ten feet from a rat.'

'Paris is beautiful. Always was.'

'Well, not in the Second World War, no.'

'Hitler liked it. Anyway, I found you! My turn to hide now!'

'Keep your voice down.'

'Oh, Solly. I've missed you.'

'Well, no, you haven't.'

She smiled. 'I know you. Listen, serious news. Let's get coffee.'

'All anyone seems to do in Paris.' he grumbled.

'So? Let's blend in.'

He enjoyed himself; lovely, lovely woman. It was the best he'd ever had. He wished it could always be like this. He took his time inside her. Penetration. There is nothing like it…

'You'll get me the sack.' he muttered, raining kisses on her exposed neck.

'What a way to go though.' She agreed. 'Moistening all of my parts. Go on, honey. You're the best!'

They conjoined some more. She lay prone and arched her back, engorged.

'What are we doing?' he wondered.

'Fucking.' she said, definitely. 'Same in any language.'

'What about the body?'

'Mmm, lovely body.' She ran her hands over him, warm and kind.

'I don't mean that. You know I don't.'

'Well, what do you suggest?'

'It's not up to me to suggest.'

'Yes, it is. You are the arm and the letter of the law. You decide what's next. After you've finished me off again.'

'Finished you off?'

'Again…'

He was on top of her again.

'What do you think I think?'

'Oh, go on then. Just once more… Pascal.'

'What?'

'Oh, nothing. Just wanted your name on my lips.'

'Which lips?' he kissed her. 'These… or those…'

'Both.'

'You have beautiful lips.'

'I know. Men have said.'

'Have you had many men?'

'Enough.'

'What about me?'

'I liked you. Fancied you. Go ahead. Take what you want.'

'I want it all.'

'Go ahead.'

He fondled her splendid breasts.

'You are beautiful.'

'I know. Aren't we all?'

'I suppose so.'

'What next, though? Wipe yourself dry and escort me to the nearest prison for the rest of my days?'

He shook his head. 'No, no. I want you to be here. Anytime I want you. Or you want me. Let's keep it like that.'

'What about the body?' she wondered.

'I will detail men. They will dispose of the body. Nobody needs to know. I won't involve you.'

'"Detail". Oh. Okay.'

'Sometimes,] with unexplained deaths there is rien, nothing, we can do. A foreign traveller slips and falls. What can we do?' Different in England, I imagine.'

'You might think.'

He lingered around her body.

'Would you do this for other men?'

'Which other men?'

'Expose yourself. Let men enjoy you.'

'Well, if it's that or go to prison, count me in.'

'Count?'

'Let me show you.' She took him between her legs, using her hands. 'I like myself like this. Freshly showered and perfumed. I imagine It's like making love to a rose bush, all prickles and thorns. Until you get to the sweet stuff. If you're not careful.'

'I always am.' he said. 'You flower in such beautiful places.'

'Ouch.' she exclaimed.

'Sorry. Slipped. So... what about me?'

284

'You? You are my pronged warrior. My unicorn. Only one thing on your mind. And that's to have your wicked way with me.'

'Hold still then.' he commanded. 'Spread your legs apart. Let's get at you.'

'Ohhh. I always dreamed there'd be a man like you one day. Just going to enjoy myself now.'

... Until there was nothing left.

They lay in the early-morning glaze. Happy and contented.

Outside, in Paris, the early morning wind blew and threatened more to come. They cuddled up close.

'Breakfast soon.'

'They come at eight.'

'What is it now?'

She stretched. Her phone was on the bedside table. 'Six-fifteen.'

'Plenty of time then, Eliza-Beth.'

She giggled. 'Love it when you call me that. "Eliza-Beth." Thought I'd lost you.'

He shrugged. 'People come, and people go. Sometimes it's meant, sometimes it's not.'

'Speaking of which...'

'Go on.'

Bad news travels slowly…

Afterwards.

'What would you like to do now?' he asked.

'All planned, as it goes.'

'What?'

She reached into her purse and drew out a pair of tickets.

'Present from the old man, insider trading. I have not seen him for ages, but sometimes he remembers who I am or what I am. Two tickets to Barbados. He's got a refinery or distillery out there. Want to come?'

'Very much so.'

'May as well.'

The bedclothes twisted and turned. They made sweet love. Time passed.

Suddenly, Barbara was thirsty. She had mineral water and mints at the bedside.

'Stop, a minute.'

'Stop?'

'Just for a minute.' She replenished herself. Get rid of the thirst. She lay back. 'Now then, where were you?'

She felt, what's the word? Vibrant. Alive! Wanted him again and again. He seemed to be pressing all of her buttons. Riding up inside her. Her unicorned stallion.

He almost sobbed, a rampant animal. How had he got here? His nerves and sinews obey his every command. Everything he did seemed to turn her on more.

After a minute or so...

'How was that? You okay?' he asked.

'You tell me.' She laughed, giggled, chortled. 'You'll do for me.'

'Thought I just did.'

'Well?'

She'd felt the fat melting from her thighs.

'Well, in Shakespearean times...'

'Shakespearean?'

'It's a word. You'd take your place at whatever theatre took your fancy and sat captivated by the many entrances and exits that the famous Bard had dreamed up: early doors. Knights forlorn, Saints unavowed, Kings and Queens vanquished and unaided. Marvellous stuff to feed the great unwashed masses.'

'I see!' she said, enthralled. 'You like English?'

'I like you.'

'Oh.'

He continued. 'And then, returned to your many and various Elizabethan hovels for a good night's sleep before morning...'

'Morning?'

'Morning.'

'Oh. So, where are we now?'

'I'm where I want to be. Between your warm and lovely legs. Who wouldn't want to be?'

'Other men have tried.' she joked. 'You'll do though. Great, big and extra-large. Fantastic!'

'Ready for another?'

'If you are.' She made herself laugh.

'You inspire me.'

'Good.'

His hand slid up her thigh, warm and comfortable.

'God, I'm such a slag. Love sex, though.'

'You should do. You're pretty nigh perfect at it.'

'Pretty nigh?'

'I'll always call you that. No one but us will know what it means.'

'Sweet. Now get inside me again and fuck me hard. I'm gagging for it!'

She loved him inside her, every inch, every stroke. She lay back and enjoyed it. Feeling his muscles contract and his hot breath on her face. He was everywhere, every place. She loved it. She loved him! Already!

She gave him everything she had. Every nook and every cranny...

Sadly, though, it was all too much for her, and her heart stopped beating in the middle of it all.

By early morning's unforgiving light, Barbara was dead and gone.

It was a rough flight - well, aren't they all?

Solomon tried to read while she slept. Thomas Wolfe's "A Man in Full", which he had picked up in Duty-Free. The trip took fifteen hours, but in time, the land reappeared, and they touched down safely at Grantley Adams Airport.

They made their way through the forecourt.

'Who was he anyway?' she asked.

'Who?'

'Grantley Adams.'

'Oh, him. Politician. He was rewarded for his efforts back in the seventies. Knighted, I think. So he must have had British origins.'

'Okay.'

On the southeastern coastline, there was a nice hotel, the Coconut Court Beach Motel. It promised much.

They checked in and made themselves comfortable.

'Bellboy said to watch out for lizards.' she said.

'Just trying to frighten you. Take no notice. They're all fairly harmless.'

'Bellboys or lizards?'

'Depends on your constitution.'

'No doubt.'

'When I was in the south of France, they littered the ground. Twenty-eight degrees Celsius most days. That is to say, eighty-two degrees Fahrenheit. I need hardly say.'

'No.'

'So, what shall we do now we're here?' She fanned herself with a towel.

'Do you think she'll miss you?'

'No. Not likely. You know how easy it is to keep in touch with people. If they don't, they don't.'

'Hot, isn't it?'

'Could you go for a swim?'

'Could do. Wait for low tide. Lots of fishing boats at this time of day.'

'You know best.'

'Humid anyway. Your body gets used to it. Like sex.'

She smiled. 'Yes. Maybe later.'

'Fancy some breakfast?'

'Yes! Good idea. What's on the menu?'

'I think it's soup, but it will wipe off.'

'Groucho Marx.'

'Could have been. What do you fancy?'

'Oh, scrambled eggs.'

'With Champagne?'

'Of course, with Champagne, silly. In Barbados, you have Champagne with everything.'

'Even sex?'

'We'll see.'

'Good to know.'

Out in the ocean, for seemingly no reason at all, a small boat exploded. It jolted them both awake.

'What the hell was that?'

The noise was terrible; an aftershock bathed the beach. Rough and rubbish began to settle all around them. Solomon grabbed a huge parasol.

'Quick! Under here!'

He gazed out of the veranda at the smoke and flames.

'What was it?' she wondered.

'I don't know. Drug smugglers, I guess. Happens a lot. Boats operated by kids, children, who hardly know what they're doing.'

'Do you think we should do something?'

'Like what? No, no. Best leave it to the emergency services. They'll take care of everything. Come on - scrambled eggs and Champagne.'

Later on, they bathed in the crystalline waters. The rest of the world could go hang.

And that was that.

The two men disentangled nets. All kinds of shredded plastic were trapped in the folds and cleats.

'Who was it anyway?'

'British police officer, they say. Female, what's left of her. Chartered the boat for two days. Obviously not well-versed in the ways of the sea.'

'Or boats. Say why?'

'Didn't ask. No business of mine.'

'No. Probably left the gas on. Lethal those things.'

'Ah, well. Too late now.'

'True.'